M000235209

ISBN: 978-1-64456-374-8 [Hardcover]
ISBN: 978-1-64456-375-5 [Paperback]
ISBN: 978-1-64456-376-2 [Mobi]
ISBN: 978-1-64456-377-9 [ePub]

Library of Congress Control Number: 2021944619

INDIES UNITED PUBLISHING HOUSE, LLC
P.O. BOX 3071
QUINCY, IL 62305-3071
www.indiesunited.net

Other Books by the Author

Looking for Laura
Secrets Can Kill
Missing or Dead

In memory of my grandfather, Joseph Beberman

A Tracey Marks Mystery

MEMORY

OF

MURDER

ELLEN SHAPIRO

INDIES UNITED PUBLISHING HOUSE, LLC

CHAPTER 1

Thoughts of the upcoming trial of Randy Stewart were on my mind when my phone rang.

"Tracey Marks."

"Ms. Marks, my name is Lisa Kane. Would it be possible to talk with you this afternoon?"

"How is 2:00 pm?"

"That's fine. I know where your office is. I'll see you then."

I was curious why Ms. Kane wanted to see me but decided to wait until we spoke in person to find out what was on her mind.

My thoughts wandered back to the trial. I shot Randy Stewart when my gun went off accidentally trying to defend myself. I was glad I didn't kill him since I didn't want that on my conscience, but it still haunts me. While investigating the murder of my client's mother, I eventually figured out it was Stewart and I became a threat to him. Next week I was the prosecution's star witness.

I never testified before and I wasn't looking forward to it. I guess I've watched too many shows on television where the attorney for the defendant tries to trip you up and twist your words. I'm afraid I'll fall into that trap.

At exactly 2:00 I heard the door open. I quickly got up from my desk.

"Lisa, it's nice to meet you," I said as she followed me into my office.

"Can I get you anything to drink, coffee, water?"

"No thank you," she said, taking a seat.

Lisa looked young, maybe in her early twenties, pretty with shoulder-length red hair and large green eyes. She was probably around my height, 5'8", dressed in jeans and a blue and white striped button down cotton shirt. She wore black flats and no socks.

Lisa was very nervous, twisting her hands over and over.

"Are you sure I can't get you anything to drink?"

"No thank you."

"Why don't we start with an easy question. Who referred you?"

"You may think this is naïve of me, but I googled private investigators. There were several in the area that came up but I liked that you were a female."

"Most people don't know any private investigators and resort to the internet."

"I briefly read about two of your cases and I thought you might be able to help me."

"Well why don't you tell me what this is about, and I'll ask you some questions after you've finished."

"Okay. When I was three, almost four, my mother was killed. I was sleeping at the time when a loud noise woke me up. I got scared and called out to my mother but she didn't answer. I was never allowed to go into my parents' room at night when the door was closed but I was afraid. I wanted my mother, so I climbed out of my bed and slowly walked to my parents' room. The door was open, but when I peeked in I didn't see my mother or my father. Everything was fuzzy after that. I must have gone back to my bed because the next thing I remembered was my father coming into my room and giving me a kiss on my forehead. At some point there was a police lady who asked me questions but I couldn't talk. They said I must have been traumatized."

"The police investigated but they never found out who killed my mother. At the time my father was a suspect, but they had no physical evidence against him. May I have a glass of water?"

I came back with a glass of water and handed it to Lisa.

"That must have been horrible for you. How can I help?"

Lisa took a big gulp before answering.

"Lately I've been remembering, though very sporadically. An image will appear and then will be gone in an instant. Maybe it's just my imagination."

"Well why don't you tell me anyway?"

"I thought I heard voices from my parents' room, but the only voice I could recognize was my mother's. She was yelling."

"Could you tell how many other voices there were besides your mother's?"

"I think just one, but I can't be sure. I'm sorry I'm not being very helpful."

"That's okay, anything else?"

"I think I heard a door slamming."

"Is that it?"

I saw a slight hesitation before she answered.

"Gray coat."

"What do you mean?"

"Again, maybe I imagined it, but I think the person who killed my mother was wearing a gray coat."

"Have you told anyone about these memories?"

"No, you're the only one. I need you to find out who killed my mother. Is that something you can do?"

I was hesitant about taking on the case. Not knowing Lisa at all, it was hard to know her state of mind and if these memories were real or not.

"Is your father still living?"

"Yes. He's only fifty-five."

"What does he do for a living?"

"He's a patent attorney."

"Did he ever remarry?"

"He did, about a year after my mother died. I have no illusions that my mother was perfect. My nanny was the one who cared for me. I need to know for sure who killed my mother."

"Why don't we do this. I'll see if I can get your mother's police file, and after reviewing it, I'll decide whether to take your case."

"Thank you, but you won't have to go to the trouble since I already have the file."

"Well that makes things easier," I said. "Why don't I stop by your place later and pick it up."

"I'm going back there now. You can come by any time."

As I walked Lisa out, she gave me her address. She lived in Soho, a fairly expensive area in Manhattan. I wondered how she could afford to live there.

I didn't know what to think. Was Lisa really remembering things or did she imagine them? It seems her father married pretty quickly after the death of his wife. I was definitely eager to see what was in the police file.

I decided to call it quits for the day and headed to my apartment on the Upper West Side. It was a beautiful September day, and I walked the fifteen blocks to my building. My doorman Wally was outside.

"Hi Tracey, you're home early," Wally said.

"It's too nice out to spend it inside. I thought I would go for a run."

"My shift is finished in a few minutes, so I'll see you tomorrow."

"Have a nice night," I said to Wally, waving goodbye as I walked to the elevator.

Wally is one of my favorite people. He's been my doorman as long as I've lived in the building, almost twelve years. Looking at him you would never know he's around seventy. He's tall and hefty with a velvety brown complexion.

When I got upstairs I changed into a tee shirt and shorts. I looked at the long scar on my arm and was glad to see it wasn't very noticeable. A few months back someone sliced my arm with the intent of killing me. I was fortunate I was able to get away before any more damage was inflicted. Lucky for me it happened near my building. Wally had the good sense to call an ambulance right away and stayed with me in the hospital.

At the park I did my usual three mile loop. When I got back I showered, and ran a comb through my straight, light brown hair that I keep cut to my chin. I slipped on a pair of jeans and a long sleeve cotton pullover and went down to my building's garage to get my car.

I drove to Lisa's apartment in Soho. I was able to find a tiny spot my little Beetle could fit into—one of the perks of having a small car when you live in the city.

The doorman let me in and I took the elevator up to the fourth floor. Lisa waved to me as I got off the elevator.

"Thanks for coming by," she said as she led me into her living room.

"You must be wondering how someone my age can live in such an expensive area."

"It did cross my mind."

"My mother was very wealthy, well her family was. I guess you can call me a trust fund baby, though I do have a profession. I'm a fashion designer. Please sit down."

I sat down on a beautiful light blue couch and Lisa sat opposite me on a blue and beige upholstered high back chair. The walls were painted in a light beige tone. There were several abstracts hanging up. Her taste seemed to be very eclectic.

"Do you have your own company?" I asked.

"Yes. I design women's sleep wear."

"I have no fashion sense. I basically wear the same thing every day. It makes life a lot simpler when I don't have to figure out what to wear when I get up."

"Well that's an interesting way to look at it."

"Are your mother's parents still living?" I said, changing the subject.

"My grandmother is. I spent a lot of my childhood at my grandparents' house in Bronxville. I always had the feeling my grandparents blamed my father for my mother's death, and they certainly were not happy when he remarried so soon after she died."

"Are you close to your father?"

"I am. I know he loves me and would do anything for me."

"Do you have a good relationship with your stepmother?"

"Yes. We're fairly close. Since I was so young at the time she married my father, she took over the role of mom. She never treated me like a stepchild."

"Lisa, do you have any thoughts on who may have killed your mother?"

6

"I really have no idea. Though the police suspected my father, I can't imagine he had anything to do with my mother's death."

I wasn't quite sure if she believed her father was innocent.

"I'll read through the file and get back to you."

"Thank you, and whether you take the case or not, I will pay you for your time."

On the way out I noticed a photo, sitting on a glass table, of a woman and a child.

"May I?"

"Yes. It's me with my mother."

"She's beautiful."

"She was. I have her red hair and green eyes," Lisa said with sadness in her voice.

I left still not sure about Lisa. But one thing was certain, someone killed Lisa's mother and this person has never been caught.

CHAPTER 2

After parking my car in the garage, I walked three blocks to the Chinese takeout place. I'm probably their best customer. I guess you can say cooking is not my strong suit, though I do have my moments, but they are few and far between.

I was digging into my Shrimp Lo Mein and watching the news on my little TV I have in the kitchen when the phone rang.

"Hey there," I said to Jack when I answered. Jack and I have been in a relationship for about a year and a half. Jack comes from a bi-racial family; his mother was black and immigrated from Jamaica and his father was white and came from a Protestant family from Massachusetts. I met him on a case that took me to Massachusetts where Jack lives. He owns a small brick house in the town of Lee which he remodeled. Downstairs is completely open and the upstairs is where his bedroom and office are. Jack is also a private investigator and works for an attorney who does only criminal work.

"Did I catch you with your mouth full?"

"Shrimp Lo Mein."

"Well as delicious as that might be, I'm in the middle of grilling swordfish."

"Show off. By the way I had a very interesting day." I went on to tell Jack about my meeting with Lisa Kane. "I'm staring at a box full of police reports and documents. It's going to take me hours to go through everything."

"It will. Look over the interviews first and write down what you think may be important. This way you can go back and look over your notes."

"That's why I keep you around."

"Not for my good looks and other amenities I have to offer?"

"Bragging is not becoming," I said, smiling. "What's going on there?"

"The usual. Locating witnesses for an upcoming trial and getting them to talk."

"Which reminds me," I said. "Stewart's trial starts next week. Friday I'm going to the assistant district attorney's office so they can prep me."

"They're going to tell you that when you're on the witness stand to keep it simple. Tell the truth and just answer the questions the attorney asks. Don't elaborate."

"Aye aye sir."

"I think my fish is burning. I'll talk to you soon. Sleep tight."

"Ditto."

The following morning I was up bright and early ready to tackle the police reports. I decided I would work from home. I turned on the coffee maker. While the pot was filling up, I sat down and had a bowl of Cheerios and milk.

I brought my coffee into the living room and began sifting through the files. As I was reading I took down notes of anything that I thought was significant. I learned that Lisa's mother, Rebecca, had a life insurance policy taken out two months prior to her death. Her husband Jason was the sole beneficiary.

It seems that the reason the police couldn't make a case against him was that Mr. Kane had a solid alibi. He was at a dinner meeting with a client while Mrs. Kane was dying.

The police interviewed several people, including family members, friends of Rebecca, and other people involved with the case, including the person who was Mr. Kane's alibi for that night, an Eric Jordan. According to Mr. Jordan's statement, he and Jason Kane met around 8 pm for dinner and then went to a nearby bar for a nightcap. They both left the bar around midnight and parted outside of the bar.

Looking into Rebecca Kane's life, the police found nothing that pointed to any other suspects. Though their marriage appeared to be solid, a neighbor who lived in the brownstone next to the Kane's said that on a few occasions she heard loud shouting, but no one else the police spoke with thought the marriage was in trouble.

My phone rang as I was pulling out the crime scene photos.

"How about dinner later? I'll meet you at Anton's at 6:00," Susie said before I even had a chance to say hello.

"See you then."

Susie is my best friend. Actually she's probably my only friend. When I was young I never reached out to make friends with other kids. I'm not sure why. I met Susie in high school. She sat next to me in one of my classes and annoyed the hell out of me. I couldn't seem to get rid of her, and somehow we wound up becoming good friends. I think we mesh because we're complete opposites. Susie is outgoing with a positive attitude, while I'm reserved with a cynical attitude.

I took out the crime scene photos and laid them on the floor. I had never seen a dead person in a photo. It was kind of weird. Her body was found in the bathroom connected to the master bedroom. Blood had seeped out of the back of her head, where she hit the side of the tub. From the angle of her body it appeared she fell backward, probably from a struggle. Her white satin nightgown was stained with blood. There was a partial fingerprint from a smear of blood found on Rebecca's neck, which led the police to believe someone else was in the room.

The toxicology results showed no signs of alcohol or drugs in Rebecca Kane's system. The coroner's report confirmed that she died from hitting her head against the tub. The police did not find any proof of a break-in. Does that mean Rebecca Kane knew her killer?

I wondered whether Lisa actually witnessed the attack or just a fleeting moment when the killer was leaving the house.

My stomach started growling. When I looked at my phone it was after 1:00. It was definitely time for a break and something to eat. I made myself a peanut butter sandwich and more coffee and went back into the living room to continue reading the police file.

What I can't understand is why someone would kill Rebecca Kane and not one person the police questioned had any knowledge why she was targeted.

According to the coroner's report, her death occurred between 8:00 pm and 12:00 midnight. Would a business meeting last that long and that late? I had no clue.

While munching on my sandwich, I went through the police interviews. They seemed to have been pretty thorough. I made a note to ask Lisa if there was anyone she could think of that was not interviewed by the police during that time period.

Rebecca Kane owned a dress shop on Madison Avenue at the time of her death. Maybe Lisa inherited her fashion sense from her mother. I was curious if the shop was still in business and who owns it now?

This was a good point to take a break and go back to reading the police reports when I could look at it with fresher eyes.

It was after 4:00 when I called it quits. I went for a quick run before meeting Susie for dinner.

When I arrived at Anton's, Susie was talking to Olivia, the hostess. Normally Susie would be at the bar waiting, but she's pregnant.

"Hi guys," I said when I walked in.

Olivia, as always, looked fabulous. She could have been a model. Susie and I are jealous of Olivia's long legs that seem to go on for miles.

"Are you sure you're pregnant?" I said smiling, as we were seated at our table. "You are still flat as a board."

"Not sure how to take that but I guess it's a compliment. I'm only two months pregnant."

The waiter came over and I ordered a Sauvignon Blanc. I hated drinking knowing Susie couldn't, but she gave me her blessing and it eased my guilty conscience. I ordered my usual linguini and clams with the house salad and Susie ordered the eggplant parmigiana, also with the house salad.

"I started having morning sickness. I was tempted to call in sick today but decided against it. You never know when I might really need to play that card."

Susie is a matrimonial attorney at a small law firm in the city. She's a wealth of information, and I pick her brain all the time when I need advice on any of my cases.

"I might have a new client with a very interesting case." I went on to tell Susie the conversation I had with Lisa Kane, and what I had found out so far from reading through the police reports.

"On the surface it appears the police did a thorough investigation, but the fact remains someone killed her mother. My guess is that some people were lying to the police," Susie said.

"But why would they?"

"Maybe they had something to hide at the time and weren't willing to reveal the truth for their own reasons."

"That's interesting. I see your point."

"Not to change the subject but Mark and I want you to be our child's godmother."

"I would be honored as long as I'm not named in your will as guardian if anything happens to you guys."

"I promise," Susie said laughing, "but I know you would be a better mother than you think. And Jack would be a super father."

"Well you're probably right about Jack, but don't forget we're not married and not even living together."

"It'll happen one day."

"Wishful thinking on your part."

After dinner and dessert I said goodbye to Susie outside the restaurant and I walked the few blocks back to my apartment. I thought about what Susie said. My relationship with Jack is the longest I've ever had. I have always shied away from committing to marriage. I know how quickly you can lose people you love and I'm afraid to go through that pain again. Jack and I have had conversations about moving our relationship forward. He's very patient for the moment, but I don't know when his patience will run out.

CHAPTER 3

The following morning I went to the gym and did my usual workout with weights and some cardio on the bike. I finished up with stomach crunches and push-ups.

I stopped on my way into the office at the Coffee Pot, a place where I buy my coffee and muffin most every morning.

"Hi Anna. How are the kids?" Anna is the manager and has known me since I started coming in more than five years ago. I always look forward to opening up the bag to see what kind of muffin Anna has surprised me with.

"They're staying out of trouble for the moment."

"Always a good thing. I'll see you soon."

The first thing I did when I got into the office, besides taking out my coffee and my surprise Cranberry Nut muffin, was to open up my computer and check for any articles on the murder of Rebecca Kane. Since it was over twenty years ago, I wasn't sure if there would be any references to the crime.

It turned out there were a few articles but no information in them that I didn't already know about. I looked up the telephone number for the precinct that handled Rebecca's case. I picked up my phone, called the precinct and asked to speak with Detective Stanley Cooper. He was the lead detective in charge of the investigation back then.

"Detective Cooper retired a few years back. Can anyone else help you?"

"Would it be possible to get in touch with him?"

"I'm sorry we can't give out that information."

"What if I give you my name and telephone number and ask him to get in touch with me?"

"I can pass on the information to him but I can't guarantee he'll call you back."

"I understand." I gave the officer my name and telephone number and the reason I wanted to speak with Detective Cooper.

My next call was to Lisa Kane.

"Hello."

"Lisa, it's Tracey Marks. I decided to take your case though I have some questions before I start my investigation. Would you be able to come by my office at some point today?"

"I could be there around 12:00 if that's okay with you."

"Fine. I'll see you then."

I was working on some administrative paperwork when Lisa arrived.

"I'm happy to hear that you're going to be investigating my mother's death," she said as she sat down in my office.

"I went through most of the police reports. I made a list of the people the police questioned. I'd like you to take a look at it and see if there may have been anyone who is not on the list that they could have overlooked," I said, handing her the names I typed up.

While I waited for Lisa to look over the list, I offered

her a cup of coffee.

"Thank you," she said as I placed the coffee down in front of her.

"Offhand, I can't think of anyone else."

"Keep the list. Someone might occur to you later on. By the way, do you know what happened to the dress shop your mother owned?"

"Yes. The woman who managed it kept the store, though I believe she's no longer there."

"You had a housekeeper. Would you happen to know where she is now?"

"Celia was my nanny and she also took care of the house. She still comes in a few days a week at my father's place and one day a week at my place."

"Would you happen to have any addresses or telephone numbers for any of these people?"

"Yes, some of them. I'm not sure about my mother's friends but you can ask my father. He might be able to help you."

"Within the next day or so can you please send me that information. Also can you provide me with a photo of your mother? I'm going to email you my retainer letter. Just sign it and return it with the retainer. You can email me the other information I'm requesting."

As I was walking Lisa out, I said: "Does your father know you're planning on hiring a private investigator to look into your mother's death?"

"He does, though I don't think he's that happy about it."

"Why do you say that?"

"He says it's to protect me, but I'm not so sure that's his main reason."

I left it at that.

My phone rang just as I was about to leave the office

to pick up some lunch.

"Tracey Marks."

"Ms. Marks this is Stanley Cooper. You called the precinct asking for me."

"Yes. Thank you for returning my call. I was told that you're retired."

"I put in my twenty years and I'm doing some security part-time. How can I help you?"

"I was hired by Lisa Kane. She's the daughter of Rebecca Kane, who was murdered about twenty years ago. She wants me to investigate her mother's death. Do you remember the case?"

"Yes, it was one that I never solved, unfortunately."

"Could we meet?"

"I guess that would be alright. I get off at 5:00. There's a coffee shop on 26th and Lexington Avenue. I think it's called Stella's." He gave me a brief description of himself before we hung up.

I recognized Detective Cooper as he was heading in my direction. He was tall with a beer belly. He looked around sixty though he may have been younger. He had a ruddy complexion. I wondered if he drank.

"Detective Cooper," I said as he approached me. "Thanks so much for meeting with me."

The waitress seated us at a booth in the back. We both ordered coffee.

"What do you remember about the case?" I asked.

"At the time I was pretty sure it was the husband, but unfortunately he had an airtight alibi."

"Is it possible the person he was with that night was lying?"

"It is, but we couldn't prove otherwise."

"I've been looking through all the police reports and the crime scene photos. It looks like you did a very thorough job. If it wasn't a robbery and she was targeted, something was going on in her life that got her killed."

"I agree. We just couldn't make a case."

"Is it possible the coroner was off on the timeline of her death?"

"If he was, it still wasn't enough time for the husband to kill his wife."

"Do you remember if you thought anybody you interviewed may have been lying?"

"Funny you should ask. I thought the woman who managed the clothing store may have been hiding something."

"Why do you say that?"

"Just a hunch. Nothing concrete."

"Besides the husband, was there anyone else you were looking at for Rebecca Kane's murder?"

"Not really. There was circumstantial evidence against the husband. Unfortunately the smear of blood found at the crime scene wasn't enough for fingerprint analysis, and again he had an alibi that we couldn't shake."

"That's too bad. Anything else you can think of?"

"Not that I can recall at the moment. If I do, I'll let you know."

"Do you remember if you spoke with anyone at the restaurant where the husband was having his business meeting?"

"I'm sure we did. If I recall correctly, they left the restaurant and continued their meeting at a bar not far from there," Detective Cooper said.

"What about the insurance policy his wife took out two months before her death?"

"I asked the husband and he said he didn't even know about it at the time."

"That's interesting," I said. "And you believed him?"

"Again, we couldn't prove otherwise."

"What about the fact that he remarried only a year after his wife's death?"

"It did look suspicious. He may have been cheating on his wife but so do millions of other men. That in itself is not a crime. We just had no evidence against him. Can I ask why Ms. Kane is looking into her mother's death?"

"It appears she has started to remember a few things from that night."

I had no reason to tell him that Lisa might be imagining these details.

"I see. Well I can certainly understand why she would want to find out exactly what happened to her mother."

"One last question. If I remember correctly from your interviews, you checked out the bar where Mr. Kane and his client went for drinks. Did anyone remember seeing them?"

"I believe the bartender said they were very busy that night and couldn't identify if Mr. Kane was there or not. Since Mr. Kane told me he paid cash for the drinks, there was no way I could prove he wasn't at the bar."

When we were leaving the coffee shop I asked Detective Cooper to contact me if he thought of anything that would be helpful to the investigation.

It was after 6:00 by the time I finished talking with Detective Cooper. I took the train back to my apartment and stopped at the takeout Italian place near me and picked up a veal parmigiana sandwich for dinner.

When I got home I changed into my sweats and made a salad. I poured myself a glass of Merlot and sat down to eat. While I was eating I made a list of people I intended to speak with regarding Rebecca Kane's murder. I was really interested in speaking with Eric Jordan, Jason Kane's alibi for the night of the murder, as well as a long list of other people. I'm hoping most of them are still in the area. Twenty years is a long time.

As I was contemplating who to speak with first, my phone rang.

"Hey Jack. Guess who I met with today?"

"Can I get a hint?"

I can envision the smile on his face.

"Okay. It is someone regarding the case I'm working on."

"Well that really narrows it down."

"You give?"

"Absolutely."

"The detective that was investigating the death of my client's mother. He retired about five years ago and works security now."

"A lot of retired police people wind up getting security jobs. Brings in money on top of their pension."

"It must be nice to get a pension."

"So what did this detective have to say?"

"He suspected the husband but couldn't prove it. He had an airtight alibi."

"What was his alibi?"

"A client he was having dinner and drinks with."

"Maybe this client had a reason to lie."

"Apparently this person stuck to his story."

"Did the detective suspect anyone else?"

"Not that he mentioned, and no other suspect was mentioned in the police report. I made a list of people to contact. I think I'll start with the husband."

"I'm wondering if you might be better off waiting and talking to him after you've gathered more information. Maybe talk to other people that were questioned at the time."

"That's a good idea."

"Would you like to come up this weekend, or would you rather me come down?" Jack asked.

"I'll come up. Us city gals sometimes like the tranquility of the country life."

Jack laughed.

"I think you like the fact that I have a barbecue and a patio."

"Though that is very true, I also like the owner of the patio and barbecue."

"Good to know. I'll see you Friday. Sleep tight."

"Don't let the bed bugs bite."

CHAPTER 4

When I got up the following morning it was raining. I skipped my run and went into the office early, stopping only for my coffee and muffin.

I pulled out my list of people I wanted to contact. I thought I would try and locate Samantha Gerard, Rebecca Kane's assistant at the dress shop. I didn't have an address for Ms. Gerard and there wasn't one in the police file. Twenty years ago the dress shop was called La Robe of Madison Avenue.

I looked it up to see if it was still listed under the same name. To my surprise it was. I dialed the number.

"La Robe of Madison Avenue, can I help you?"

"I hope so. My name is Tracey Marks and I'm looking for a Ms. Samantha Gerard."

"Oh, Ms. Gerard no longer owns the store."

"Would you happen to know where she is working or where she is living?"

"I believe she is still in her apartment on the east side in the sixties. Is there anything I can do for you?"

"No. You've been very helpful. Thank you."

After hanging up I did a search for Samantha Gerard on one of my databases. I found an address and cell phone number for her.

I called Ms. Gerard but it went straight to voice mail. I left a short message without telling her the reason for my call.

As I was looking through my emails I saw Lisa Kane's email. When I opened it up there was a photo of her mother which I downloaded and printed out along with the addresses and telephone numbers for some of the people on the list I had given Lisa.

There were a few people I decided to wait before speaking with, including Jason Kane's alibi, Eric Jordan and Jason's law partner, Howard Stein.

My phone rang. "Tracey Marks."

"Ms. Marks this is Samantha Gerard returning your phone call."

"Yes, thank you. Ms. Gerard I'm investigating the death of Rebecca Kane. Her daughter has hired me to find out who murdered her mother."

There was silence on the other end.

"I'm sorry. You've taken me by surprise. It was such a terrible time for me. Rebecca and I were so close."

"Would it be possible to meet at some point today?"

"Why is this being dredged up now?"

"As I said, her daughter is interested in finding out who killed her mother."

"I guess we can meet. Can you come to my apartment, say around 11:30?"

Ms. Gerard provided me with her address before we hung up. I didn't bring up the fact I already had it.

I thought I would contact Lisa's grandmother next.

She picked up the phone right away.

"Mrs. Martin, my name is Tracey Marks and I was hired by your granddaughter to look into her mother's death."

"Lisa told me she was hiring a private investigator.

23

Maybe you can do a better job than the police. They investigated for months and never found out who killed my poor Rebecca."

"I would like to meet if you had some time this afternoon?"

"Yes, of course. Can you come by around 3:00? Do you have my address?"

"I do. I'll see you then."

I took the train to Ms. Gerard's apartment building on the Upper East Side. The doorman called up to Ms. Gerard and I was told to take the elevator to the ninth floor.

I rang the bell and was greeted by a woman probably in her fifties, very well dressed with short blond hair. It looked like she kept herself in very good shape.

"Thank you for seeing me. I know this can't be easy for you after all these years."

I followed Ms. Gerard into the living room. It was tastefully done with a mixture of antiques and modern furniture.

"Please sit," she said. "I was caught off guard by your telephone call."

"Why don't you tell me about your relationship with Rebecca."

"Well we met at school, the Fashion Institute and became good friends."

"How did the arrangement at the dress shop come about?"

"Rebecca wanted to open the shop but she didn't want the responsibility of running it by herself. She had just given birth to Lisa so I assumed she wanted to spend time with her daughter. I was very happy when she asked me to manage the shop."

"Did you both finance it?"

"Actually Rebecca financed the shop. She had family money and wasn't concerned that I couldn't afford to contribute. I would be the one taking on most of the responsibility of running the shop."

"What happened if Rebecca wanted to sell the store?"

"Rebecca and I had a verbal arrangement. If she was going to sell it, she would give me the opportunity to buy it before she offered it to anyone else."

"Why was there only a verbal arrangement?"

"I trusted Rebecca completely. We were good friends and I had no reason to believe Rebecca would renege on her word. When Rebecca died the landlord came to me and I entered into a new lease for the dress shop. By then I was ready to take on the financial responsibility."

"Do you remember if there were any problems in her marriage?"

I noticed a slight hesitation before she spoke.

"I guess now it doesn't matter if I tell you Rebecca was having an affair."

"Did you tell the police?" I said, knowing full well she never did. I was surprised she withheld such important information.

"I didn't. Rebecca confided in me. She was already dead so I didn't see any reason to smear her name."

"Did it occur to you that the person she was seeing could have killed her?"

"From what Rebecca told me about him, he would never have harmed her."

I didn't dignify that remark.

"Did she tell you his name?"

"No. I do know that he was married. Rebecca's husband was no saint either. She thought he was having an affair but had no proof."

"And you never mentioned any of this to the police?"

"No."

"Did you think it might have been her husband who killed her?"

"I thought it was a possibility but I was told that he had an alibi."

"Would you happen to remember if Rebecca was acting any differently before she died or mentioned she was worried about something?"

"Not that I can recall, but it was over twenty years ago."

"Do you recall the names of any friends of Mrs. Kane?"

"I'm sorry it was a long time ago."

"Here's my card. If you think of anything else please contact me."

Riding down in the elevator I couldn't help but wonder why she would lie to the police just to protect the reputation of someone who was dead.

CHAPTER 5

I headed back to my office and wrote up the conversation I had with Ms. Gerard. By the time I finished it was almost 1:30. I needed to pick up my car and drive up to Bronxville to speak with Lisa's grandmother.

Before leaving the office I went next door to my Cousin Alan, who owns an insurance company. The brownstone my office is located in has three suites on the main floor, the third one is now occupied by a criminal attorney.

"Hey Margaret, how are the rug rats?" That's my affectionate term for her two kids. Margaret is Alan's assistant, a gem of a woman.

"They're fine. Both still in one piece. He's all by his lonesome so go ahead in."

"Hey cousin."

"Glad you stopped by. How's everything?"

"Good. How's my little man?" Alan and his wife Patty had Michael almost fifteen months ago. Michael was a welcome surprise since Patty was almost forty-five when he came along.

"Getting into a lot of mischief around the house.

Why don't you come by next week for dinner? I know Michael misses you."

"I miss him too. Just let me know when. By the way I got an interesting case which I will tell you all about at dinner next week."

"Thanks for the tease. Be careful."

"Always."

The town of Bronxville is right off the Bronx River Parkway, a very narrow winding, two lane road. Fortunately I'm only on it for a minute before exiting the parkway.

I found Sylvia Martin's colonial style home without getting lost. It was enormous. It was painted white with green shutters. There were planter boxes below the upper and lower windows with red and purple flowers. There were several workers tending to the landscape.

I drove into the circular driveway and parked. I went up to the door, rang the bell and was greeted by someone I assumed was the housekeeper.

"Hello. I'm here to see Mrs. Martin."

"Yes, she's expecting you. Please come this way."

I have to say this is the first time I've ever been welcomed by the help. I found myself in a sitting room off of the kitchen. I was waiting to be offered tea and butter cookies like I see in the movies.

"Mrs. Martin will be right with you. Can I offer you tea or coffee?"

I smiled to myself.

"No, I'm fine thank you."

While I was waiting I looked around. The sitting room had floor-to-ceiling windows. It was furnished with a two-seated couch with white cushions and two upholstered chairs in a green and white checkered pattern. There was a colorful throw rug lying on the white stone floor. The sun was lighting up the room. But the main attraction was the spectacular swimming pool that I was looking at through the windows.

"Ms. Marks, thank you for coming."

I stood up to shake hands with Mrs. Martin. Though she was probably in her late seventies, she was still very beautiful and dressed impeccably. Her face looked baby smooth. I couldn't tell if she had any work done.

"Please sit down," she said. "Did Genevieve offer you anything to drink?"

"She did."

Mrs. Martin sat opposite me on one of the chairs.

"I have to say I was extremely disappointed when the police never found out who killed my daughter."

"Was there anyone that you suspected at the time?"

"Only her husband. I warned Rebecca not to marry him. But of course children never listen to their mothers. There was something about him that I didn't trust. Did you ever feel that way about someone?"

"I know what you mean."

"And when he married so soon after Rebecca died, I just knew he killed her."

"Did he inherit any money when she died?"

"My daughter had taken out a two million dollar life insurance policy and Jason was the beneficiary."

"Did you know about the policy?"

"No. He must have talked her into it."

"Did he get any other monies?"

"Just the townhouse that he's still living in. The bulk of her estate went to my granddaughter in a trust fund that he could never touch."

"Do you know if your daughter was upset about anything prior to her death?"

"I was sure she knew her husband was cheating on her, but there was no way she would confide in me because of how I felt about him."

I decided not to mention that her daughter may have been having an affair of her own.

"What can you tell me about your daughter's life?"

"Rebecca was a troubled child and I blame myself. My husband and I were busy growing the business and we neglected Rebecca and her brother David. Rebecca was a sensitive child and it seemed that she suffered the most because of our busy life. There were times when she was withdrawn."

"She seemed happy when she married Jason, and she did love her daughter. About a year after Lisa was born, Rebecca opened up a dress shop with another woman. She was very excited about it. Her degree was in fashion."

"Was her husband on board with her opening a dress shop?"

"If he wasn't, she never told me."

I didn't think I was going to find out anything more about her daughter's relationship with her husband. I decided to change the subject.

"When I was talking with Lisa she told me she spent a lot of time here when she was growing up. According to the police reports, Lisa couldn't remember anything from that night. Did she by any chance say anything to you, maybe something she recalled later on?"

"We never spoke about it."

"May I ask when your husband passed away?"

"It was a few years after our daughter's death. It hit him very hard and he had a heart problem prior to her death."

"What type of business do you own?"

"We import toys from China and sell to various companies in the toy industry."

"Who runs the business now?"

"When my husband died, my son David took it over. We have over thirty employees."

"I see. Would you happen to remember any of your daughter's friends, maybe someone she was very close to?"

"There was one friend Rebecca spent a lot of time with. Let me get back to you with her name."

"Thank you. I would appreciate that."

"I would be forever grateful to you if you found out who murdered my daughter."

"I will do my best ma'am."

Except for the fact that she couldn't stand her son-in-law, Mrs. Martin knew very little about her daughter's life.

My phone rang as I was getting into my car.

"Tracey Marks."

"Ms. Marks, my name is Jason Kane. I'm Lisa's father. I think we should talk."

"Unless you have some free time around 6:00 today, I can't meet with you until Monday afternoon."

"Can you come to my office around 6:15 pm?" he said.

I decided I wanted to make it a little inconvenient for Mr. Kane.

"The only way I can see you is at my office."

"Fine. Give me your address," he said in an annoyed tone.

Jason Kane hung up as soon as I gave him my address. He did not seem happy that I wasn't cooperating with him. Well too bad.

I found a parking spot two blocks from my office. I was starved and stopped at the deli to get a turkey sandwich and french fries.

I ate my sandwich and fries while I was writing up

the conversation I had with Mrs. Martin since I was expecting Mr. Kane in forty-five minutes. I was a little curious why he needed to speak with me right away.

I heard the door open, got up and walked into the reception area to meet Mr. Kane. He was sort of what I pictured in my head, attractive, tall and slim, with dark brown hair. He was dressed in a gray suit, white shirt and a gray and black silk tie. There was an arrogance about him.

"Glad to meet you Mr. Kane. Please take a seat," I said, as we walked into my office.

He got right to the point.

"My daughter told me she hired you to investigate the death of her mother."

"And your wife," I added.

He brushed my comment aside.

"I want you to stop."

"Why is that?"

"I don't want to see my daughter hurt. Bringing up the past will only make things worse for her."

"I'm not sure I know what you mean."

"Lisa has been in and out of therapy for most of her life. The death of her mother has taken more of a toll on her than I realized. I'm afraid digging up the past will only hurt her more."

"Mr. Kane, I don't see how finding out the truth can be worse than never knowing what happened to her mother unless that truth…"

"I don't think I like what you're implying," he said before I had a chance to finish.

"Whether you like it or not, Lisa hired me. If you have nothing to hide then it shouldn't be a problem. Now why don't we start over again. Tell me about your relationship with Rebecca?"

I can tell he wanted to resist but decided against it.

"I loved Rebecca but she wasn't easy to live with. I didn't realize when I married her that she was very needy. Everything had to center around her. Sometimes it became too much."

I got the feeling Mr. Kane didn't like the fact he wasn't in charge of this interview. That was okay by me.

"Tell me about the night she died."

"I was at a dinner meeting with a client. When we finished we walked to a nearby bar and had some drinks."

"What time did you meet at the restaurant?"

"I think around 8:00 pm. We stayed till approximately 10:00 and then left. We were at the bar for about two hours. When I got home I found Rebecca and called the police."

"How can you be so sure of the times?"

"I have a habit of checking my watch every so often."

I guess that could be true but I was a skeptic by nature.

"Do you normally take clients out for dinner and drinks?"

"Sometimes. It's good business practice."

"How did you get home?"

"I walked. I was having trouble getting a cab."

"How far did you have to walk?"

"Maybe ten blocks. I'm not quite sure."

"I was told you were the beneficiary of your wife's insurance policy."

"Yes, two million dollars. I didn't know about the policy until after her death."

"So you never discussed it?"

"We had talked about it, but that's all. Her will left me the brownstone. Everything else went to our daughter in a trust fund that Lisa couldn't touch until she was twenty-one, but I had no idea she took out the policy and how much it was for."

"Were you having an affair at the time of your wife's death?"

"No," he said a little too quickly.

"How did you meet your present wife?"

"A friend introduced us."

"Can you give me your friend's name?"

"It was so long ago. I don't remember the person's name."

"If someone introduced me to the person I wound up marrying, I think I would always remember their name."

"Well guys are different."

"Look, I don't know if you're hiding anything or not, but if you're not guilty it would be better just to cooperate for your daughter's sake."

"Are we finished?" he said.

"One last question. Can you think of anyone who wanted your wife dead?"

"No I can't."

"Oh, by the way, did you know your wife was having an affair?"

"Who told you that?" he said in an angry voice.

"Why does that matter?"

"I was just curious. People shouldn't spread rumors around."

"So what you're telling me is that you didn't know."

"That's what I'm telling you."

"Here's my card. If you remember your friend's name or anything else that may be important, please contact me. Also, would you happen to know the names of any friends of your late wife? If so I would like their names."

"If I remember I'll let you know," he said.

Why did I get the feeling he wasn't going to be contacting me, at least with what I just asked him for.

Mr. Kane got up and walked quickly to the door before I had a chance to see him out.

As soon as he left I wrote up our conversation, not wanting to forget anything. I knew he was lying; I just didn't know if it was about an affair or his wife's death, or both.

CHAPTER 6

I was at the courthouse the following morning by 9:00 am. Assistant District Attorney Joseph Dean greeted me and brought me into the courtroom where the trial was going to take place. Mr. Dean was maybe two inches taller than me, medium build with a confidence about him.

"I've never been inside a courtroom except when I watch Law and Order episodes on TV."

He laughed.

"So you're probably a pro at this," he said smiling.

"I know enough to give just the facts, nothing else."

"The attorney will try and trip you up. That's his job. Don't let it rattle you. Take your time before you answer his questions."

We spent the next couple of hours going over the questions Mr. Dean would be asking me, and what he thought the attorney for Randy Stewart would be asking. By the time we finished it was almost noon.

When I left Mr. Dean I was less anxious about testifying. He thought I would probably be called to testify the following Wednesday.

Leaving the courthouse I called Lisa's nanny/housekeeper. Lisa had mentioned that Friday was

Celia's day off.

"Hello."

"Is this Celia Ramirez?"

"Yes."

"My name is Tracey Marks. Lisa Kane hired me to find out what happened to her mother. I'd like to talk with you this afternoon if you're available?"

"It was so long ago and the police had questioned me."

"Lisa said I should speak with you."

"Well if Ms. Lisa wants me to, I will. I live in Washington Heights."

"Is 2:00 good?"

"That will be fine."

Celia provided me with her address before hanging up. I took the train back to my apartment, threw some clothes in my backpack for my weekend with Jack, got my car and drove to Ms. Ramirez's place.

I found a spot three blocks from Celia's apartment building. It was a walk up. Her apartment was on the third floor. I rang the buzzer and Celia buzzed me in.

A short woman with light brown skin, on the chunky side, in her sixties, opened the door.

"Come in, please."

Her apartment was small but very neat. We sat in the kitchen. Though it probably hadn't been updated in years, it felt very homey.

"Thank you for seeing me on such short notice."

"I called Ms. Lisa and she said it was okay to talk with you."

"What country are you from?" I asked. Though she's probably been in this country for many years she still spoke with a heavy accent.

"I'm from Honduras. I came here almost thirty years ago. The Kane's were kind enough to hire me, first to look after their house and then to look after Ms. Lisa when she was born."

"You must be very devoted to them."

"Oh yes. They sponsored me so I could become a citizen."

"When did you become a citizen?"

"That was fifteen years ago. It was one of the happiest days of my life when they swore me in," she said proudly.

"You mentioned the police questioned you at the time of Mrs. Kane's death?"

"Yes, it was horrible what happened to her. I was so sad and I felt terrible for Mr. Kane and Ms. Lisa, poor child. Every night I would rock her to sleep and she would cry in my arms. My heart broke for her."

"Do you remember what the police asked you?"

"They wanted to know how Mr. Kane and his wife got along."

"And what did you tell them?"

Mrs. Ramirez was silent and turned her head away from me.

"What's the matter?" I said.

"I did something bad, but I was afraid if I said anything Mr. Kane wouldn't sponsor me."

"Well don't worry about that now. I just want you to tell me the truth. You're not in any trouble."

"I don't want Ms. Lisa to know."

"She won't. Actually would you mind making me a cup of coffee?" I thought if she was busy doing something it would put her more at ease.

"That's a good idea. I'll join you."

I waited patiently as she finished making the coffee.

"Can I call you Celia?"

"Please. I told the police that Mr. and Mrs. Kane were very much in love," as she looked down towards her coffee cup.

"But that wasn't true?"

"No. They fought a lot."

"What did they fight about?"

"Mr. Kane didn't like that his wife was controlling the money. He said she was keeping tabs on how much he was spending."

"Was he spending a lot of money?"

"He would buy whatever he wanted even though he was just starting out as a lawyer. He thought that since they were married, her money was his."

"Do you know if he was having an affair?"

"I wasn't sure but I know Mrs. Kane accused him."

"Did you think Mr. Kane killed his wife?"

"I know Mr. Kane had many faults, but I don't think he would ever hurt the missus. And the police said he had an alibi so he couldn't have killed her, right?"

I let that question slide.

"What was Mrs. Kane's relationship like with her daughter?"

"I know she loved Lisa but it was hard for Mrs. Kane to show her love. I don't know why but I felt bad for Mrs. Kane."

"What did you think of Mr. Kane?"

"He was always kind to me. He told me jokes and made me laugh."

"Do you remember how soon after Mrs. Kane's death he started to see his wife Danielle?"

"I don't remember but it wasn't that long after Mrs. Kane died."

"What do you think of Danielle?"

"She has always been good to me and was loving towards Ms. Lisa."

"Well I appreciate your time."

"I always felt very bad that I lied to the police but I

was so afraid at the time. I hope you can understand."

"If you think of anything else, here's my card."

Part of me was angry at Mrs. Ramirez for lying, but I can understand what a terrible position she was in at the time. I'm not sure I wouldn't have done exactly the same.

On the drive up to Jack's I remembered what Susie had said to me; there are reasons why people lie. Both Rebecca's assistant and Mrs. Ramirez both lied to the police for reasons they believed were justified. How many more people lied about that night?

CHAPTER 7

I made it to Jack's place in record time. He was pulling up to his house just as I got there. I walked over to him and he wrapped his 6'3" solid frame around me. When he let me go I looked into his large dark brown eyes and felt weak in the knees. Jack has that effect on me.

"Is this a special occasion I'm not aware of?" Jack asked.

"Oh you mean the slacks."

"That would be correct."

"My meeting with the assistant district attorney. I didn't want him to think his star witness was a slob."

"I'm sure he gave you some suggestions about what to wear when you testify."

"He did."

"Are you hungry?" Jack asked.

"I am, but not for food at the moment," I said looking into Jack's eyes.

Jack took my hand and led me upstairs to the bedroom. By the time we finished, I was really hungry.

"What's for dinner?" I said as I was nestled against Jack's shoulder.

"Baby lamb chops."

"You're the best boyfriend ever."

"The saying goes, 'the way to a man's heart is through his stomach.' I think you might be the only woman to defy that mold."

An hour later we were sitting on the patio enjoying our dinner and sipping on a glass of Cabernet Sauvignon. The September evening air was cool.

"So how did it go with the attorney?"

"I think it went okay. We spent at least two hours going over questions and my answers. I'm as ready as I'm going to be."

"It could be stressful. The most important thing to remember is to answer truthfully. You won't get into any trouble if you do."

Changing the subject I said: "I was going to wait to interview the husband but he contacted me and practically demanded to meet with me."

"What did you tell him?"

"I told him when and where. He wasn't happy about it but I left him no choice. When we met he stuck to his story that he didn't know his wife took out an insurance policy on her life and that he was the beneficiary."

"Do you believe him?"

"I'm reserving judgment."

I told Jack about the conversations I had with the nanny and Mrs. Kane's manager at the dress shop, and how they both lied to the police.

"Are you going to interview the current Mrs. Kane?"

"I am, and I won't give her any advance warning."

The rest of the evening we sat enjoying our wine and the quiet surroundings.

In the morning Jack and I fixed a scrumptious

breakfast of pancakes topped off with fresh strawberries and local maple syrup. I poured us coffee and we sat down to eat at a rectangular antique wooden table in Jack's kitchen.

"I was thinking once the case you're working on is over, we could go on a vacation," Jack said.

"Really," I said surprised.

"You don't sound too excited. Is something wrong?"

"I just never thought about it much, but I'd be willing to entertain the idea."

"If you could think of one place, where would it be?"

"I always wanted to go to the Grand Canyon. My parents were planning a family vacation there the spring before my father died. Have you ever been?"

"No, but I'd love to go. I'll look into it. When was the last time you took a vacation?"

"I'm embarrassed to say, probably never. You don't know what you're getting yourself into hanging around with me."

"I'll take my chances," he chuckled.

"Have you traveled much?" I asked.

"After college I backpacked through Europe with a friend. Since then I've been mostly exploring places in the states and Canada."

"Well if you plan it I'll show up as long as it's not around the time Susie is supposed to give birth."

"I'll keep that in mind. In the meantime, I thought since it's such a beautiful day we could take a drive to the Berkshire Botanical Gardens and walk around."

"I didn't realize I was hanging out with such a cultured person."

"There are a few things you don't know about me just like I'm sure there may be one or two things I don't know about you."

"Well now I'm intrigued. Please enlighten me."

"If you reciprocate."

"You got a deal."

"My given name is Jackson."

"Hmm. I like Jackson. Would you prefer I call you by that name?"

"I think we'll stick to Jack."

"Did your mom call you Jackson?"

"Only when she was mad at me. Then she would recite my full name, Jackson Michael Baldwin, and not in that tone. Now what's your secret?"

"Well it's not really a secret, it just never came up. When my father was a boy he used to read Dick Tracey comic books. When I was born he said he took one look at me and the rest is history."

"Did you become a private investigator because of your dad?"

"That never crossed my mind but maybe I did," I said, thinking to myself why it never occurred to me.

After cleaning up we drove to the botanical gardens in Stockbridge. As Jack gave me a guided tour I was amazed at all the different variations of flowers. Walking around I was very impressed that Jack was able to point out the names of the flowers.

"How do you know so much?"

"They give courses here. I've gone to a few."

"I can't even tell you the name of the flowers I buy at the market. Well maybe I know tulips but not much beyond that."

"I have a book at home about different variations of flowers and plants I can give you."

"You're too kind."

It was nearly 4:00 by the time we left the gardens. On the way back to Jack's we stopped at an upscale market in the town of Pittsfield called Guido's Fresh

Market place. They had everything from fresh meat and seafood to organic produce. They even sold crepes to order.

It was fun going through the different aisles and looking at all the interesting foods they had. We bought fresh trout for dinner and chicken for tomorrow night. At the deli counter Jack introduced me to several types of olives. First we selected two different kinds of cheeses and then I chose olives that were not too salty. At the produce section we bought several kinds of lettuces and some vegetables. By the time we finished our cart was filled to the brim and I was getting hungry.

When I woke up Sunday morning rain was hitting hard against the bedroom windows. Jack opened up his eyes.

"Hey beautiful."

"That kind of language can get you in trouble."

"I hope so," he said smiling broadly.

"Well if you insist."

The next hour or so we sweated up the sheets.

"So what do people in this part of the country do when it rains?" I said lying next to Jack.

"Well, first we get all the townspeople together, and then we choose one to sacrifice to the rain gods. It's a gruesome sight. I hope it stops raining before there's a knock on the door."

"Very funny. I guess we could sweat up the sheets some more," I said as Jack gently kissed the scar on my arm.

After a late breakfast, Jack suggested playing Chess.

"Okay but you play at your own risk," I said.

"What is that supposed to mean?" he said suppressing a smile.

"I'm very competitive."

"I think I figured that one out about a year ago," Jack said.

"Smarty pants."

"Too much talking, let's play."

Two hours later we each had won a game.

"I have to say for a girl, you're pretty good," Jack said with a grin.

"You're jealous that I beat you."

"I admit it. Where did you learn to play?" Jack asked.

"In college. I played with the boys." My emphasis on boys. "I was probably a better chess player than a student. You know there's some male chauvinism lurking in you."

"You got me."

I hadn't played chess in a while and forgot how much I loved the game. The afternoon went by as we were engrossed in our chess moves. We came out tied.

"I believe the rain has stopped. I guess we're safe from the village people. I think I'll set up the barbecue and roast the chicken," Jack said.

"I'll wipe off the table and chairs outside and break out the wine and cheese."

After dinner we watched an old movie and conked out by 10:30.

In the morning Jack and I hugged right before he opened the door to my car. The drive back was easy. No traffic. I was sitting in my office by 11:00. My phone rang.

"Hey, how was your weekend?" Susie said.

"Very relaxing. Jack didn't know what hit him when I beat him at chess."

"So you never told him you're a closet chess player."

"Of course not. How about dinner later? I want to pick your brain about the case."

"I'll meet you at Marco's at 6:00."

I was very interested in talking with Eric Jordan, Jason Kane's alibi for the night his wife was killed. Twenty years ago Mr. Jordan had his own manufacturing business according to what I read in the files. I googled him. There was a listing for an Eric Jordan who had an office in midtown. It looks like he manufactures something kids play with in the bathtub. I decided I would just show up. If he was lying about that night I didn't want to give him advance notice to contact Jason Kane, assuming they still were in communication.

CHAPTER 8

I took an Uber instead of my car. His office was off of Sixth Avenue on 52nd Street. I walked into the building and signed in.

I took the elevator to the twentieth floor and walked through the halls until I found his office.

"Hello," I said to the receptionist.

"Can I help you?"

"I'd like to see Mr. Jordan. I don't have an appointment, but tell him I'm a friend of Jason Kane." A little white lie never hurt anyone.

Two minutes later I was seated in Mr. Jordan's office. Mr. Jordan was maybe in his late fifties, though he looked older. He carried more than forty extra pounds on his medium size frame. He was probably nice looking in his younger days but the extra weight was not flattering to his face.

"So you said you're a friend of Jason's. I haven't seen Jason in many years. How is he?"

"Actually he's more like an acquaintance."

"I don't understand."

"I was hired by Mr. Kane's daughter to look into the death of his late wife Rebecca."

Mr. Jordan's brows shot up. I'm sure I completely surprised him.

"Well how can I help you?"

"I was told you were Jason's alibi for the night of his wife's death."

There was a slight shift in his seat.

"It was a long time ago. I don't remember much of that evening. Like I mentioned, it was a long time ago."

I believe a sign that he was nervous was the fact that he had repeated himself.

"I would think you would remember that night. Why don't you tell me what you do recall?"

"I was a client. Jason took me to dinner and then we left and went to a bar near the restaurant and had a few drinks."

"Did you leave the bar together?"

"From my recollection we did."

"Do you remember what time that was?"

"Maybe around midnight."

"How did Jason get home?"

"I can't recall, maybe he walked or took a cab."

"But you're not sure?"

"Like I said, it was a long time ago. I think we're done here. Good luck."

Riding down the elevator I knew Mr. Jordan was lying about something. I needed to go back over the detective's notes to find out if he asked Eric Jordan how Jason Kane got home that night.

Susie and I arrived at Marco's at the same time and we were seated right away. People in New York tend to go out for dinner later so it's pretty easy to get a table around 6:00.

"Can I get you ladies anything to drink?" the waiter asked.

"A Cabernet Sauvignon. My friend here is on the wagon."

He gave us a peculiar look and left.

"So now I'm an alcoholic," Susie said, trying to suppress a smile.

"That's more fun, at least for me, than saying you're pregnant."

"Oh what the hell," Susie said. "How's Jack?"

"He asked me if I wanted to take a vacation after the case is over."

"The dirty bastard," Susie said with a straight face. "What did you tell him?"

"I said I would. I didn't want him to think I was a complete nut job, though I did mention that vacations are not normally on my agenda."

"Well that's true."

"I thought if I was coerced I would like to see the Grand Canyon. Maybe we can go as a foursome."

"Only if it's before I have the baby. Maybe Jack would rather have you all to himself."

"I'll ask him."

"Are you ready to order?" the waiter asked as he placed my drink down on the table.

"I'll have the spaghetti bolognese with a house salad," I said.

"And I'll have the same, thank you."

"So what's going on with the case?"

I filled Susie in on everything, including the interviews I had conducted so far and some of what I read in the police reports.

"You were right. Everyone I interviewed so far lied to the police."

"Well we know why the nanny and Rebecca Kane's manager lied. If Mr. Kane knew about his wife's affair that might give him a motive for murder. We're still not sure if the client Mr. Kane was dining with that night lied. That might be something to explore. You also need to talk to more people that knew the Kane's," Susie said.

"How am I going to find out about the man she was having an affair with?"

"You have to keep talking to people related to the case. Somebody knew."

"Why? Maybe she kept it private."

"That's possible, but in my experience as a divorce attorney, people normally tell someone. It's just human nature."

"Let's hope so," I said. "By the way, Mr. Dean, the assistant district attorney, thinks I might be testifying at Randy Stewart's trial on Wednesday. I'll certainly be glad when it's over."

"Would you like me to be there for moral support?"

"Can you get off from work?"

"It won't be a problem."

"That would be great."

"Well I guess I should take myself and this little person inside of me home. Let me know about Wednesday."

"Will do."

The next morning I got up early and went for a run. I hadn't exercised in a few days and I was feeling guilty. Instead of doing my usual three mile loop, I pushed myself to do an extra loop. By the time I finished I was out of breath and sweating.

After showering and scarfing down my Cheerios, I picked up my surprise muffin and coffee before going into the office.

As I was taking a bite of my cranberry walnut muffin, I went through the police reports again to see what Eric Jordan told the detective about that night he was with

Jason Kane. It looked like Mr. Jordan told Detective Cooper that Kane walked home. I wondered why he wasn't sure when he spoke with me. Maybe twenty years clouds your mind. From what the maître d' said that night, they left together but he didn't see in what direction they went.

I decided to take a chance and see if Danielle Kane was home. I took a cab over to her apartment building. When I spoke to the doorman he told me she wasn't in.

"That's strange I thought we were suppose to meet here at 11:00." Another white lie. "You wouldn't happen to know when she's expected back?"

"I'm sorry I don't."

"Well thank you."

Then I remembered that Lisa said her stepmother usually goes to the gym in the mornings.

"You know," I said to the doorman, "it slipped my mind that Danielle said she was going to the gym this morning."

"Yes, the Equinox. It's two blocks from here."

"Thanks."

I wondered if there was a hell would I'd be going there for telling all my white lies.

I walked over to the gym and waited outside for Danielle Kane. I knew what she looked like from a photo I saw at Lisa's apartment.

After waiting for about thirty minutes, I spotted her coming out of the gym.

"Mrs. Kane, my name is Tracey Marks. Your stepdaughter Lisa asked me to speak with you."

"Oh, sorry, you kind of startled me. My mind must have been somewhere else."

"Do you have time for a cup of coffee?"

"Is this about Rebecca's death because I really don't

know anything about it."

"I need to ask you some questions anyway. It won't take long."

"There's a café right around the corner. Why don't we go sit there," she said.

Danielle was very pretty with straight blond hair down to her shoulders, beautiful skin, and a perfect nose. She was a little taller than me and definitely in good shape. She looked like someone who watched everything she ate.

We found a table and we each ordered a coffee. I ordered a bacon and egg sandwich on a croissant. In my defense, it was just about lunchtime.

"Lisa has me worried, dredging up that horrible night her mother died."

"It seems that she might be remembering some things that she suppressed at the time of her mother's death," I said.

"Does that really happen?" she said looking up at me.

"I'm not a psychologist but I've heard it's possible. Did you know Lisa's mother?" I asked her.

"Not really. We actually went to the same high school though I was a year behind her."

That's interesting, I thought to myself.

"May I ask how you met your husband?"

"An acquaintance of his introduced us."

"So you must have known this person also."

I could see the wheels turning in her head.

"At the time, but it's been so long ago I can't recall the name."

I let that slide.

"How long after Rebecca Kane died did you meet Jason?"

"I don't know exactly, a few months maybe."

Danielle seemed a little ill at ease.

"Weren't you afraid that it was too soon after his wife's death to start a relationship?"

"I didn't think about it at the time."

"Do you know if Mr. Kane knew about his wife's affair?"

I could see the nervous look on her face.

"I have no idea. If he did, he never discussed it with me. I'm sorry to cut this short but I have another appointment."

She took a few dollars out of her bag, tossed the money on the table and left.

I sat there eating my bacon and egg croissant not knowing if Danielle Kane was in the dark about her husband or she was somehow involved.

CHAPTER 9

Back at my office I took out my cork board and 5x7 index cards and wrote down each person's name I interviewed so far on an index card. I tacked Rebecca Kane's card in the middle with her husband as my primary suspect. The others I tacked up to the side of the board, not exactly sure where they fit yet in the investigation.

I heard a shout hello from the reception area. I got up and saw Gary Roberts, the criminal attorney now occupying the third suite.

"Sorry for barging in. I didn't have your number handy. Are you in the middle of something?"

"A case I'm working on. Actually a cold case."

"Sounds intriguing. Let me know if I can help in any way."

"Thanks. Did you need something?" I said.

"I'm trying to locate someone that was a witness in a robbery. Would you be able to help me out?"

"What do you have on the person?"

"A name of course, a last known address and a partial birth date. The guy who usually does my locate searches had some sort of family emergency."

"Here's my card with my number and email address. Send me the information. When do you need it by and don't tell me yesterday?"

"How about today?" he said sheepishly.

"I'll see what I could do. Tomorrow I have to appear in court to testify on a case I was involved in and I don't know how long it will take."

"I'll send you the information in about five minutes. Thanks."

As he was leaving my phone rang.

"Ms. Marks this is Mr. Dean. You're on for tomorrow. Please be at the courthouse by 9:00 am. You're up first. Remember just answer the questions without elaborating or filling in any silences."

"Got it. See you tomorrow."

I picked up the phone and dialed Susie.

"Hey, I'm on for tomorrow at 9:00 am," I said when Susie answered.

"I'll be there. You'll be great."

When I hung up, I was feeling a little anxious. To alleviate some of my anxiety I delved into looking for this guy that Gary Roberts wanted me to find.

Two hours later and after several database searches and phone calls, I was able to locate him at a house in Bayside, New York. I sent Roberts my findings and packed up for the day.

On the way home I stopped at the fish market for some shrimp. My next stop was to the Corner Sweet Shoppe. When my anxiety level goes up, so does my consumption of ice cream.

"Hi Mr. Hayes, how are you?"

"Tracey, so nice to see you. I'm fine. How are you?"

"I'm testifying at a trial tomorrow so I am in desperate need of ice cream. Hopefully it will soothe my nerves."

"Well I'll be sure to pack extra ice cream in the container. Do you want your usual?"

"Yeah, though put more of the pistachio in."

"Good luck tomorrow." Mr. Hayes handed me the paper bag with my ice cream.

"Thanks. I'll see you soon."

I was just finishing up dinner when Jack called.

"What are you doing?" he said.

"I'm finishing up a glass of wine from dinner and trying to relax. I have to testify first thing tomorrow morning."

"And what's your excuse other times?"

"I have none. You might be dating a closet alcoholic. Just warning you."

"The sacrifices I make for a good lay."

"I'm testifying tomorrow. The good news is Susie is going to be in the peanut gallery."

"I'm glad she can make it. Maybe look at her when you're giving your answers."

"Good suggestion. I spoke with the current Mrs. Kane. She, of course, claims she does not remember who introduced her to her husband, and had no idea whether Jason knew anything about an affair his first wife was having. I'm thinking Jason Kane and the current Mrs. Kane were having their own affair before his wife died. That's why they both can't recall who introduced them."

"Even if they were having an affair that doesn't mean he killed his wife."

"I know. I'm wondering if Eric Jordan covered for him."

"What would be his motive to lie for Jason?"

"I don't know. That's what I have to find out."

"Good luck tomorrow. You'll be great."

At 9:15 the following morning I was seated on the witness stand. I was dressed in a navy suit and a white silk blouse. I was wearing a pair of black high heels.

Joseph Dean, the assistant district attorney, took me through my testimony leading up to my encounter with the defendant, Randy Stewart, and his attempt on my life. The recording from my phone was played for the jurors revealing that Randy Stewart killed Stephanie Harris and raped Maddie Jensen when he was in high school. His career running for Congress would have been over if Stephanie had gone to the papers exposing that she witnessed Randy Stewart raping Maddie. It may have been hard to prove but he couldn't take that chance.

When the attorney for Randy Stewart was questioning me, I focused on keeping calm. As expected, Stewart's lawyer tried to trip me up but he couldn't budge me on my account of what happened. I made sure I answered the questions without going into any long explanations. It was over before I knew it. Leaving the witness stand I let out a sigh of relief. Susie gave me a thumbs up and followed me out of the courtroom.

"You were fantastic," Susie said as she hugged me. "Stewart's attorney must have been so frustrated with you."

"Ms. Marks," I heard from behind me.

I turned around and saw Mrs. Jensen, Maddie's mother. She looked so much older than the last time I saw her.

She walked towards me.

"I just wanted to tell you how thankful I am that you caught Maddie's rapist," she said as tears slowly ran down her cheeks. "I don't think I can forgive myself for not paying closer attention to Maddie before she killed herself."

"I think Maddie knew you loved her and she would want you to forgive yourself."

"Thank you for those kind words."

I watched Mrs. Jensen as she slowly walked away.

CHAPTER 10

As Susie and I were leaving the courthouse, I couldn't help but feel angry all over again for the pain Randy Stewart caused to so many people.

"Well it's times like this I wish I could drink," Susie said as we walked outside and down the courthouse steps.

"If I decided to have a baby, I might have to go the surrogate route since I don't know if I could give up wine for nine months."

"Now why didn't I think of that," Susie said.

"It's almost lunchtime. Why don't we get a bite to eat. My treat," I said.

"Okay, as long as I'm back in the office by 2:00 for a consultation with a new client."

"Another couple who's headed for divorce. Another reason to stay single," I said.

"Stop your whining and let's find a place to eat."

We found a coffee shop near the courthouse.

"I'm so relieved it's over," I said, after we were seated at a booth. "I may have looked calm but I had to keep my hands on my knees to stop them from shaking."

"Well I'm sure no one knew."

"Do you think they'll find him guilty?"

"Without a doubt. I hope he gets the maximum for killing Stephanie Harris and for the attempt on your life. He'll be going away for a long time," Susie said.

"I hope so. I still can't get the image of Mrs. Jensen out of my head. She's suffered so much."

"I hope she finds some peace in knowing Maddie's rapist is going to jail," Susie said.

"Somehow I doubt it."

Susie and I shared a cab to our respective offices.

Before going into my office I opened the door to Cousin Alan's Insurance firm.

"Hi Margaret."

"Well don't you look nice. What's the special occasion?"

"I had to testify in court today."

"How did it go?"

"I think it went okay. Hopefully the jury thought so too."

"Go ahead in."

"I thought I heard your voice," Alan said.

"You look great. I can't remember the last time I saw you in a skirt."

"Well don't get used to it."

"I have the perfect wine to celebrate your courthouse appearance. Patty is cooking up something special."

"Anytime Patty cooks, it's special," I said.

"We have a surprise for you tonight."

"Really, I can't wait. How's my little man?"

"We told him you were coming over and he's very excited."

"It's nice to have a man excited to see me, even if he can't pronounce my name."

"We'll see you around 6:00."

As I was walking across to my office, I saw Mr. Roberts.

"Hi Tracey. I'm glad I bumped into you. I wanted to thank you for locating the witness. I didn't get your invoice."

"No charge. You never know when I might need your services. The rate I'm going, anything's possible."

"Well maybe I can repay you with lunch sometime."

"Sure."

I walked into my office with the intention of going over everything I learned so far about Rebecca Kane's murder, when my phone rang.

"Hello."

"Ms. Marks, this is Sylvia Martin. I found my daughter's high school yearbook. Her best friend was Jacqueline Woods. I have no idea what happened to her."

"Where did Rebecca go to high school?"

"She went to Bronxville High School. Unfortunately Jacqueline and I didn't keep in touch after Rebecca died."

"Thank you for calling me."

"If you find out anything please let me know," Mrs. Martin said.

I hung up and immediately googled Jacqueline Woods. If she married google might not help me. There was one Jacqueline Woods who was living in Connecticut. I found a telephone number and called.

"Hello."

Hi, my name is Tracey Marks and I'm trying to get in touch with a Jacqueline Woods who went to Bronxville High School in New York."

"I'm sorry you have the wrong person. I went to high school in Connecticut."

"Well thank you."

A bummer. Now what? If Jacqueline's parents are still living they might be in the Bronxville area.

I went into one of my databases and found a Charlie and Ethel Woods listed. They were in their early seventies, which would be about the right age range.

I dialed their number, crossing my fingers I had the right family.

"Hello," a woman's voice answered.

"Is this Ethel Woods?"

"Yes, can I help you?"

"I'm trying to get in touch with an Ethel Woods who has a daughter by the name of Jacqueline."

"Yes."

"My name is Tracey Marks. I wonder if you might remember a friend of your daughter's named Rebecca who died about twenty years ago."

"Of course, my Jacqueline and Rebecca were inseparable. She was devastated when Rebecca died. What is this about?"

"I was hired by Rebecca's daughter Lisa to find out who killed her mother."

"Oh my, little Lisa. She was adorable."

"I'm interviewing everyone that knew Rebecca and I'd like to speak with Jacqueline."

"She lives in North Salem. It's about fifty minutes north of Bronxville."

"Would it be possible to have her telephone number?"

"Of course." Mrs. Woods provided me with her daughter's telephone number before we hung up.

I quickly dialed. It went straight to voice mail and I left a message.

By this time it was after 4:00. I packed it in and walked the fifteen blocks to my apartment building. I forgot how uncomfortable it is to walk in heels. I was practically limping by the time I stopped at the Hungarian bakery near me and bought Michael the animal cookies he loves and an apple strudel for the adults.

I was able to get in a quick run before going to Alan and Patty's house. After showering I slipped on my jeans and boots, a welcome relief from a skirt and high heels.

I took an Uber over to Alan's house, a brownstone he inherited from his grandfather, who at one time had a seat on the New York Stock Exchange.

When Patty opened the door I saw Michael's chubby face light up as he reached out his hands to me.

"My little man," I said taking him from Patty right after I dropped the bakery bag on the table in the foyer.

"Tracey," Michael said.

"I don't believe it. You can finally say my name," giving Michael a big hug.

"We practiced for the last two days. It's not an easy name to pronounce," Patty said.

"That's the best present ever," I said.

"Why don't we put Michael in his high chair and I'll fill up his bottle with milk to have with the elephant cookie," Patty said.

Just as I was adjusting Michael in his chair, my phone beeped. I nodded to Patty that I had to take the call.

"Hello."

"Ms. Marks, this is Jackie Donovan. My mother mentioned you might call. I was just thinking of Rebecca the other day. I have a horse farm and when we were growing up Rebecca and I used spend time at the horse stables near where we lived."

"Can we meet tomorrow? I can come up to your place," I said.

"I'd love to. Can you come around noon?"

Jacqueline gave me directions to her farm before hanging up.

"Is everything alright?" Patty asked when I hung up the phone.

"Yes, just someone I'm looking forward to interviewing."

I heard Alan's voice from a distance. He was coming down the stairs looking fresh from a shower.

"Hey, did you get your surprise yet?" Alan said to me.

"I did, the best surprise ever."

"Well now we can't get Michael to stop saying your name. Just a little annoying."

"You poor thing," I said to Alan. "The utter torment hearing my name over and over."

"Well if you two have stopped your bickering back and forth, why don't you take Michael into the living room and have some fun while Alan helps me in the kitchen."

"Come on little man; it's fun time."

Michael's new game was playing horsey. Guess who was the horse? We played for about fifteen minutes till I was tired, and then we went up to his room and took out his building blocks. Michael and I were on the fast track to building a skyscraper when Alan announced it was bedtime. He could have been talking to me since I was exhausted from playing with Michael.

I gave Michael a big hug and kiss and went downstairs.

"Something smells amazing," I said to Patty as I walked into the kitchen.

"I made a fish stew. Why don't you open up the wine and then we're all set to eat."

"So I want to hear all about your new case," Patty

said as we were seated at the dining room table.

Patty is an attorney and works as an advocate for children's rights.

"It's a twenty-two year old cold case."

I went on to tell them about the investigation and what I've learned so far.

"This stew is unbelievable," I said. "Are you sure you never went to cooking school?"

"I love cooking for my boys, but watching you eat is something to behold. Are you ready for seconds?"

"Absolutely," I said helping myself.

"I find it so curious that people lie to the police," Alan said.

"I don't. I think the only reason more people don't lie is that they're afraid they'll get caught," Patty said.

"You may be right," I said. "Any thoughts on the case?"

"What would have been the husband's motive to kill his wife?" Patty asked.

"Well maybe he found out about the insurance policy. And if he was having an affair that might be a motive," I said.

"I think it would be more of a motive if he thought his wife was going to divorce him and cancel the life insurance policy," Alan said.

"That's a thought. Any other suspects besides the husband?" I asked.

"Her lover. Maybe he wanted more and she rejected him. From what you told us, it appears it was more of a crime of passion than premeditated," Patty answered.

"I'm hoping this friend of hers might know the name of the person she was having the affair with," I said.

"And if she doesn't, what then?" Alan said.

"I have no idea."

I was tempted to have another helping of the fish

stew but decided against it. I needed room for the apple strudel.

CHAPTER 11

When I woke up the next morning instead of going into the office I decided to leave from my apartment to see Jacqueline Donovan in North Salem.

I was on the road by 10:30. My GPS took me on I-684 to Exit 7 and from there I followed the directions. The countryside was beautiful. It appeared the houses I passed were on several acres of land. I saw the entrance to Jacqueline's horse farm. I drove in on a gravel road till I came to the main farm house and parked. I saw Jacqueline coming towards my car. She was dressed in what looked like riding pants and boots. Her blond hair was hidden under a cap.

"Hello," I said as she approached me.

"Hi Tracey, nice to meet you. Why don't we go inside. I made us some lunch."

"You must have a sixth sense. Eating is probably one of my favorite pastimes."

I walked into a huge kitchen with a fireplace. The kitchen was remodeled all in white but it still had the feel of a farm kitchen, pots and pans hanging from a wrought iron structure, a long wooden antique table and lights hanging down from the ceiling. I loved it.

"This kitchen is amazing," I said.

"I like it. When I bought the place it needed a complete update, everything from new wiring to central heat and air. Take a seat and please call me Jackie."

The table was set with bright colored floral patterned dishes. Jackie had laid out a feast of tuna fish, smoked salmon, sliced tomatoes, cream cheese, fresh fruit and bagels.

"Can I get you a glass of wine?"

"I probably shouldn't since I am officially on duty."

"Well I won't tell if you don't."

"What the heck. Exceptions should always be made."

After pouring us each a glass of white wine, Jackie sat down.

"Please tell me what's going on?" Jackie said.

"Rebecca's daughter Lisa contacted me. She wanted me to look into her mother's death."

"Wow, after all these years. I was angry that no one paid for killing Rebecca. Lisa must be around twenty-five now."

"She is."

"How is she?" Jackie asked me.

"She's okay. She has her own company designing women's sleep wear."

"I remember Lisa. She was the cutest kid, beautiful thick red hair and green eyes just like her mother. It's hard remembering Rebecca without getting emotional. She was my soul mate."

"Are you married?" I asked.

"I was but it didn't work out. My horses keep me pretty busy."

"I'd like to ask you some questions about Rebecca and her husband Jason."

"Go ahead."

"Tell me about Rebecca?"

"Rebecca was shy, maybe even naïve in some ways. She didn't see herself as other people did. She could have used her beauty to her advantage but it never occurred to her. Yes, her family was very wealthy, yet Rebecca was not a snob and didn't flaunt her good fortune. She wanted me to open up the dress shop with her but that wasn't where my passion lay. I always wanted to raise horses. She opened the dress shop with a friend she met in college. It seemed like it worked out pretty well since Rebecca didn't have to go into the store every day and it gave her time to spend with Lisa."

"What about her husband, were there any problems?"

"I never thought she should have married him, but Jason was charming and Rebecca fell for him."

"What didn't you like about him?"

"I thought he was marrying Rebecca for her money. I got the feeling he wanted the finer things in life and saw Rebecca as a way to obtain them. As a lawyer starting out he didn't have any money. Rebecca didn't seem to care, but I thought she had blinders on when it came to him. Eventually she saw through Jason and she was going to divorce him."

"Did she know he was having an affair?"

"She knew."

"I didn't see your name on the list of people the police interviewed."

"That's because they never interviewed me."

"Why was that?"

"I'm not sure. After Rebecca's funeral I left town for a few weeks. They may have tried contacting me when I was away, but by the time I got back, I never heard from them."

"I was told Rebecca was having an affair. Is that

true?"

I noticed Jackie had an odd expression on her face.

"She was. It turned out it was someone working for her father."

"Did she tell you his name?"

"She never told me."

"Did she tell you why she was having an affair?"

"Not in so many words. I think at some point in her marriage she was feeling neglected and reached out to someone to fill a void in her life. I don't think it would have lasted with this person."

"I got the feeling from talking to a few people, Rebecca had some emotional problems."

"Despite everything she had in her life, I always thought there was a sadness that I can't explain," Jackie said to me.

"I know it was a very long time ago, but can you remember if Rebecca was acting strangely or seemed different in any way a few weeks before her death?"

"To tell you the truth I hadn't spoken to Rebecca for several weeks before she died. We had a fight. It was my fault. The man she was having the affair with was married. I told Rebecca how I felt about her seeing a married man and she was angry at me. I may have come on too strong. It still haunts me that she died before we had a chance to make up."

I didn't know what to say to Jackie. That must be hard to swallow.

"Oh, just one more question. Was Rebecca close to her brother David?"

"They were, but I believe Rebecca might have had some sort of falling out with her brother. She didn't elaborate and I didn't ask."

"Well thank you. You've been a big help."

"I'd love to show you around if you have some time.

I'll introduce you to my prize possession."

I couldn't refuse. There was something very infectious about Jackie. She reminded me of Susie.

After meeting Sanford, her prize horse, she gave me a tour of the stables and asked if I would like to go riding with her. I declined. Being that high up on an animal is not my idea of a good time.

On the trip back I had time to think about the conversation I had with Jackie. I wondered if Martin Imports, the company now run by David Martin, has any employee records going back about twenty years. Is it possible the person who had an affair with Rebecca could still be working for the company? I was hoping twenty years ago there were a lot fewer people employed by the Martin's. I decided not to mention to Mrs. Martin the real reason I was interested in speaking to past employees.

As soon as I got into my office, I called Mrs. Martin.

"Hello."

"Mrs. Martin it's Tracey Marks."

"Did you speak with Jacqueline?"

"Yes." I didn't want to divulge any information that Jackie told me. "I was wondering if you had a list of employees from twenty years ago?"

"Those records would be in storage. If you contact my son David, he could help you."

"Thank you. By the way were David and Rebecca close?"

"Very close. David was inconsolable when Rebecca died."

Before hanging up Mrs. Martin provided me with her son's cell phone number. I thought it was interesting that Mrs. Martin didn't mention any problems between her two children. Maybe she had no idea that Rebecca and David were having any issues, that or she didn't want to say.

CHAPTER 12

As soon as I hung up from Mrs. Martin I called David Martin.

"Mr. Martin my name is Tracey Marks. Your mother gave me your telephone number."

"She mentioned that Lisa had hired a private investigator to look into my sister's death. How can I help you?"

"Your mother told me you have employee records going back over twenty years in storage. I'd like to take a look at the records of the employees that were working for the company at the time of Rebecca's death."

"May I ask why?"

"Sure. I'm talking to everyone in Rebecca's life and that might include people from your company. I won't know until I talk to them."

"I see. We have a storage facility in Yonkers. I can meet you there tomorrow morning, say around 8:00 am?"

"That would be great. Also, are there any employees that were working back then that are still employed with you now?"

"Maybe. I'll have to check with Human Resources and let you know."

"I would appreciate that."

Mr. Martin gave me the location of the storage unit before hanging up.

Depending how many employees there were twenty years ago, I might be in for a tedious and time consuming process. Hopefully I can eliminate some of the employees if their marital status was listed on their employment application.

I was looking forward to meeting David Martin. I had questions for him but thought it would be better to wait and speak with him at his home or at his office. When I looked at my watch it was after 5:00. I called it quits and left for the day.

At home I changed and went for a run. On the way back I picked up some crispy chicken with walnuts and broccoli and a shrimp roll.

After a quick shower and throwing on a pair of sweats and a tee shirt, I sat down to eat. I turned on the TV in my kitchen, flicking through the channels till I found something besides the news. There was an old rerun of the show Friends that I watched while skillfully eating my Chinese food with chopsticks. My favorite character on the show was Joey. He played a character that wasn't too bright but made me laugh.

As I was cleaning up my phone rang. It was Jack.

"Am I interrupting anything?" Jack asked.

"Nope, just finished. Guess where I was today? Never mind, I'll put you out of your misery and just tell you. I was at an actual horse farm. I met Rebecca Kane's best friend, Jackie. She has this amazing farm house."

"What did she have to say?"

"Well she wasn't a fan of Rebecca's husband. She thought he was a gold digger and only married Rebecca for her money. Jackie was sure Rebecca was having an affair with someone who worked for her father, and according to Jackie, Rebecca was planning to divorce him but she never got the chance. I'm meeting with David Martin tomorrow morning at their storage facility to get the employment records of everyone who worked for Martin Imports going back twenty years. It would be a miracle if this person still worked there."

"See if any of them left soon after Rebecca died."

"That's a thought. Guess what the biggest news of the week is?"

"I give."

"Michael can officially pronounce my name."

"I don't know if I'm happier for him or you."

"Me silly."

"Of course. My mistake."

"So what's happening there?"

"Well nothing as exciting as your news. It seems everyone I speak to can pronounce my name."

"Well if my name was Jack that would probably have been Michael's first word."

"I don't doubt it. My boss is taking on a partner. We're getting swamped here."

"Does that mean you'll have to work more hours?"

"I discussed it with Mr. Morgan and they're going to hire another investigator. They realize it would be too much work for me."

"When is this all happening?"

"Next week. Actually I know an investigator who's interested in coming aboard. If they like him it means they don't have to go through the whole process of advertising and interviewing people."

"I hope this guy works out so you're not overloaded. How do you feel about the practice getting bigger?"

"At first I wasn't too keen on it. I kind of like that it's just my boss plus Charlene, but the more I thought about it, there would be someone else to share the load. Charlene's the one who will have more work since she's like super human, taking care of the office and making sure things run smoothly."

"What are you up to this weekend?" I asked Jack.

"A group of us are getting together for my friend Kevin's birthday. We'll probably go to a few bars. Nothing too exciting."

"Isn't Kevin married?"

"Yeah, but it's kind of a tradition with the guys."

"I'm dating a real red neck."

"Are you jealous?"

I could picture the smile on Jack's face.

"Do I even have to dignify that with a remark?"

"I'll miss you," Jack said.

"Now that gets you brownie points."

"I'll be sure to collect."

"Have fun with the boys."

"Love you."

"Me too."

I drove up to Yonkers in the morning and met with David Martin. He was a good looking man. Instead of red hair and green eyes like his sister Rebecca, David had dark brown hair, almost black with brown eyes and an olive complexion. The only similarity between his sister and him was their straight nose.

"Mr. Martin, thank you for meeting me," I said shaking his hand.

I didn't get the feeling he was happy to see me. Maybe I was interrupting his day. It seemed liked the only member of the family that was glad I was investigating Rebecca's death besides Lisa was Rebecca's mother.

We walked into the storage unit and started sifting

through the boxes until we found the one that was marked employment records.

"Would you mind if I took the box back with me since it would be too difficult to go through it here?"

"I wouldn't normally let the records leave this room but if it's important to my niece, go ahead, just please make sure they don't get lost and you return them sometime next week. You can drop it off at our midtown offices."

"Thank you. By the way where is your warehouse located? If there are any employees around from twenty years ago, I might want to talk with them."

"It's in Patterson, New Jersey."

David gave me his business card with the address of the warehouse.

"Did you by chance find out who was working back then that is still in your employment?"

"I haven't had the chance yet, but I'll email you the information as soon as I get it."

"Thank you. Maybe we can meet at your office or home sometime next week. I'd like to ask you some questions."

"Sure, when you return the employment records we can figure out a time to talk."

We walked out in silence. I thanked him again for meeting me.

CHAPTER 13

I carried the box to my car and headed back to my office. Thinking back to what Jackie said, I was curious what David and Rebecca had a falling out over.

My phone rang as I was getting into my car.

"Hey Susie, what's going on?"

"Just getting ready to go into our weekly staff meeting. Listen, Mark has to work part of the weekend. Are you interested in doing anything?"

"Sure, let's talk in the morning."

I was happy to find a parking spot only a block away from the office since I didn't want to schlep the box of records too far and didn't want to leave it in the car.

I dropped the box in my office and went out to get something to eat since I was starved. When I got back I switched on the coffee maker and started going through the records. Well there was one good thing, the employment application listed marital status but no box to check for children.

I filled up my mug with coffee and took a bite out of my bacon and egg sandwich. Unfortunately there were numerous employment records and I had to go through each one.

Two hours later I sifted out all the employees that were hired after Rebecca's death. That eliminated quite a few. There were ten employees left that were working for the company prior to Rebecca's death, three of which worked in the Manhattan office and the others worked at the warehouse in New Jersey.

Of the ten only five were married at the time they were hired. These records did not include anyone that is still working for the company since Rebecca's death. Hopefully I'll have that list by the end of the day. I'm betting it's a very short list. I noted there were two people who had left not long after Rebecca was killed, one worked in the warehouse and the other in the Manhattan office.

For the next several hours I attempted to track down former employees. By the time I was ready to call it quits, I had found current addresses for four of them.

Before shutting off my computer I noticed an email from David Martin. When I opened it up there was only one person on it. He was working at their corporate offices prior to Rebecca's death and is still employed with the company.

I shut all the lights, grabbed my backpack and the box with the records and walked to my car. I think my brain had expired with the last person on the list I was trying to locate. I couldn't wait to veg out and do nothing except eat and have a glass of wine.

It was after 7:00 pm when I opened my apartment door. I took a long shower and got into my sleeping attire, boxer shorts and a tee shirt. I poured myself a glass of wine and heated up the leftover Chinese food. I was feeling lazy and decided to eat in the bedroom while reading the latest Harlen Coben mystery book. By 10:00 my eyes were closing. I turned off the light and fell fast asleep.

The next thing I heard was the sound of buzzing. At first I didn't know where it was coming from until I realized it was my phone.

"Hello," I said still groggy.

"I woke you. It's 9:00 am. Should I call you back?"

"No, I'm up now."

"Who sleeps till 9:00?" Susie said.

"Well apparently not you. Aren't expectant mothers supposed to get a lot of sleep?"

"Is that some sort of rule?"

"I don't know. Maybe I read it somewhere," I said.

"Anyway, there's a walking tour of Central Park at 1:00 pm. I thought it might be interesting. If you get your ass out of bed we can meet and get a late breakfast before the tour starts."

"No problem. I'll meet you in front of your building at 10:30."

"See you soon."

I dragged myself out of bed and went directly to the coffee maker. While the coffee was dripping I showered and dressed. My morning coffee is one of the pleasures I look forward to especially on the weekends.

I brought my mug filled with coffee into the living room enjoying the quiet when my phone rang. I didn't recognize the number.

"Hello."

"Ms. Marks, it's Lisa."

She sounded scared.

"What's the matter Lisa?"

"I think I remembered something."

"What is it?"

"When I got up this morning I had a memory of something that happened that night. I'm afraid the more I remember the more I think it might be my dad and I don't want it to be him."

"Tell me what it is?"

"I must have drifted back to sleep after I went looking for my mother. I remember my father coming into my room and kissing me on my forehead. I didn't open my eyes. I heard him walking out of my room and then I heard him whispering on the phone."

"He could have been calling 911."

"I guess, but why would he be whispering?"

"Do you recall how long after the call the police arrived?"

"I don't know."

"When you first came to me you told me you couldn't imagine your father had anything to do with your mother's death."

"I know what I said but I wasn't sure, and the thought of him killing my mother is too horrible to imagine."

"It's much too early in the investigation to know who was responsible for your mother's death. Try not to worry and we'll talk after the weekend."

When we hung up I thought about what Lisa said. It's possible Lisa was asleep when her father called 911, and I still wasn't convinced that Lisa wasn't imagining what she saw or what she heard.

CHAPTER 14

Susie was waiting in front of her building when I arrived. We walked over to Sarabeth's on 59th Street and Central Park South, where we sat at an outside table.

When the waitress came over I ordered the Lemon and Ricotta pancakes with a side of crispy bacon, and Susie ordered a spinach and goat cheese omelet.

"So what names do you have in mind for the baby?" I asked Susie after the waitress left.

"I'm leaning towards Sophie and if it's a boy Sam."

"They're great names. Are those Mark's picks also?"

"Well it might be a toss-up between Sophie and Jordan. We both like Sam."

"All three are winners," I said.

The waitress came and set down our plates and refilled our coffee cups.

While we were eating I filled Susie in on everything I found out since we last spoke.

"What does your gut say? Do you think these images are real or imagined, and why do you think they are coming up now?" Susie said.

"That's a good question. I'm just not sure. She was

really young at the time. It could be as simple as her subconscious telling her what she has wanted to know ever since she was little, who killed her mother. I'm not sure the reason matters anymore. Someone killed Rebecca Kane and her killer is still out there."

"As far as finding the man Rebecca was having an affair with, I would start with Jack's suggestion and look into anyone who left the company not long after Rebecca died. I also doubt she would be having an affair with someone working in the warehouse. She would more likely meet this person at their offices in Manhattan."

"Well that narrows it down to three people, though I wouldn't rule out someone working in the warehouse, but I'll start with corporate."

"By the way, because I'm going to be this baby's godmother does that mean I'm the one in charge of throwing you a baby shower? Cause you know how that might work out."

"Heaven forbid. I wouldn't want to traumatize you," Susie chuckled. "I think one of my other friends could handle it."

"That's a load off my mind," I said biting into a piece of crispy bacon.

"Though you do have to show up."

"I guess that's the least I can do."

It was a beautiful September day for a walk in Central Park. I'm not sure why we needed to have a guided tour but I had left it up to Susie. I thought I could endure two hours of listening to someone tell me about Central Park though my attention span is probably not that long.

"I'm ready to sit somewhere," Susie said after the tour.

"Why don't we go to the Boat House. I can have a glass of wine and I'm sure there's something you can drink."

"I can always have a Shirley Temple."

"There you go, always looking on the bright side."

We made our way over to the Boat House which is in Central Park. We had to wait a few minutes before a table was available. Once we were seated I ordered a glass of Sauvignon Blanc and Susie had a lemonade.

"Shall we get the cheese plate?" I said.

"Yes, I think this baby is going to take after you when it comes to food. I can't seem to stop eating."

"Yet you refuse to gain weight."

When the waitress came back with our drinks we ordered the Cheese Plate.

"Jack's boss, Mr. Morgan is taking in a partner. They're hiring another investigator to help with the additional workload they're expecting."

"How does Jack feel about that?"

"At first he wasn't too happy about it but he's come around. I think having another investigator to share the work with might relieve some of the pressure he sometimes feels. And he'd have someone to bounce ideas off of."

"He might have more free time to spend with you," Susie said.

"Is that what you heard out of everything I said?"

"I like Jack and I don't want you to screw things up."

"Why would I? I like him too."

"Your track record sucks."

"Don't use such foul language in front of the baby," I said.

Susie laughed.

"Stop worrying about us, we're doing fine."

I dived right into the cheese and crackers when it

came. When I looked up, Susie's face was completely white.

"What is it? What's the matter?" hearing the alarm in my voice.

"Somethings not right. Oh my god, I'm bleeding," Susie said looking down. "I need to get to the hospital," she said panic stricken.

"It's going to be alright," I said as I called for an Uber.

"Can you stand?"

"The pain in my back is unbearable."

"Hang on to me."

The Uber was waiting for us when we got to the street.

Take us to Lenox Hill Hospital," I said as soon as we climbed into the Uber.

"I'm scared Tracey. I don't want to lose the baby."

"I know sweetie," holding her close.

"Mark. You have to call Mark and tell him to meet us at the hospital. Oh, it hurts."

"What's going on back there? Is everything alright?"

"Just drive quickly!"

I was so afraid that Susie would lose the baby, I could hear my heart pounding in my chest. I just kept holding her.

When we got to the emergency room they took Susie right away.

"Can I be with her?" I asked.

"The doctor is going to examine her. As soon as he's finished, I'll let you know."

As I turned around I saw Mark rush in.

"The Doctor is examining her now."

"What happened?"

"I don't know. Everything was fine and then she just turned white and said she was bleeding," the tears streaming down my face.

Mark started pacing, making me more anxious. Fifteen minutes later Mark went back to see her. He came out and told me they were admitting her. They were taking her to the third floor, Room 312. We both went upstairs. Mark went in and I waited outside the room. About five minutes later, Mark came out. He was crying.

"The doctor told me they were taking her to the operating room to do a D&C. She lost the baby. She doesn't know yet."

I didn't know what to say to him. Everything I could think of sounding like a cliché, 'it'll be fine', 'you could try again.'

While Susie was having the procedure, Mark and I sat in the waiting room, neither of us talking, consumed with our own thoughts. I didn't realize until this happened how much Susie wanted this baby. I mean I knew she was happy about the baby, but what I saw on her face was devastation. Susie was always the strong one, comforting me through all my near death experiences and was there for me when my mother died. Nothing terrible ever happened to Susie that she needed me to be a rock for her. I wasn't sure I could handle it.

It seemed like we were sitting there for an eternity when the doctor finally came out.

"Your wife is fine. She's perfectly healthy."

"Can she still have children?" Mark asked nervously.

"Yes. There is no physical reason why she can't. You can wait for her in her room. She should be there in about thirty minutes."

"Do you want me to be there with you when she wakes up?" I asked Mark.

"Yes. I don't think I can face her alone."

When they wheeled Susie into the room she saw our

faces and knew.

"I lost the baby, didn't I?"

Mark leaned over and tried to comfort Susie.

"I'm so sorry sweetie," I said.

At that point the doctor came in and spoke to Susie, telling her this is not uncommon, and she is perfectly fine and could have other children. Just what someone wants to hear after they've lost their baby. The doctor said she could go home in the morning and to rest for a few days.

I thought Mark should be alone with Susie. I leaned over and kissed her and told her how much I loved her. I gave Mark a hug and said I would come by tomorrow and left.

I didn't step into my apartment until after 10:00 pm. I was emotionally and physically exhausted. I changed and got into bed. I called Jack but it went straight to voicemail. I left a message for him to call me. When I hung up I remembered he was out with some friends celebrating a birthday.

I turned off the light and fell fast asleep.

A buzzing sound woke me up. I fumbled around for my phone.

"Hello."

"I woke you. I'm sorry. When I finally got your message, it sounded urgent. What's the matter?"

"What time is it?"

"It's 12:30 am."

"Susie lost the baby."

CHAPTER 15

I went on to tell Jack what happened.

"I'm sorry babe."

"I feel so bad for her. I've never seen Susie like this ever."

"Well she never had such a loss."

"I know but to me she was invincible. I was the one that always needed her."

"Now it's your turn to be there for her."

"What if I can't?"

"I know how much you love her. It might not be perfect but it will be your way."

"Thanks. How was the birthday party?"

"Just a bunch of guys getting drunk."

"I need to go back to sleep. I'll talk to you tomorrow," I said.

"I love you."

"Right back at you."

Even though I was exhausted, I didn't sleep well after Jack called. I was up by 6:00 am and turned on the coffee maker. In the meantime I showered. I thought I would call Mark around 10:00. I was hoping Susie would want some company for a little while.

I had planned on doing some work on the case today, though now I wasn't sure if I was up for it with Susie not far from my thoughts. Maybe work might take my mind off of the baby.

I took out the three employment records of the men who worked in the corporate offices of Martin Industries over twenty years ago, two of which left not long after Rebecca's death, Simon Mack and Daniel Tucker, and the third, Leonard Woods, was still employed with the company. All three were married when they were first hired.

I was able to locate Daniel Tucker. He was living in the town of Pound Ridge in Westchester County. From the report I pulled up on him it appeared he was divorced about five years ago and remarried. I was able to obtain a cell phone number for Mr. Tucker.

I was having a hard time finding Simon Mack even though I had his date of birth from his employment record. The address listed for him twenty years ago was also a dead end. What now? Could he be dead? I searched on the death index but there was no match with his name and date of birth. It was odd that he wasn't coming up on any of my databases. Where can you be Simon Mack? According to his employment application he was married back then. His wife's name was Amelia Mack. Well at least Amelia is not that common of a first name, but is her last name still Mack?

I did a search for Amelia Mack inputting the same address I had for her husband from over twenty years ago. Bingo. I got a hit on her. She was living right in Manhattan. From what I can tell from the report she is no longer married to Simon. I found a telephone number for Amelia. I was debating when to call her. Sunday's were not always the best day for a warm reception from a stranger, and especially from one that wants information about her ex-husband.

When I looked at the time, I dialed Mark.

"Hi Tracey. We just got home from the hospital."

"Is she up for visitors?"

"You're not a visitor. Why don't you come over around 2:00. I think she's tired right now. She'll probably sleep for a while."

"Okay, can I bring you anything?"

"No. See you later."

Mark sounded depressed. I knew there wasn't anything I could do to make things better. It was frustrating.

At the moment there was nothing else to take care of involving the case. I thought I would call Leonard Woods in the morning, the person who was still employed at Martin Industries from twenty years ago, and make an appointment to see him away from the office tomorrow. I decided to wait to question the people who worked at the warehouse.

I fixed myself a tuna fish sandwich and called Jack.

"Hi, I was just about to call you. How are you doing?"

"Trying to keep busy to avoid feeling terrible about Susie and Mark. I'm going over to their apartment around 2:00. Mark said Susie was tired and resting. He sounded tired himself."

"I can only imagine."

"Do you regret not having a child?" I asked Jack.

"Up to this point I chose not to have a baby but you never know what the future will bring."

I decided not to go there at the moment.

"I'm afraid to say the wrong thing to Susie."

"I don't think Susie is expecting you to say anything.

She just wants you to be there."

"I went through the employment records," I said to Jack, wanting to change the subject. "There were three in corporate that might be possibilities, two of which left after Rebecca's death and the third who is still employed at the company."

"That'll keep you busy for a while."

"Susie thinks we should spend more time together," I blurted out.

My remark took me by surprise. Too late to take it back.

"What do you think?" Jack said.

"I forgot I'm talking to Sigmund Freud here."

"You still didn't answer my question."

"I haven't had much time to think about it since other things got in the way."

"If you're asking for my opinion, I think she's right," Jack said.

"Got it. Well, nice chatting. Have stuff to do."

"You started it and you will finish it. Love you."

"Ditto."

As I was walking to Susie's, I wondered why I mentioned to Jack what Susie had said. Though I've never been in therapy, I know it wasn't a slip of the tongue. I wanted to know how Jack felt about the relationship. Did he really want more?

The doorman at Susie's building let me in and I went straight up.

When Mark opened the door we hugged. He said to go into the bedroom. Susie looked so small lying in bed. I didn't say anything. I just laid down next to her and held her.

"You know what I remember," I said. "When we were, I think seventeen, we walked past this pet store and stopped to look at this adorable, tiny dog that was in the window. Your eyes lit up. 'Let's go inside,' you said to me. Even though your mother would never allow you to have a dog, you didn't care. You decided to take him home with you. You thought if your mother saw the dog, she would change her mind, but your mother wouldn't budge no matter how much you pleaded. Your father was on your side but that didn't matter. You yelled and screamed and refused to take the dog back. The next day when we were at school your mother returned the dog to the pet store. I remember you came to my house and were inconsolable."

"It took you a long time to get over the dog even though you had it for only a day. Eventually as time went on it got better," I said.

Susie and I laid together without speaking for a while.

"Jack called. He's a man with few words. I like that about him," Susie said.

"Me too."

Mark came into the room. I thought it was my cue to leave.

I kissed Susie goodbye and told her I loved her. She was drifting off.

On my way back I stopped at my neighborhood bookstore and browsed around. My next stop was to the Corner Sweet Shoppe. Unfortunately, Sunday is Mr. Hayes' day off. I bought my usual, a pint of pistachio with some dark chocolate added in.

At the fish store I picked up two pieces of lemon sole. I thought I would try something different for dinner.

CHAPTER 16

I woke up to a gloomy Monday morning. It was raining and the temperature outside was only fifty degrees.

I got ready to go to the gym, stuck a change of clothes in my backpack and headed out. At the gym I did my usual routine, weights, the treadmill and finished up with abdominal exercises.

On the way to the office I stopped at the Coffee Pot. Anna greeted me.

"Hi Anna,"

"You don't sound like your usual self. Everything alright?"

"Yeah, I'm fine. Just a gloomy day."

"Believe it or not we get more customers on rainy days. Can't figure it out."

"That is weird. See ya tomorrow."

When I got in I went straight to Cousin Alan's office. Margaret wasn't at her desk. Since the door was open it was a good indication Alan was in. I knocked.

"Come in. I'm glad you stopped by. How's the case going?"

"Susie lost the baby."

"She must be devastated."

"She is. I was with her when it happened. They couldn't save the baby."

"How is Mark?"

"The same. I think once Susie became pregnant, he was looking forward to the baby just as much as she was."

"Do you think they'll keep trying?"

"I hope so. How's my little man?"

"A terror, but an adorable terror. You know you're always welcome to see him. You don't have to stand on ceremony."

"Thanks. I appreciate that. I'm going back to my wigwam to fight crime."

"Alright. Always here for you."

I took out my computer and my notes from the employment records. I opened up my bag from the Coffee Pot and took out my surprise cranberry/blueberry muffin and coffee.

First order of business was to call Daniel Tucker. He answered right away.

"Hello."

I guess I wasn't expecting him to pick up so quickly. He kind of caught me by surprise.

"Mr. Tucker my name is Tracey Marks. I'm sorry to bother you but I'm looking into the death of Rebecca Kane."

"Wow. I hadn't heard that name in many years. Are the police reopening her case?"

"Actually her daughter Lisa hired me."

"I remember little Lisa. Sometimes Rebecca would bring her into the office when Rebecca came to see her father. Sweet kid. How can I help you?"

"I would like to meet and ask you some questions about Rebecca."

"I don't know if I would be much help, but I'd be glad to answer any questions you have."

"That would be great. What is your schedule like?" I asked him.

"Can you come by my office say around 1:00 today?"

"I'll see you then." Mr. Tucker worked for a title insurance company in midtown.

My next call was to Leonard Woods. It went straight to voicemail. I left a message.

I still needed to locate Simon Mack. That meant calling his ex-wife Amelia. I picked up the phone, not sure what I was going to say to her when she answered.

"Hello."

"Yes, I'm trying to get in touch with Amelia Mack."

"You have the right person. What is this about?"

"My name is Tracey Marks. Do you remember a woman by the name of Rebecca Kane."

"Yes, she died a long time ago. I believe she was murdered."

"The case has been reopened and I'm investigating her death."

"Well I didn't know her. My husband at the time worked for her father."

"I'm talking to everyone who knew Rebecca back then. Would you happen to know where Simon is living?"

"I can't help you. I haven't seen or heard from Simon in many years. The last thing I heard about him he was living in Pennsylvania. When we were together Simon started drinking heavily. That's one of the reasons I divorced him."

"Do you know why he left Martin Industries?"

"It was fairly sudden. If I recall he said he was having some disagreements with his boss."

"You didn't believe him?"

"It was hard to know with Simon."

"Would you happen to have any idea where in Pennsylvania he might be living?"

"The town of Morrisville rings a bell, but I can't say for sure. I think he had relatives living in that area."

"Do you recall what he was doing at Martin Industries?"

"He was part of the sales team."

"Thank you for your time."

As I was hanging up, my phone rang.

"Tracey Marks."

"Ms. Marks this is Lennie Woods returning your call."

"I don't know if David Martin mentioned to you that I'm looking into the death of his sister Rebecca. I'm talking to everyone who knew her, and I was informed that you worked for the company prior to her death."

"I see."

"I'd rather we talk away from the office if that's okay with you."

"There's a bar right across the street from the office. Why don't we meet there, say at 6:30 this evening."

"Sure. I'll see you then."

I did a search for a Simon Mack in Morrisville, Pennsylvania. The address listed was from more than a year ago. When I checked the address, it came up to some sort of rehabilitation center. I jotted down the number.

When I called I was told they couldn't give me any information. Now what? If I went there would I have any chance of learning any more about Simon Mack?

It was almost 12:30. I needed to get to Daniel Tucker's office pronto. I called for an Uber and locked up on my way out.

I made it to Tucker's office with two minutes to

spare. The receptionist was very nice and told me to go right in.

"Ms. Marks, glad to meet you. Please sit down."

Mr. Tucker was probably around sixty. He did not look like he aged well. The sagging skin on his face reminded me of a specific kind of dog whose jowls hang down.

"As I mentioned to you I'm talking to everyone who knew Rebecca Kane."

"I didn't really know her all that well. Every once in a while she would stop in to see her father. The only other times I saw Rebecca was at the Christmas parties the Martin's hosted."

"May I ask why you left the company?"

"I didn't see any future for me there and I wanted to be independent."

"What can you tell me about the family?"

"What do you want to know?"

"Were you aware of any problems in Rebecca's relationship with her husband?"

"Well I guess after all this time there's no reason to hold back. I didn't think the two of them got along. Whenever I was in her presence I sensed a loneliness about her. There was nothing specific."

"Do you know if either of them were having an affair?"

"If they were, I didn't know anything about it."

"I was told there was some friction between Rebecca and her brother."

"Again, if there was, I wasn't aware of it."

"Do you have any idea who would have wanted Rebecca dead?"

"I wish I can help you. The police couldn't find her killer. Maybe you'll have better luck."

"I believe the police thought her husband killed her

but there just wasn't any physical evidence against him. Do you think it could have been her husband?" I said

"I prefer not to speculate."

"Here's my card. If you think of anything, please call me."

"I will."

Leaving his office I didn't believe Mr. Tucker was Rebecca's lover. I have been wrong before but I don't think this time.

On the way back into the office I picked up a salad for lunch. Every once in a while I try to have something healthy. It's always a battle.

As I was digging into my salad I picked up the phone and called Susie. Mark answered.

"Hi Tracey."

"How are you managing?"

"I'm trying to work from home but it's difficult."

"How's my girl doing?"

"She's putting up a brave front for me but she hasn't strayed too far from the bedroom. You might have better luck coaxing her to get out of bed and to maybe take a shower."

"I have to meet someone at 6:30. Why don't I stop by around 4:30 and see what I could do? Do you guys have food?"

"We're alright."

"Okay, see you soon."

I spent the next two hours writing up all my interviews so far and sending my report to Lisa.

I hurried out of the office and stopped at the bakery on the way to Susie's and picked up her favorite dessert, a lemon tart. Since I thought Mark liked tiramisu, I got him a piece and got myself a chocolate cupcake.

Mark answered the door and gave me a big hug. We went into the kitchen where I placed the lemon tart and the cupcake on a plate and went into the bedroom. I propped myself up on the bed next to Susie.

"Remember when I was sick," I said. "I think I was just getting over the flu and hadn't been in school for a few days. You came by with these amazing looking cupcakes. I stuffed one of them in my mouth, swallowing it practically whole. You were hysterical laughing even when I proceeded to throw up. I can still hear the sound of your laughter."

"I remember. I think you hid the rest of them so your mother wouldn't find them."

"That's right. I forget I did that. I smell coffee brewing. Are you game?"

Susie nodded her head slowly up and down. A small victory.

As we were having coffee and Susie was picking at the lemon tart, I told her what was happening with the case and what I learned so far. I wasn't expecting any feedback but I wanted us to feel some normalcy.

"I'm not sure how Mark feels, but you might need to spray one of those fresheners you see on TV if you don't manage to get out of bed and take a shower soon."

"I'll take it into consideration."

I kissed Susie goodbye and gave Mark a hug as I left.

When I arrived at the bar Leonard Woods was sitting at a table in the back. I recognized him from his description. He stood up as he saw me approaching. Mr. Woods was approximately 6'4" and solidly built. He was a good looking man, bald, though he may have shaved his head. I couldn't help but notice the steely look in his eyes.

"Thanks for seeing me," I said as I sat down opposite him.

"What would you like to drink?" he said as the

waitress came over.

"I'll have a Sauvignon Blanc."

"And I'll have a scotch on the rocks."

"How long have you been employed at the company?" I asked.

"It's been almost twenty-five years. I started with them a few years after I graduated from college. My degree was in marketing. I basically oversee sales for the company.

"That's a long time to be at one place."

"John Martin, David's father, was a good man. It's a shame he died so young."

"Were there any problems when his son took over?"

"Not really. Mrs. Martin, David's mother, was still in charge and to some extent still is. When Mr. Martin died David had already been learning the business, going to China and dealing with companies there that manufactured children's toys."

"Did you think you might take over the business at some point?"

"Absolutely not. My expertise was in marketing. I did help grow the company and was always generously rewarded for my contributions."

"Who do you think killed Rebecca?"

"I have no idea."

"Someone mentioned that Rebecca and her brother had some sort of falling out before she died. Do you know anything about that?"

"If they did, they kept it private. Can I get you another drink?"

"No thank you."

Excuse me," he said to the waitress as she went by. "Can I get another scotch on the rocks?"

Mr. Woods looked at me and asked if I wanted to order something to eat. I got the impression he was flirting with me.

"I think I'll pass on the food. Thank you."

The waitress brought over Mr. Woods' drink.

"Can you bring over some munchies?" he said to the waitress.

"It appears that Rebecca was having an affair with someone at the company," I said.

"Really?"

"You had no idea at the time?"

The waitress came back with potato chips and an assortment of mixed nuts.

I picked up a potato chip waiting for his answer.

"I had no clue, but Rebecca was hot, really hot. She gave off a very sensual vibe."

"So you would have slept with her if you had the opportunity?"

"Maybe, but I was married and I didn't want to jeopardize my job."

"Are you married now?"

"Why, are you interested?"

What a sleaze ball, I thought to myself.

"I don't mix business with pleasure, if you know what I mean," I said giving him a seductive look. Let him think it's a possibility.

"What about Simon Mack? What do you remember about him?"

"His name brings back memories. We started about the same time. I'm not sure what happened to him. He was doing pretty well and then he just quit."

"Did you ever find out why?"

"No. Never did," he said, looking at me with lust in his eyes.

"Do you think he could have been having an affair with Rebecca?"

"If he was, I wasn't aware. But lucky dog if that were

true."

My skin was crawling and I was running out of questions to ask this jerk.

"Well thanks for your time," I said taking out some money and putting it on the table.

"Hey I thought we could continue this over dinner at a nearby restaurant."

"Sorry, have to get home to a sick dog," I said as I got up and left him sitting there.

Leaving the bar I thought if Rebecca had hooked up with this guy she would have been desperate, and that didn't fit with the image I had of her.

CHAPTER 17

When I walked into my apartment I stripped off my clothes and took a hot shower trying to get the stink of that man off of me.

I was starved. I went into my refrigerator and saw there wasn't much. I didn't want to go to sleep on an empty stomach so I cut up an apple and sliced some cheddar cheese. I grabbed some crackers and sat down to eat.

The picture I'm getting of Rebecca is of someone who was unhappy, maybe even destructive. Could she have involved herself into something that got her killed or maybe her husband had enough, but divorce was not an option? Too much money to lose. I finished eating and went straight to bed. I realized it was too late to call Susie.

My internal clock woke me at 6:30 am. While eating breakfast I decided to track down Simon Mack. I knew it wouldn't be easy and I wasn't looking forward to traveling to Morrisville, Pennsylvania. For all I knew I could be going on a wild goose chase.

I threw a toothbrush, my charger and a pair of

panties in my backpack in case I might have to stay overnight.

I programmed my GPS for directions when I got into my car. As I was leaving the garage my phone rang. I didn't recognize the number.

"Hello."

"Tracey, this is Joseph Dean. I know you didn't want to be at the courthouse when the jury read the verdict but I thought I would give you the good news. They convicted Randy Stewart on 2nd degree murder."

"What does that mean?"

"It means he'll be going to prison for a minimum of fifteen years."

"That is good news."

"Well if it wasn't for you solving Stephanie Harris' murder, he would still be walking free."

"Thanks, I appreciate that."

"We hire investigators in our department if you're ever interested."

"I'll keep that in mind."

When we hung up I felt relieved. I was glad Stewart got what he deserved. It's too bad they couldn't charge him for Maddie's rape, but at least he'll be in prison for a long time.

As I was driving and listening to Beatles music my mind kept wandering. I wondered how Susie was doing. I think my biggest fear is that she would never be the same, the exuberant, fun person she was before. Would she and Mark decide to try again? I wanted the old Susie back. Did that make me a selfish person?

When I finally got to the area on the New Jersey Turnpike where trucks were not allowed to drive, my body relaxed. Big trucks practically on the back of my little Beetle made me nervous. My GPS said it's approximately a little over an hour and a half to Morrisville. Before going into the rehab center I needed to come up with a story that they would buy into in order to get information about Simon Mack.

Traffic was pretty heavy and it took me almost two hours before I parked in front of the Sarah Larsen Rehabilitation Center. I got out of my car slowly, still trying to come up with a story.

I was assessing the person at the front desk as I entered the building.

"Excuse me," I said, "my name is Cindy Mack and I'm here to see my brother Simon Mack. I hope I've come at a good time since I didn't know when visiting hours are. I've driven a long way to see him."

"I'm sorry you've come a long way for nothing."

"What do you mean?" I said sounding disappointed.

"Simon left over a year ago."

"Really. I can't believe it. I haven't been in touch with Simon for a few years, and I had just found out how bad things were for him. Do you know where he went?"

"I'm sorry we don't keep track of anyone after they leave."

"Is it possible he told someone here before he left? Maybe someone he was friendly with?"

"I wouldn't know."

"Well thank you for your time. Actually why don't I leave you my number in case you happen to run across someone who might know where he is."

"Well I guess I can ask around. It couldn't hurt."

"That would be such a big help. I really want to know if he's alright."

Where to now? I can't wait around here just on the off chance someone might have information on Simon. My stomach was growling so I thought I'd find a diner and get some lunch. Maybe an idea would come to me as I'm eating.

I found a cute looking diner about a mile from the rehab center. Before going in I called Susie.

"Hi"

"I'm so happy to hear your voice. I miss you," I said.

"I'm glad you called. Where are you?"

"I'm in Morrisville, Pennsylvania. I'll explain later."

"Mark dragged me into the shower."

"It was time, sweetie."

"That bad, huh?"

"Well I don't have to sleep next to you."

"It still hurts."

"I know. It will get better though. I almost forgot to tell you, Randy Stewart was convicted of 2nd degree murder. He'll spend at least fifteen years in prison."

"He deserves that and more."

"So you have any plans for today?" I asked Susie, hoping she wasn't going to stay cooped up another day.

"I think Mark is going to hound me until I agree to go for a walk with him."

"That's a great idea. It's so beautiful out."

"Don't push it."

"Okay. I'll call you later. You can hear about my thrilling time in Morrisville, PA. Love you."

"Hi there," the waitress said, handing me a menu.

"Can I get you a cup of coffee while you're waiting?"

"Always want coffee," I said to Heidi, her name tag attached to her uniform.

"Why don't you look over the menu while I bring your coffee."

"Thanks."

I opened the menu. Diner menus are so big, even bigger than Chinese menus.

"Here you go," placing a mug of coffee down. "So what can I get you?"

"I should eat something healthy but I think I'll go with an order of your pancakes with fresh blueberries and bacon crisp."

"You're skinny enough to afford the calories."

"I know this may be an odd question but would you happen to know a guy by the name of Simon Mack?"

"Is he wanted?" Heidi asked laughing.

"No, not quite. He was a friend of someone close to me. He was at the rehab center down the road but I was told he's no longer there."

"Are you local?"

"No. I'm trying to find him before I go back to New York."

"Well maybe someone around here knows him. Why don't you give me your name and number and if you're lucky somebody might have run into him."

"Thanks, I appreciate it," I said as I handed Heidi a piece of paper with my telephone number.

"Let me get you those pancakes."

While I was sipping my coffee, I called Jack.

"Guess where I am?"

"I love these guessing games you play with me," he said laughing.

"You're no fun. I'm in Morrisville, Pennsylvania trying to track down this guy I think Rebecca Kane was having an affair with."

"That was going to be my very first guess."

"Ha ha, very funny. Anyway, when I tried to locate him I couldn't find him anywhere. I was able to track down his ex-wife and she mentioned the last time she heard anything about him he was in Morrisville, PA, but wasn't positive. When I pulled up a report on him it listed an address from over a year ago that turned out to be a rehab center in Morrisville."

"Did they give you any information?"

"I was very creative and gave the receptionist some bullshit story that I was his long lost sister. Anyway it turns out he left about a year ago. I gave her a made up name and my telephone number, and asked her if she would be kind enough to inquire whether anyone knew him."

"I'm proud of you. You're turning into a first rate PI."

"Well thank you," I said pleased with myself.

I saw the waitress coming with my food.

"Here you go. Hope the bacon is crisp enough for you."

"Thanks Heidi."

"What was that about?" Jack asked.

"I'm at a diner having lunch."

"Did I hear bacon?"

"And pancakes with fresh blueberries. The blueberries count for something, don't they?"

Jack laughed.

"Are you coming back today?"

"Most likely. I doubt if anyone is going to know where he is before I head back, unless you have any ideas."

"Are you crunching in my ear?"

"Sorry. So you got something?"

"A long shot. Find out where the Clerk's office is and see if anyone with his last name has any property in the area. Maybe his parents live around Morrisville."

"A genius. By the way the assistant district attorney called me this morning. They found Stewart guilty of 2nd degree murder."

"That's great news. You should be really proud of finding the person who killed Ms. Harris."

"Oh, and even better news, Susie took a shower."

"We should celebrate when I see you on Saturday."

"I'd like that."

"I have some good news also. They hired Jake, the private investigator I recommended."

"Mazel Tov. A triple celebration."

"I gotta go. Let me know if you find this guy. I love you."

"Ditto."

After finishing my delicious lunch, I made a quick stop at the ladies room. On the way out I thanked Heidi for everything.

When I got into the car I pulled out my computer and looked up the Clerk's office. I added the address in my GPS and drove the five miles to their offices and parked in their parking lot.

The building was small, only two floors. The property records I was told was on the second floor. When I opened the door I went straight to the counter where there was a gentleman looking as if he wanted to be any place but where he was. Maybe he was at this too long or his dreams of a more fulfilling life were a distant memory.

"Hello," I said. "I hope I'm not disturbing you."

"Oh no, how can I help you?" he said trying to perk up.

"I'd like to check property records."

"I can help you with that. What's the last name?"

"It's Mack."

"Do you have a first name?"

"Why don't you first look under the last name, since I don't have a first name."

"No problem."

I drummed my fingers on the counter as he was doing whatever he was doing.

"There are two properties owned by someone with the last name of Mack, one is James Mack and the other is owned by Gail Mack. Would you like a printout?"

"Yes that would be great."

"Is there anything else I can do for you?"

This guy must be really bored.

"No, I'm good, thank you."

He handed me the printout and I left.

When I got back into the car I looked up both James and Gail Mack. James was between seventy-five and eighty years old. It could be Simon's father. Gail Mack was forty-eight. Maybe Simon's sister but I could be completely wrong. I don't even know if either of these people are related to Simon. I thought I would drive over to James Simon's place first.

The house looked kind of run down. Every house on the block looked the same. All small ranch style homes. The only way you could tell them apart was from the color they were painted. One was pink, another yellow. The Mack's house was white. The lawn needed mowing. I parked in front and knocked on the door. An elderly lady answered.

"Can I help you?"

"I hope. I'm trying to get in touch with Simon Mack. Are you related to him?"

Before she had a chance to answer I heard a man yelling from inside the house.

"Who is it Sylvia?"

"Some lady looking for Simon."

Well at least I knew I had the right people.

"Tell her he's not here and shut the door."

"I'm a friend of Simon's from New York," I said quickly, hoping she would tell me where he is.

"We haven't seen Simon in several years."

"Have you spoken to him on the phone?"

"He does call every so often but I have no idea where he's living."

Before I had a chance to leave my name and number, the door slammed in my face. I walked back to my car thinking it wasn't a total waste. If he was in communication with them I could try to obtain their phone records, though I thought it was odd that Simon was in a rehab facility in the area and they had no idea where he currently lives.

I drove over to Gail Mack's place. It took me about twenty minutes. Gail lived in a garden apartment development. Though the grounds were well maintained, the outside of the buildings were in desperate need of a paint job.

I spent a few minutes looking for Gail's apartment. When I finally found it no one was home. I had no idea when she would be back and I had no intention of waiting. I left my name and number on a piece of paper and stuck it by her door. I thought if I left my card it might scare her that a private investigator was looking for her.

The ride home was a nightmare. The traffic was heavy most of the way back. By the time I reached my garage it was almost 7:00 pm. Before going upstairs I stopped at the Thai place near my building and bought a chicken dish in a fairly spicy sauce with broccoli and rice.

Upstairs I changed into my sweats, emptied my dinner in a large bowl, grabbed my chopsticks and turned on the TV in the bedroom.

I was raising my chopsticks to my mouth when the phone rang.

"Hello."

"Is this Tracey Marks?"

"Yes."

"This is Gail Mack."

"Thank you for getting back to me," I said as my chopsticks fell on my lap. "I'm trying to get in touch with Simon Mack. Is he your brother?"

"Yes. Why are you trying to reach him?"

"When Simon was in New York he worked for Martin Industries."

"I vaguely remember that Simon worked for a company while he was living there."

"John Martin, Simon's boss, had a daughter by the name of Rebecca. She was killed about twenty years ago."

"I don't understand. If his daughter died a long time ago why would you have to speak to Simon now?"

I didn't really want to tell her why, since if she knew where he was and got in touch with him he might not want to talk with me.

"Rebecca Kane's daughter Lisa has hired me to look into her mother's death since the police never found out who killed her mother. I'm talking to everyone who knew Rebecca at that time."

"Why did my brother know her?"

"Rebecca used to visit the corporate offices to see her father. She knew everyone who worked there, and every year the Martin's would host a Christmas party at their home."

"I have no idea where my brother is. We're not speaking. The last I knew he was getting sober at a place in Pennsylvania where we're from, but I haven't had any contact with him in a long time."

"If you happen to hear from him, can you please pass on my information?"

"I doubt if I will," she said and hung up.

It didn't surprise me that Gail wasn't speaking with her brother especially if he was an alcoholic. I just wasn't sure if she was telling me the truth.

CHAPTER 18

It was still pitch black out when I got up the next day. I wanted to go for a run but I was a little leery about running in the dark since the last time I did I was almost killed by my attacker on my last case. I decided to brave it anyway.

Instead of running in the park, I ran on my neighborhood streets. By the time I finished my run I saw the first signs of life, people walking their dogs and buying coffee at Starbucks.

After showering and turning on the coffee maker, I sat down to have my usual breakfast, Cheerios and milk. I had told David Martin that I would get the employment files back to him by the middle of the week. I thought I would bring them back today and hopefully get a chance to talk with him.

While drinking my coffee, I remembered that I needed to obtain the telephone records for James Mack, Simon's father. I emailed my contact and gave him Mr. Mack's information and requested his telephone records for the past six months. Now I just had to wait about two days and hope one of the numbers listed belonged to Simon Mack.

I hauled the box with the employment files down to my car and drove to David Martin's office. As I got off the elevator I was greeted by a male receptionist, probably in his twenties.

"May I help you?" he said in a husky voice.

"My name is Tracey Marks and I'm here to see David Martin."

"Do you have an appointment?"

"Sort of. I'm supposed to return these files to him."

"Let me see if he's available."

Five minutes later David Martin was walking towards me.

"Ms. Marks, I see you've brought back the files. Thank you," he said taking the box from me and placing it down on the receptionist's desk.

"I thought as long as I'm here we could chat for a few minutes."

David looked down at his watch.

"I guess I could spare a few minutes. Come this way."

David Martin had a great view of the city from his window. He sat down at his beautiful Mahogany desk and I sat across from him.

"I know it must be hard on the family after all these years bringing up the memories of your sister's death. I'm sorry to have to open old wounds, but as you know your niece has hired me to see if I can find out who killed her mother."

"What makes you think you can if the police never did?"

"I don't know if I can. I know the police were focused on your sister's husband Jason, but he had an alibi for that night. Except for the alibi, there only circumstantial evidence."

I saw no need to mention the information withheld

from the police by Lisa's nanny and Rebecca's friend.

"What can you tell me about your sister and her relationship with her husband?"

"I really wasn't involved in my sister's life at that time. I was busy learning the business from my dad. I didn't see Rebecca that often. Once in a while she would show up at the office."

"What about family dinners?"

"Are you kidding? My parents worked 24/7. It was rare that we all got together."

"So you don't know of any problems between your sister and her husband?"

"Do you mean did Jason marry my sister for her money? Maybe that might have been part of it, but I think he loved her. Whether that changed I don't know."

"Were there any problems between you and your sister?"

I noticed a slight hesitation when he began speaking.

"No, like I said we didn't see each other that often."

"It was mentioned that your sister was angry with you."

"Really. I'm not sure who you were speaking with. I did voice my opinion to Rebecca about Lisa. I told her she was a terrible mother."

"Well that might do it. Why did you think that?"

"She left Lisa with the nanny most of the day. I was kind of sensitive to that since our parents were never there for us. I thought Rebecca should have taken more of an interest in her daughter knowing how we were treated."

"I can see where that might be a sore spot for you. Well if you think of anything else, please give me a call."

What David Martin said made sense but I wasn't convinced that's why he and his sister had a falling out.

Before driving to my office, I called Susie from the car.

"Hey," I said when Susie answered. "How about I bring over some lunch in about two hours? I'll surprise both of you."

"Mark went into the office for a few hours so it's just you and me."

Instead of going into the office, I went straight home. I opened up my laptop to conduct a search on a Tommy Black, one of the two people working at the warehouse prior to Rebecca's death. The other person was Miguel Cortez who I had already located living in Astoria, which is in Queens, not too far from where I grew up.

From an old address of Tommy Black's employment file I was able to track him to Yonkers in Westchester County.

On the way to Susie's I picked up tuna fish sandwiches at my local delicatessen, along with coleslaw and a bag of potato chips.

When Susie opened the door she looked a lot better than the other day. I was glad to see she was showered and dressed.

I gave her a big hug and told her to sit down at the kitchen table. I opened up all the drawers and cabinets looking for plates, silverware and glasses. Susie just sat there, not saying a word.

"In my defense," I said, "I'm not used to the new kitchen."

Susie gave me a little smile.

While I was eating and Susie was picking at her sandwich, I caught Susie up to date on the case.

"As you can see I'm not making much progress." I wasn't sure if Susie was listening to me.

"I'd go back to the guy who was Jason's alibi."

"Why?" I said surprised.

"Because he wasn't sure about the detail of how Jason got home. I would think even after twenty years you would remember what occurred that night. I would press him. If he did lie, he probably won't give it up so easily, if at all. You have to be persuasive."

"Got it. Anything else?"

"Keep digging. Something will show up eventually."

Then she said: "I'm having a hard time concentrating. I started reading a book but had to put it down since my mind kept wandering."

"Each day will get a little better, I promise. Jack is coming down on Saturday. How about we get together and play cards."

"As long as it's not bridge. You have to concentrate too much."

"Thank you. My concentration is just fine and I still have a hard time playing that game," I said.

"It takes practice."

After cleaning up, I kissed Susie goodbye.

Walking back to my apartment I thought about what Susie said. Maybe she was right and this guy Eric Jordan, Jason Kane's alibi, had something to hide. I doubt if Mr. Jordan would be looking forward to speaking with me again. I guess I'll have to pay him an unannounced visit.

CHAPTER 19

The first thing I did when I got back home was to look up Eric Jordan's home address. According to the internet he was living in Scarsdale, New York, a place I got to know on one of my cases. I wasn't sure where to approach him. Going to his house might not be such a good idea, especially if his wife was home. If he did lie to the police, he might not be inclined to confess his sins in front of her.

A better idea might be to meet him for a drink to get him comfortable. But why would he accept my invitation? I would have to give him a phony story. That wouldn't be too difficult.

I picked up the phone and called his cell number.

"Eric Jordan speaking."

"Mr. Jordan this is Tracey Marks."

"What can I do for you?" he said cautiously.

"I found out some information that is quite disturbing about Jason Kane. Is it possible to meet for a drink later? I want to run some things by you."

"I'm not sure I can help you. I was a client of his but didn't really know him all that well."

"I understand but I'm kind of desperate here. I'll take any help I can get."

I could hear the wheels turning in his head. I was hoping my 'damsel in distress' cry for help would soften him up.

"There's a place near my office. It's a small bar that has a few tables. I can meet you there at 6:15 pm."

When I hung up I had just enough time to go for a quick run.

The bar was as advertised, small with a few tables with dim lighting. I sat down at a table furthest from the door. The waitress came over and I ordered a glass of wine. Just as the waitress was about to leave, Eric Jordan sat down and ordered a beer.

"Thanks for meeting me," I said after the waitress left. It did not go unnoticed that Mr. Jordan was staring at her breasts while he was giving her his drink order. In his defense they were practically falling out of the top of her uniform. It was probably a ploy to get men to keep ordering drinks.

"So what is it that you need to tell me?"

"In speaking to some people that knew both Jason and his wife Rebecca, it seems their relationship was not as perfect as the police were led to believe. For reasons they divulged to me, they did not reveal this information when they were originally questioned. It appears Jason was having an affair at the time of his wife's death."

I noticed a slight body shift in Eric Jordan.

"What I'm saying is that people lied when they were questioned by the police. Maybe if they hadn't Mr. Kane would have been looked at more closely in his wife's death. It was your alibi that got him off the hook."

The waitress brought over our drinks.

"Thank you," I said as she walked away. I noticed

Mr. Jordan did not leer at her breasts when she set the drinks down. Instead he looked as if he was somewhere else.

"If you did lie to the police you must have had a good reason," I said, trying to get him to open up.

"I didn't lie."

"This is between us. I have no intention of getting you in trouble. I'm just trying to get justice for Rebecca Kane and her daughter."

I could see that Mr. Jordan was weighing what to do.

"When we left the restaurant Jason told me he was meeting a woman for drinks. When I found out his wife had been murdered it didn't even occur to me that Jason had anything to do with her death. He asked me to lie because he said it wouldn't look good to the police if he was out with another woman, so I went along with it. I didn't see the harm at the time," he said sheepishly.

"The only harm in it was if he wasn't meeting someone else, but was going home to kill his wife."

"If I had thought at all that Jason killed his wife I never would have lied for him."

"I'm sure you believe that."

"What now?" Eric asked me. "Are you going to tell the police I lied?"

"As I told you I don't plan on going to the police, but do you have any proof that he didn't kill his wife?"

"No, not really. Can't you find out who this woman was and ask her?" Eric said practically pleading.

"If it's his current wife, do you think she would tell me the truth?"

"I see your point. What now?"

"I don't know."

"To tell you the truth, it's always weighed on my mind that I lied to the police, but I still don't think he did it."

"I'm glad you can be so sure."

When we parted outside I knew Eric Jordan would be wondering if I was going to rat him out to the police even though I told him I had no intention of reporting him. Let him have something to worry about. This was certainly an interesting development. The more I investigate, the more Jason Kane looks guilty. It's very possible he was meeting a woman that night, and if he was, I can understand why he wouldn't want the police to know.

When I got home I heated up my leftover Thai food. While I was eating a million thoughts were swirling around in my head. If his current wife Danielle had been his alibi and they weren't together that night, would she have lied for him? She may have, but would she have married him knowing it was possible he killed his wife? Too many questions. No answers.

CHAPTER 20

When I woke up the following morning I saw an email with an attachment for the phone records I had requested for Simon Mack's father. I showered and went straight to my office only stopping for my muffin.

First thing I did when I arrived at my office was to set up the coffee maker. Second was download the phone records of James Mack. I had six months of records to go through. It was not a task I was looking forward to. My phone rang just as I was about to dive right in.

"Hey lover boy."

"You're in a good mood," Jack said.

"As if most of the time I'm not?"

"I plead the fifth."

"Well as long as you're pleading. I had lunch with Susie yesterday at their apartment. She was dressed and I believe, showered."

"That's good news."

"When I hear her infectious laugh I'll feel a lot better, which is why I took the liberty of inviting us over to their place Saturday night for a hot game of poker.

No bridge, don't even mention it."

"So you know how to play poker. Another facet of your life I didn't know about."

"I play strictly according to Hoyle or is that blackjack. Oh well."

"I get it. I guess I won't be playing for money with you. You would rob me blind."

"I have some very interesting news. We can add one more person in the lying column. I spoke with Jason Kane's alibi and you will be stunned to know he was not with Jason after 10:00 pm the evening of Rebecca's murder."

"Shocking."

"My sentiments exactly. Mr. Jordan fessed up that Jason asked him to lie to the police because he was meeting a woman and he knew it would look bad for him. I could see why this guy Jordan lied for Kane," I said. "If he didn't think Jason had anything to do with his wife's murder what would be the harm in a little white lie."

"Now you have a problem. With the other information you recently found out about Kane, he might have killed his wife."

"Possibly, but I'm still not sure. It's very plausible if he was having an affair he might have been with this woman the night his wife died."

"Even if you found out who the woman was he allegedly was meeting with that night, she's never going to tell you the truth."

"Yeah, I kind of figured that out. So where do I go from here?"

"Right now Kane is your main suspect. He's not going anywhere. Find this lover boy of Rebecca Kane. He might be able to shed some light on the situation. Keep working the case and keep an open mind."

"Will do. I'll see you bright and early Saturday morning."

"Yes ma'am. Love you."

"Ditto."

I knew Jack was right. I had to keep plugging along.

I turned my attention back to the phone records. Fortunately the Mack's did not make or receive many phone calls. That made it a lot easier. I was looking for a telephone number that was listed maybe only once or twice in the past six months. According to Mrs. Mack she rarely heard from her son. Nice guy.

I went through each month methodically. There were a couple of numbers that fell into that category. I wrote each one of them down on a notepad.

I started calling. One turned out to be a doctor's office, one was to a plumber, the third was from a bank. Hopefully the Mack's weren't getting thrown out of their home. None of the others I called panned out except for one possible number. When I called a man's voice said to leave a message, nothing else. Maybe that was Simon. It was a 516 area code.

I attempted to find the person connected with that number but I was having difficulty. I emailed the company who handles those types of problems for me, hoping they would have better luck obtaining an address and name from the telephone number I gave them.

In the meantime I had promised Lisa I would call her. I thought I would keep the information I learned about her father to myself for now until I was sure he killed Rebecca.

"Lisa, how are you?"

"I'm glad you called."

"Did you happen to remember anything else from that night?"

"No. Did you find out anything?"

"There are some things that have come to my attention but I prefer to wait and see what happens before I share them with you."

"I see. I spoke to my father yesterday. He's still upset that I hired you. He thinks it's a waste of time."

"Lisa, do you remember hearing your parents argue? I know you were very young but I'm curious if there's anything you can recall?"

"I'm sorry."

"Don't be sorry."

"I have to go. A client just walked in," Lisa said.

"Call me anytime."

The next call I placed was to Molly Kane, Jason's sister. Maybe she can tell me more about Jason.

"Hello."

"Is this Molly Kane?"

"Are you selling something because I'm not interested?"

"No, my name is Tracey Marks. I was hired by Lisa Kane to look into the death of her mother, Rebecca Kane."

"Really. This is news."

"So you didn't know?"

"My brother and I haven't spoken in quite some time."

"Are you in touch with your niece?"

"We've had very little contact over the years which is unfortunate."

"Why is that?"

"I'm right in the middle of painting. If you would like to come by my studio we can talk there."

"Where is your studio?"

"It's in Chelsea. Why don't you come around 2:00 pm? I should be ready for a break by then."

"Thank you."

I don't think I've ever been to an artist's studio in Chelsea, an area in New York that has numerous art galleries. Actually I was pretty excited. It's too bad Susie wasn't up for it. She would love to see the gallery.

I took an Uber down to Molly Kane's studio.

The first thing I saw when I walked in was a large abstract in very vibrant colors. I loved it. I waved to Ms. Kane as she came over to me. Ms. Kane did not resemble her brother in any way. Where Jason is always neatly dressed and his demeanor guarded, Molly Kane was warm, vivacious and covered with paint.

"Please look around while I make us some coffee."

I loved her already.

Looking around the gallery, I was very impressed with her paintings though I have no knowledge of whether a painting was a work of art or painted by an amateur.

"If I could afford your paintings, you would have a buyer right now."

"An artist always likes to hear praise."

We sat down in a separate area from the studio that had a couch and a lounge chair.

"Black is fine," I said.

"This is a banana nut bread that I made. Usually around this time I take a break and have something to eat."

"It's delicious," I said after taking a bite.

"Now let's talk about why you're here."

CHAPTER 21

"May I ask when the last time you spoke to your brother?"

"Let me see, it's been about ten years."

"That long ago?"

"It is. We've always kind of locked horns. Our lifestyles, as you can probably tell, are very different. We never saw eye to eye on much. When our parents died Jason tried to cheat me out of money from the sale of our parents' house. It wasn't much but it was supposed to be divided fifty/fifty. In the end it wasn't worth the fight."

"Were you and Rebecca friendly?"

"I liked Rebecca, though I thought she had some problems and was probably not a good match for my brother."

"What kind of problems are we talking about?"

"Nothing specific. Sometimes she seemed as if she was somewhere else, not present. I don't think it was conscious on her part. When the three of us were together, I thought there was a distance between the two of them."

"Did you know Jason was having an affair before Rebecca died?"

"I didn't, but it doesn't surprise me."

"Why is that?"

"As I said, I didn't think they were suited for each other. She came from a very wealthy family and Jason envied her, or let me say her money. I don't think that combination makes for a good marriage."

"What about Lisa?"

"Unfortunately Lisa was a byproduct of my relationship with my brother. I rarely saw her. I do follow her on Facebook, and it appears she has turned into a lovely young lady and a very talented one. It's too bad what happens in families. I think Lisa and I would have a lot in common."

I wanted to tell her to reach out to Lisa but it wasn't really my business. I felt bad for both Lisa and her aunt.

"Please tell me why after all these years Lisa has hired a private investigator to look into her mother's death?"

"Lisa needs to know who killed her mother. It might help her to move on. Also she started to remember some details from that night. Can I be blunt?"

"Of course."

"Do you think Jason killed Rebecca?"

"I really have no idea. I don't know what my brother is capable of. I'm sorry I don't have a better answer for you."

"Well I appreciate your time. I have a friend who would love to see your gallery. Would it be alright to call you when she's available?"

"Absolutely. I wish I could have been of more assistance, and I hope for Lisa's sake you do find out who killed her mother."

As the Uber was headed back to my office, I thought about what Jason's sister told me. None of it further incriminated Jason Kane. Though he was my number one suspect, actually my only suspect at the moment, I needed to continue talking with other people that might be able to shed some light on the case.

I wasn't expecting the information back on the telephone number that would hopefully lead me to Simon Mack until tomorrow. In the meantime I wanted to look into the two people who were working at the warehouse at the time Rebecca died. They were long shots but I didn't know what else to do at the moment.

The first call I made was to Tommy Black. It went straight to voice mail and I left a message to have him contact me.

My next call was to Miguel Cortez.

"Hello."

"Is this Miguel Cortez?"

"Yes," he answered.

He spoke with an accent. Maybe from Mexico, but I wasn't sure.

"My name is Tracey Marks. I'm sorry to bother you. Would you happen to remember a woman by the name of Rebecca Kane? She was killed about twenty years ago."

"Yes, But I know nothing about her death."

"I understand but I'm trying to gather information about the family and you had worked for the Martin's for a few years."

"That was a long time ago. I can't help you. I have to go now."

The next thing I heard was silence. What was that about? Was he afraid to speak to me and if so, why?

My phone rang.

"Tracey Marks."

"This is Tommy Black."

"Mr. Black. I'm looking into the death of a woman

named Rebecca Kane who died about twenty years ago. Do you remember her?"

"I remember."

"Would it be possible to meet? I'm trying to find out as much as I can about the family."

"I would like to help you but I never even met Mrs. Kane and the only person in that family I vaguely knew was David Martin."

"Can I ask why you left after working there for several years?"

"My friend opened up his own auto body shop and wanted me to come and work for him. It meant more money."

After hearing his answers I didn't see any reason to pursue speaking with him in person unless I was completely wrong about him.

"Well I appreciate your time and if you happen to remember anything, please get in touch with me."

I was ready to call it quits for the day when my phone rang. I didn't recognize the number.

"Tracey Marks."

"Ms. Marks, this is Celia Ramirez. I need to tell you something."

CHAPTER 22

"I'm listening?"

"I would rather not tell you on the phone. Can you come over now?"

It was already almost 6:00 pm, but I was anxious to hear what she had to say.

"I can be there in twenty minutes depending on traffic."

As soon as I got off the phone, I called for an Uber.

I arrived at Mrs. Ramirez's apartment by 6:40 pm.

"Thank you so much for coming to my home. I thought it would be better to tell you in person."

We sat down in the living room. I waited for her to speak.

"So much was going through my head when you questioned me last week, that I forget to tell you about the argument. It was terrible. They were screaming at each other."

"Who was screaming?"

"Rebecca's friend Jackie."

"What was she screaming about?"

"I just heard bits and pieces. Ms. Jackie was so upset. She was yelling at Ms. Rebecca, 'how could you do it' she said over and over again."

"Do you know why Jackie was yelling at Rebecca?"

"I think Ms. Rebecca took Ms. Jackie's husband."

"What do you mean?"

"You know, had sex with him."

My mind was racing.

"Did you hear Jackie say that?"

"I heard her say, I'm so angry I could kill you."

"Did you hear what Rebecca said?"

"She was yelling also but I couldn't understand what she was saying. And then Ms. Jackie slammed the door so hard as she was leaving I swear the house shook."

"Do you remember anything else that was said?"

"They were in Ms. Rebecca's bedroom and I was downstairs. It was hard to hear."

"Did Ms. Rebecca say anything to you about the argument?"

"She never brought it up."

"How long before Rebecca's death did they argue?"

"Maybe a couple of weeks. It was so long ago I don't remember exactly."

"And you never mentioned any of this to the police?"

"No, never. I was too afraid to get involved."

Well if this is true, I thought to myself, then Jackie lied to me why Rebecca and her were not speaking prior to Rebecca's death. Well actually she partially lied. She did tell me she was angry at Rebecca for sleeping with a married man. Maybe it slipped her mind it was her own husband.

"If you remember anything else about their fight, please contact me."

"I promise. I won't forget."

Getting into my Uber ride home, I wondered if anyone told the truth about that night. From what Ms. Ramirez told me it still wasn't clear what the argument was about. If Rebecca and Jackie's husband were having an affair, I may have another suspect. I can envision Rebecca and Jackie fighting, and somehow it got out of control, and Rebecca fell backward and hit her head.

When the Uber dropped me off in front of my apartment Wally was already gone for the day. Our other doorman, Roberto was on duty.

"Hi Roberto."

"Hi Ms. Marks. How are you today?"

"I'm fine, but I'm glad to be home."

"I know what you mean. Goodnight," he said as he opened the door for me.

While trying to figure out what to eat, I called Susie. Mark answered.

"How's my girl?"

"She seems to be doing better. We went out for lunch today."

"Did she tell you that Jack and I are coming over on Saturday for a hot game of poker?"

"Yeah, she did mention it. I think it will be good for her to have you guys around."

"Can we bring dinner?"

"Nah, we'll order from here."

"Okay, I'll bring the dessert and wine. Is she up for talking?"

"Hold on a second."

"Hey sweetie," I said, when Susie got on the phone. "I can't wait to beat you at poker Saturday night."

"Don't hold your breath."

I thought I'd fill Susie in on the latest developments when I saw her on Saturday.

"I'll see you soon. Love you."

"Love you back."

When I got off the phone I made myself an egg sandwich and ate it in the bedroom after changing into my sleeping attire.

As I was about to call Jack, my phone rang."

"I was just about to call you," I said to Jack.

"I bet you say that to all your special friends."

"Only the ones I'm dying to sleep with."

"I see."

"Unfortunately the one I want is not available. What do you think I should do?"

"You have quite a dilemma on your hands my friend. How about if this guy who's not available right now makes it worth your while to wait?"

"That could work, though he has a lot to live up to."

"I'm sure he can manage."

"Sounds like a plan."

"Not to change this scintillating conversation, but Jake starts working on Monday. He's been a PI for a few years so he knows the ropes."

"Well maybe next time I'm up there I can meet him. Is he married?"

"He is."

"You know we've never gotten together with any of your friends. Is there something you're hiding from me or you don't want them to know about me?" I said smiling.

"You got me. I told them you were just someone I picked up at a bar and I'm using you for wild sex."

"Well part of that is true."

Jack laughed. I went on to tell him about Celia Ramirez's admission.

"Oh what a tangled web we weave when we practice to deceive."

"How original."

"You have to confront her. Don't expect an

admission of guilt if she did kill her friend."

"That would be a first."

"I'll see you Saturday. Sleep tight."

"Don't let the bed bugs bite."

When I woke up Friday morning I went for a run first thing. When I got back I showered and pulled on my jeans and a long sleeve cotton pullover. As I was sitting down to have breakfast I opened up my computer. There was an email with the information on the telephone number I was checking out. I was totally surprised that it belonged to Simon Mack since I thought it was a long shot. His address was listed in Long Beach, New York.

I looked on google to see where Long Beach was located. It was in Nassau County, a little over an hour from the city on the south shore of Long Island. Well I guess I was taking a ride to Long Beach.

I threw a bottle of water and a couple of health bars in my backpack and headed out. At this time of morning, traffic was heavy with commuters traveling to work. I arrived at Simon's address at 10:00 am. It was a small house, almost looked like a cottage, painted yellow that was in walking distance to the ocean. It was situated on a narrow plot of land and was in serious need of a lawn mower.

I parked across the street and assessed the situation. There was one car parked in the driveway. I decided to wait and see if anyone comes out.

About a half hour later a woman around thirty with dark hair in a ponytail, walked out of the house and drove off in the car that was in the driveway.

I waited a little while longer then got out of my car and knocked on the front door not expecting anyone to answer. The door opened and I was staring into the face of a man maybe in his early fifties. At one time he was probably very handsome but now looked like someone that had taken a few too many punches from life. When I looked into his big dark brown eyes I knew how Rebecca could have fallen for him. Though he had lost his youth and good looks he was still quite attractive with high cheek bones and a dimple in the middle of his chin.

"Can I help you?" he said.

"My name is Tracey Marks. Do you happen to remember a woman named Rebecca Kane?"

The surprise look on his face gave him away.

"Yes," he said slowly. "She died a long time ago."

"I know. Her daughter Lisa hired me to look into her death since the police never found out who killed her. Can I come in and talk with you?"

"Sure," he said, drawing out the word 'sure.'

I followed Simon into the living room. The furniture looked old but in fairly good condition. I sat on the couch opposite Mr. Mack who sat down on a brown leather recliner.

"You're a hard man to find. I guess you've moved around a lot."

Simon looked like he hadn't shaved in a few days. He was still in his undershirt but had pants on.

"What happened to Rebecca was terrible," he said.

I could see the pain in his eyes.

"How well did you know her?"

"I'm not going to lie to you, Rebecca and I had an affair. I loved her and I was heartbroken when she died."

"Was the affair going on when she was killed?"

"Yes. I can't imagine who would have wanted to kill her except maybe her husband."

"Do you think he knew about the affair?"

"If he knew he probably didn't care. He was having

an affair with the second Mrs. Kane."

So it was her who Jason was allegedly seeing the night his wife was murdered.

"Why do you think he might have killed her?"

"For her money. It's as simple as that."

"Do you know if Rebecca was planning to divorce him?"

"She was but she never got the chance."

"Were the two of you planning to marry once her divorce was finalized?"

"I wanted to marry her but I'm not so sure what she wanted. Rebecca needed a lot of attention. I thought I could make her happy."

"Were you married at the time?"

"I was."

"Are you still married?" I asked, knowing the answer already.

"No. My wife couldn't live with me when she found about Rebecca. I started drinking and left the company about a year after Rebecca died. I was in and out of relationships and rehab for years. I finally got sober and met the person I'm living with now."

"Do you have a job?"

"I have some real possibilities. I hope something pans out soon."

"Besides her husband is there anyone else you can think of that would want to harm Rebecca?"

"Not that I can think of."

"I heard that Rebecca and her brother David had a falling out before Rebecca died."

"If they did, Rebecca never said anything to me."

I decided not to mention the possible affair Rebecca was having with Jackie's ex-husband.

"Didn't it make you angry that Rebecca didn't want to marry you?"

"She died so I don't know what would have happened between us. I want you to know I had nothing to do with Rebecca's death."

"Well I appreciate your time. Here's my card in case you think of anything that might help with my investigation."

"Wait. How is Rebecca's daughter?"

"I think she would be better if she knew who killed her mother."

"I see."

We shook hands and I left. Walking back to my car I wasn't sure if I believed that Simon Mack had nothing to do with Rebecca Kane's murder. From the picture I'm getting, he was crazy about Rebecca. If he knew she wasn't going to marry him, would he be able to let her go?

CHAPTER 23

I drove over to the boardwalk and sat down on a bench looking out over the ocean. With no one around it was peaceful. The September sun warming my face.

In the distance I noticed a mother and her young child laughing as they were running in and out of the water. They seemed so carefree.

When did life get so complicated? I thought to myself. The investigation, Susie losing the baby, my struggle committing fully to Jack. Sometimes it feels overwhelming.

For now I turned my thoughts back to the case. Though Jason Kane is still my prime suspect, I can't rule out Jacqueline Donovan or Simon Mack. I didn't completely buy Simon's story. He knew Rebecca was never going to marry him even if she did divorce Jason. But would he have killed her if he couldn't have her? And if he did, would that have sent him into a downward spiral and lead him to drink?

As for Jackie, she could have killed Rebecca in a moment of rage. I might have done the same if I was in her shoes.

The problem is how does any of this get me closer to finding out the truth, though I now know that the current Mrs. Kane was in the picture when Rebecca died. Another reason for Jason to kill his wife.

I stayed a little longer and then walked back to my car. I was getting hungry but not for a health bar. It would be at least an hour and probably longer before I got back to the city. I decided to pick up a sandwich and eat it in the car before heading back.

I found a coffee shop in the town and ordered a burger and fries to go. While I was eating and listening to music in the car, my phone rang.

"Hello," I said not recognizing the number.

"Ms. Marks, this is Jason Kane. I was wondering if you were making any progress on the case?"

That's interesting. He didn't want me on the case in the first place and now he wants to know if there are any developments.

"I'm sorry but the only person I can talk to about an ongoing investigation is your daughter since she's the one who hired me."

"Well I'm sure she wouldn't mind."

"Until I have that in writing from her, that's my policy. By the way, I found out that you were seeing Danielle while you were married to Rebecca."

I decided not to mention that his alibi was blown.

"Who told you that?"

"That's private information, but since you didn't deny it, I will assume it's true. Is there anything else I can do for you?" I said, happy to have put a damper in his day.

"This matter is not over," he said as he hung up.

What a pompous ass. I wondered if he's cheating on the second Mrs. Kane. I wouldn't put it past him.

The drive back was as tedious as the drive there. The

traffic was horrendous. It took me almost an hour and a half before I was sitting in my office.

When I got in I wrote up the conversations I had with Simon Mack and Jason Kane. The day was slipping away. I wanted to go up to North Salem and confront Rebecca's friend Jacqueline, but since it was almost 4:00 pm it would have to wait till Monday.

On my way home I stopped at a small mom and pop supermarket near my apartment building to pick up some groceries so Jack doesn't think I'm poor. I was out of everything including toilet paper. I thought over the weekend I would try my hand at making a red sauce to have with pasta. I wanted to surprise Jack with my culinary skills which were in all honesty, non-existent. What's the saying, fake it till you make it. A big ask for me.

CHAPTER 24

Saturday morning I woke up bright and early since I wanted to do some cleaning before Jack announced himself. Afterward I showered and turned on the coffee maker. The doorbell rang as the coffee started dripping.

"The coffee smells delicious," Jack said as he wrapped his arms around me.

"You sure it's not me."

"That goes without saying," he said, kissing me hard on the lips.

"Good recovery."

"Though the coffee is tempting I think I'd like something else even more."

"And what could that be," I said, as Jack lifted me over his shoulder and carried me into the bedroom and gently tossed me on the bed.

"You do make good choices," I said.

Those were the last words spoken for the next forty-five minutes.

"I spoke with Simon Mack," I said, as Jack held me close to him. "He didn't deny that he was in love with Rebecca. As a matter of fact, he wanted to marry her. He said that Rebecca needed attention that Mack didn't think any one man could give her. Who knows if that's even true."

"How do you assess this guy?"

"I'm not sure. He seemed to be honest with me and truly saddened about Rebecca's death, but that doesn't mean he didn't kill her. If he thought Rebecca wouldn't marry him would that make him mad enough to kill her? I don't know."

"The suspects are just lining up."

"I still think it's the husband, especially now knowing that his second wife, Danielle was in the picture prior to his wife's death. It gives him opportunity and motive, actually several motives. Let's not forget about the insurance policy that he says he knew nothing about."

"But we're still not sure if he did have opportunity."

"That's true. Unfortunately we don't know if he was with either Danielle or another woman that night. We may never know, but the fact remains that he had his client lie for him so he'd have an alibi."

"Something will eventually shake out."

"I love that you have such confidence in me."

"Always," Jack said, as he kissed my neck and then proceeded to slowly go lower and lower.

By the time we finished, I was drained but famished.

"Let's eat. I'm starved."

"I'm right behind you."

I toasted some bagels and placed smoked salmon and sliced tomatoes on a plate. I poured us each a cup of coffee and we sat down to eat.

"I hope you brought your poker face with you for tonight," I said as I forked a piece of salmon onto my bagel.

"Do you think I need it?"

"I'm not sure about Mark and Susie but if you want to beat me, you'll definitely need it."

"Well, aren't you the presumptuous one."

"We'll see tonight."

"How do you think Susie's doing?"

"I'd feel better if I heard her laugh."

"It's only been a week."

"It feels like forever," I said.

"To you, but probably not to Susie."

"We know patience is not my strong suit."

"Yes we do. By the way, do you have a bike?"

"I actually do. I bought it in a moment of weakness when I wasn't thinking straight. At the time I thought it was a good idea. It's been sitting in my storage unit probably covered with dust."

"I thought if you're game I could bring it back with me so the next time you come up we could go bike riding, unless you don't like to ride."

"Hmm. I loved riding when I was a kid. It's not that I don't like it, it's been a long time."

"Well since it's wasting away down here, why don't I bring it back and if it's not your cup of tea, my garage will have another bike?"

"Sounds like a plan. And speaking of plans, how about a jog in Central Park?"

After cleaning up we both changed into our running clothes and walked over to the park. The leaves were just beginning to turn colors. In another week October would be here. It was a nice time of year though it meant winter would not be far behind.

We arrived at the spot where we were starting our run.

"Okay, before we go, this is not a competition, right?" Jack said.

"Of course not," I smiled.

Jack gave me a sideward glance as if to say he didn't believe me.

We ran for three miles. When we stopped I was huffing and puffing only to mess with Jack. He just smiled at me.

"What? My allergies are bothering me," I said.

"I didn't say anything," Jack said grinning.

"I'm starved. How about getting something to eat? There's a little café a few blocks from here."

"Lead the way," Jack said.

On the way back we stopped at a French bakery and bought some delicious looking pastries, and then to my neighborhood wine shop for a bottle of red and a bottle of white wine.

When we got back to my apartment we had just enough time to shower and have a little fun before walking over to Susie and Mark's place.

"I'm so glad you guys could come," Mark said when he opened the door.

"Hey, there you are," I said hugging Susie.

I noticed Susie had put on a little makeup. I was overjoyed.

Jack embraced Susie and whispered something in her ear that made her smile. I was dying to know what he said.

After eating take-out from a Greek restaurant nearby, we got down to our serious poker game, which is always more fun to play while drinking wine.

Susie and Jack were winning most of the hands. We were playing with poker chips instead of money. I think I was the only one taking the game seriously. While Jack was dealing he was telling a story about some guy he had to interview on one of his cases. It turned out he did the interview while the guy was taking a crap. Susie burst out laughing. It was the first time since she lost the baby that I heard her laugh. I was so happy I could have kissed Jack.

After dessert and coffee, Jack and Mark played chess and Susie and I went into the living room with our wine.

"I went to a gallery in Chelsea that I can't wait for you to see. I know you're looking for artwork for the apartment. Her paintings are so vibrant. I think you'll really like them."

"How come you were there?"

"The woman who owns the gallery is Jason's sister, and she did not have kind words about him. They haven't spoken in ten years."

I updated Susie on what I had found out so far.

"The case is cold. I think whoever did it thinks they got away with it and they may be right."

"The daughter for whatever reason is remembering some details?" Susie asked.

"Yeah, but very little and nothing that significant."

"How about a hypnotherapist? They might prove helpful in this situation," Susie said.

"Why didn't I think of that?"

"That's why you have me."

I gave Susie a big hug.

"I wonder if Lisa would be willing to entertain the idea."

"No harm in asking. It isn't something you should rely on even if she agrees. It's very possible she won't remember anything else," Susie said yawning.

"I think it's time Jack and I left so you can get your beauty sleep. By the way I mentioned to Jack that you thought we should be spending more time together."

"Thanks a lot."

"He thought so too. Lately I've been thinking of maybe seeing someone to figure out why I'm having such a difficult time committing to Jack. I'm crazy about him."

"I'm all for therapy."

On the walk back I told Jack about the conversation Susie and I had, leaving out the therapy part.

"I think a hypnotherapist is a great idea if she'd be willing to do it."

"Where would I even find someone who's reputable?"

"I'm not sure if they have to be state licensed but if you start googling hypnotherapists, you'll find out where you need to go."

"That might work."

When Jack and I were in bed I asked him what he had said to Susie when he hugged her.

"Aren't you the nosey one."

"Out with it."

"I told her she looked great."

"I see. By the way I owe you big. You made Susie really laugh with that story you told. It was true wasn't it?"

"Would I make something like that up? But I do like the fact that you owe me."

"Do you want that in writing?"

"Yes, please."

"I don't think that's necessary but can it wait till the morning? I'm pooped."

"Absolutely."

In the morning Jack collected on my debt.

While we were eating breakfast I said to Jack: "It's rainy out, how about an afternoon movie?"

"As long as it's not too scary," Jack said with a straight face.

"Don't worry, I'll protect you."

By the time we got out of the movie theatre, the rain had let up. On the way back we stopped at a gourmet cheese shop near me to buy some Parmigiano-Reggiano cheese and a crusty loaf of Italian bread for the pasta meal I was preparing this evening.

I had searched online for a recipe I thought I would attempt, one that I couldn't butcher too badly.

With the sauce cooking, I had Jack put together a salad and I tried my hand at making garlic bread. Jack poured us each a glass of red wine and we sat down to eat.

Dinner was a huge success. We devoured every last morsel and went to bed happy campers.

On Monday before Jack left we retrieved my bike from my storage unit downstairs in the basement and maneuvered it into the backseat of his car. Right after Jack left I went straight to the office.

First thing on my agenda was to find out how to get in touch with a reputable hypnotherapist. After poking around, I found a list for Board Certified Clinical Hypnotherapists. Searching further, it appears you do not have to be licensed by the State of New York to be a hypnotherapist. It was good to know there would be some place to contact if Lisa is willing to undergo hypnosis.

Next was to contact Lisa.

"Hi Lisa, it's Tracey. How's everything?"

"My father called me. He told me he spoke with you and you wouldn't provide him with any information about the investigation. He wasn't too happy."

"As I mentioned to him it's not my policy to provide any information on an ongoing investigation except to the person who hired me."

"I'm glad you didn't. At the moment I'm not concerned about his feelings."

"I'd like you to consider something."

"What is it?"

"Since you've recently had some repressed memories of the night your mother died, I wonder if going to a hypnotherapist might help."

"It never occurred to me. I've only seen that on TV and in the movies, but I don't know anything about it."

"That makes two of us. Is that something you might consider?"

"I think so."

"Why don't I try and get as much info as I can and I'll get back to you."

"You hear about all the reasons people who've had traumatic experiences and have no recollection of what happened, or that there are pieces that are missing from their memory. For all I know I witnessed what happened and have repressed it."

"Let's hope so, but in the meantime I'll see what I can come up with."

After hanging up I contacted the Board of Certified Clinical Hypnotherapists. The person I spoke with was pretty helpful. He provided me with the names of three people in New York City that are certified clinical hypnotherapists. He suggested I speak with each one before making a decision.

I set aside the list. Right now I wanted to pay an unannounced visit to Jacqueline Donovan, Rebecca's friend, and find out if there was any truth to what Celia Ramirez overheard. Is it possible that Jackie's husband slept with Rebecca?

CHAPTER 25

When I arrived at Jackie's horse farm in North Salem I parked and went up to the main house and knocked. The door was open. I shouted her name but there was no answer. I stood outside for a minute and then walked over to the stables since I didn't see Jackie anywhere outside.

"Hello," I yelled, peeking my head into the stables. No answer. There was a black truck parked near the house. I wasn't sure if I should leave or wait a little bit. Then I saw Jackie riding towards me on a horse.

"Hi, I wasn't expecting you," she said climbing off her horse.

"It was last minute."

"Wait here while I get Buddy settled back in his stall."

Ten minutes later we were sitting outside on the wraparound porch.

"So what's on your mind?" Jackie said to me.

"You remember when I asked you why you weren't speaking to Rebecca. You said it was because she was angry at you for voicing how you felt about her affair with a married man?"

"Yes, that's true," she said cautiously.

"Is that because it was your husband?"

"Where did you hear that?" she said nonchalantly.

"Does it matter?"

"Would you like some lemonade? It's homemade."

"If you're having."

"A few minutes later Jackie came out with two glasses of lemonade."

"This tastes really good," I said.

"Look, it's obvious that you know something since you wouldn't have come all this way just to shoot the breeze."

"I know Rebecca slept with your husband." I wasn't positive but Jackie didn't know that.

"I'm not going to deny it. When I had found out I hated her, but I also knew Rebecca and I knew what she was capable of. I actually blamed Rick more than her. According to Rebecca they slept together twice."

"Did you believe her?"

"Yes. This may sound weird to you but Rebecca would have no problem sleeping with my husband but she could never lie to me. I know that doesn't make sense. You would have to understand Rebecca."

"How did you find out?"

"I was visiting my mother who lives in Connecticut. I was supposed to stay for two nights but decided to come home a day earlier. Rebecca wasn't here but I smelled her perfume on the bedroom sheets. He denied it of course. I didn't believe him. I was so angry. I went straight to see Rebecca. Rick must have called her to tell her I was on my way. When I got to her house she kept saying over and over how sorry she was. But I knew she wasn't really sorry."

"Did you threaten her?"

"In the heat of anger I might have said words I

didn't mean. If there was anyone I wanted to kill it was Rick. I threw him out and we divorced soon after. I did not kill Rebecca. I loved her in spite of everything."

"Do you still think it was her husband?"

"If it wasn't for his damn alibi, he'd most likely be rotting away in a jail cell right now."

I wanted to believe Jackie. I liked her, but I didn't want my feelings to cloud my judgment.

On the way back I wondered who else Rebecca slept with. Maybe she hooked up with the wrong person and got herself killed. I hadn't even entertained the idea that while she was seeing Simon Mack she might have been sleeping with someone else. Maybe Mack found out and killed her. Too much speculation. I have to stick to facts.

I picked up some lunch before going back to the office. While unwrapping my turkey sandwich I took the list of hypnotherapists from my desk drawer and started calling. I left messages since none of the people I called answered.

I was thinking about Rebecca when my phone rang. I didn't recognize the number.

"Tracey Marks."

"This is Thomas Samuels returning your call."

"Yes. Thank you for getting back to me. I'm a private investigator and I'm working on a twenty year old murder case. My client is the daughter of the person who was murdered. She was only three years old when it happened. Maybe I need to explain in person."

"You're doing fine, continue."

"The police never found out who killed her mother. When she came to me she said she started remembering a few details of that evening. It wasn't much. A friend of mine suggested seeing someone like yourself who might be able to help."

"What are you trying to accomplish?"

"Basically to find out if there's anything else she remembers that might assist me with the investigation."

"I see. To be honest, there are no guarantees. There are people who are not as susceptible to hypnosis, though most people are to some extent. It will depend on the person and how much they actually witnessed or heard, and will they allow themselves to remember or is it too painful for them."

"That makes sense. If my client decides to go ahead, how does this work and what are the fees?"

Mr. Samuels explained to me what was involved and the cost. He said it might take more than one session but that was not uncommon. I told him I would talk to my client and get back to him.

Before the end of the day I had spoken with the other two hypnotherapists. Without anything to base it on, except for one conversation, my intuition said to go with Samuels. Maybe he came off more trustworthy than the other two.

I called Lisa and we decided I would make the appointment and we would go together. After meeting with him Lisa would make the decision whether she wanted to go forward or not.

Before leaving for the day I had one more call to make.

"Hi Tracey,"

"Hi Patty. Did I catch you at a bad time?"

"No, I was just getting ready to bathe Michael before dinner. What's up?"

"I'd like to talk to you about something and I'd rather do it in person. Do you have any time tomorrow?"

"How about meeting for breakfast at 8:30 am? I have someone who comes in and watches Michael while I'm working. We can meet at the café on the corner of 71st Street off of Lexington. Is everything okay?"

"Yeah. I'll see you tomorrow. Thanks and give the little man a big hug and kiss for me."

"Will do."

Before meeting Patty the following morning, I did my three mile loop around the park, came back, showered, dressed and grabbed my backpack and computer bag and rushed to meet Patty.

"Hi," I said, hugging Patty before sitting down.

"What can I get you ladies?" the waitress asked.

"Definitely coffee," I said.

"Make that two, and I'll have an omelet with whole wheat toast, hold the home fries."

"I'll have the same except with the home fries."

"Thank you ladies," she said while picking up the menus.

"So what's going on?" Patty asked me.

"Do you remember when you thought you were never going to get pregnant, and you were having a hard time accepting that fact?"

"Yes. It was a terrible time."

"Before Michael was born you said you went to therapy to help you deal with the situation. I love Jack but every time I think about us having a life together, all that comes up for me is how scared I am. The past keeps following me and it's like I have no control over my feelings."

"Do you want to know if therapy helped me?"

"Yes."

"It did. She helped me sort out my feelings and she showed me another way to look at my life."

"Here you go ladies. Just let me know if you want a refill on the coffee."

"Thank you," Patty and I said in unison.

"Would you like the name and number of the therapist I went to?"

"Do you think she could help me?"

"I think you need to talk to a professional, so yes, I believe she can help."

"Thanks."

As we were eating I told Patty about the case and what was going on. I mentioned the hypnotherapist and she thought it was a good idea.

"How is it working out having someone watch Michael in the house while you're working?"

"Well I can tell you that before I hired Maggie to come in and watch Michael it was a disaster. I thought I could work and still keep an eye on him, but it was too much of a distraction and I wasn't getting any work done. Now, the only time I see Michael is when I choose to."

"I could see where it would be hard to watch Michael and try to work also."

"Let me know what you decide about therapy?"

Patty and I said goodbye outside the café since we were going in opposite directions. Though my office was across town instead of taking a cab or an Uber I walked back to my office. Walking helps me think. I knew it was time to see someone about my commitment issues. Neither Susie or Jack could fix my problems. What scared me the most was that I wasn't sure whether a therapist could fix me.

CHAPTER 26

I called Thomas Samuels as soon as I got into my office. We made an appointment for the next day at 11:00 am. I told him we would be there unless I contacted him otherwise.

I then called Lisa and we arranged to meet in front of Mr. Samuels' office a few minutes before 11:00.

I took out the piece of paper with Dr. Davidson's telephone number, the therapist Patty recommended. I kept staring at it, my hand shaking a little. Was I doing the right thing? Do I really need to see a therapist? Tracey, just make the call. I dialed her number quickly not giving myself a chance to back out.

"Dr. Davidson's office."

"I'd like to make an appointment."

"Why don't I just take a little bit of information first."

"Okay. What do you want to know?"

"Well for starters, what's your name?"

"Tracey Marks."

"Did someone refer you to the doctor?"

"Yes, Patty Marks."

"Have you ever seen a therapist before?"

"No, does that matter?"

"Not at all. The doctor can see you on Monday at 5:00 pm."

"I should be able to make that."

"If I can have your email address I can send you some forms for you to fill out so you won't have to do it when you get here."

I gave her my address and hung up. I was hoping the doctor was booked up for a couple of weeks. My luck she could see me in a few days.

In the meantime I had wanted to speak with Howard Stein, Jason Kane's law partner. The problem was I wanted to talk with him when Jason wasn't around.

"Lisa, it's Tracey. Would you by any chance know when your father is usually out of the office?"

"Friday afternoons, why?"

"Just curious." I didn't want to mention that I actually wanted to speak with his law partner.

"Why is he out then?"

"He and Danielle have a place in Spring Lake, New Jersey that they go to on Friday afternoons trying to beat the traffic."

"It's almost October. Are they still going?"

"Absolutely. As long as the weather is fairly nice they usually go through October."

"Thanks. I'll see you tomorrow."

Well that solved that problem. Now I just have to hope Mr. Stein is in on Friday.

The next day I met Lisa in front of Mr. Samuels' office. I could tell she was nervous by the way she was fidgeting with her hair.

"Remember Lisa you have a choice. If you're not comfortable for any reason you don't have to go through with it."

Mr. Samuels greeted us and we went through the

introductions. He wasn't exactly how I pictured him from the sound of his voice on the phone. You know how sometimes you have a mental image from someone's voice; mine didn't fit at all with Mr. Samuels. For one thing he was younger than I thought, maybe forty. I pictured him more like in his fifties. He was on the shorter side, but wiry, not tall as I had imagined.

The three of us sat down in his office. He went through everything, explaining how some people remain fully aware during the experience, while others may experience states of relaxation that are so deep they feel detached from what is happening.

"Does that mean I might reveal something that I experienced but when I come out of it I may not remember?"

"Yes, that does happen. That's a way of protecting yourself."

"You see on these TV shows how people are getting very agitated while they're under. If that happens to me will you stop the process?" Lisa asked.

"It will depend. I might be able to calm you and continue or I might go in another direction. Be assured that as soon as I feel we need to stop, I will. Would you like to give it a try?"

"I guess," she said with hesitation.

I had previously explained to Mr. Samuels what had happened twenty years ago and what Lisa had recently remembered. I also gave him some questions to ask Lisa while she was under hypnosis.

Mr. Samuels took Lisa into an adjoining room while I waited in a different room, though I was told I would be able to hear what was going on.

"Now Lisa, try to relax. Close your eyes and listen to the sound of my voice. Think of a place that makes you feel happy and pay attention to my voice."

While I was listening to him I wondered if accidentally I would be put under hypnosis. I think I'm getting carried away.

Mr. Samuels started off by asking Lisa questions that had nothing to do with the death of her mother. That went on for a little while. He then brought Lisa back to that night. I was getting anxious knowing where he was leading Lisa.

"Now Lisa, I'm going to take you back to the night your mother died. Do you remember where you were?"

"I was in bed sleeping."

"Good. What happened next?"

"I heard something and it woke me up."

"Do you remember what you heard?"

"Yelling."

"Who's yelling?"

"I think it's my mother."

"Can you hear what she's yelling about?"

"No."

"Can you make out anyone else's voice?"

"I can't. It was only for a few seconds and then it stopped.

"Okay Lisa, What did you do then?"

"I was scared. I called out to mommy but she didn't answer."

"What happened next?"

"I climbed out of my bed and slowly walked to my mommy's bedroom. I heard footsteps running down the stairs."

"Could you see who was running?"

"I saw someone as they were opening the door to leave."

"Do you remember anything about the person?"

"I think they had on a gray coat."

"Can you remember anything else about this

person?"

"I can only see their back."

"Okay, that's good. Is there anything else you remember?"

"There's a smell."

"Where is the smell coming from?"

"Outside mommy's room."

"Try to remember what kind of smell it was."

"It was strong like mommy or daddy smells."

"Like perfume or cologne?"

"Yes, I think so."

"Do you think you would remember the cologne or perfume if someone was wearing it?"

"I don't know."

"What did you do then?"

"I wanted my mommy. I wasn't supposed to go into her room unless she said I could."

"But you did?"

"I didn't want her to be mad at me."

"Of course. What happened next?"

"I want to go back to my room!" Lisa said raising her voice.

I could tell she was getting agitated.

"Lisa, stay with me. What do you see?"

"Please, I want to go back to my room!" Lisa was becoming hysterical.

"Lisa you can open your eyes now. You're fine. Just relax for a few minutes."

"What happened?"

"You did great."

"Did I remember anything important?"

"I think it would be best if Tracey discusses what you remembered."

"I don't think I want to have another session."

"That's fine. It's your decision."

"Thank you."

"You did fantastic," I said to Lisa as we were leaving Mr. Samuels' office.

"Did I say anything that was helpful?"

"You said that in the hallway by your mother's room there was a strong scent and it may have been cologne or perfume. It's possible you might recall what the scent was."

"How will that help?"

"If it does come back to you, it might trigger who wore that cologne or perfume."

"Maybe."

"Either way, don't put any pressure on yourself to remember."

Lisa took the train back to her office and I grabbed an Uber. It would have been helpful if she could have identified anyone else's voice, damn. Though Lisa remembered a few more details, there were still too many questions that remained unanswered.

CHAPTER 27

It was almost 3:00 pm when I finally got into the office. I had stopped for a salad. While the hypnotherapy session was fresh in my mind, I wrote it up, along with my interview with Jackie Donovan. Though Celia Ramirez heard Jackie threaten Rebecca, the jury was still out whether Jackie was a suspect. At this moment I had only one viable suspect, Jason Kane, though I was reserving judgment on Simon Mack.

I picked up the phone and called Susie.

"Hey, had it go with the hypnotherapist?"

"Interesting. Lisa remembered a smell that was in the hallway by her mother's room. She thinks it was perfume or cologne. It must have been strong for her to recall that memory. She couldn't remember anything about the person who was leaving the house except that they were wearing a gray coat."

"Can you find out what kind of cologne her father uses?"

"We're talking over twenty years ago. He probably doesn't use the same cologne."

"That's true but does he use cologne that has a strong scent? If he does, most likely he did back then."

"Or maybe I can just ask him what he used back

164

then," I said jokingly.

"That could work."

"I think she saw her mother lying in the bathroom."

"How do you know?"

"She never said she did, but something really frightened her. She became hysterical and was crying, saying she wanted to go back to her room. I think she went into her mother's bedroom even though she wasn't allowed and saw her mother lying on the bathroom floor covered in blood."

"Do you think she remembered what happened?"

"No, and I have no intention of telling her. If she can't remember on her own there's a reason. No need for her to relive a traumatic experience."

"You did the right thing."

"Where's Mark?" I asked.

"He went to work. He should be back soon. I'm thinking of going back to work next week. Staying home doesn't help. If I'm at work at least I'll be keeping busy and have less time to think about anything else."

"That's probably a good idea. And being around other people might be helpful."

"I know we can try again and it's not uncommon to have a miscarriage. I know all that intellectually, I'm just not sure if I want to take another chance."

"Patty was depressed for quite a while because she thought she may never have children."

"What did she do?"

"She went to see a therapist and she said it helped. I think she had a different perspective after seeing someone. Maybe they might have adopted if Michael hadn't come along. And Patty was in her middle forties when she had him."

"Is that your subtle way of saying I should see someone? You of all people who thinks she can solve her own problems, and just the thought of going to a therapist gives you anxiety."

"I made an appointment to see Patty's therapist."

"I'm shocked. What's going on?"

"I'm not going to tell Jack yet. I want to see how it goes first, so please don't say anything to Mark."

"My lips are sealed. What made you do a three-sixty?"

"If Jack hadn't come along, I might not have. I can't get past the commitment issue. It's not fair to Jack."

"Jack's a big boy. It's not fair to you. You deserve more."

"Well let's see what happens. Stay tuned."

"I love you."

"Love you."

When I got home I made one of my famous peanut butter, hold the jelly, sandwiches. My phone rang.

"Hello."

"Are you trying to cause my daughter to have a nervous breakdown?"

"What the hell are you talking about?" I was getting tired of Jason Kane's lectures.

"Lisa told me you took her to a hypnotherapist. She was practically in tears."

"First of all, none of it is your business and secondly, Lisa wanted to go."

"But it was your idea. You're messing with her head and I want this stopped."

"Maybe you want it stopped because you have something to hide."

"What are you implying?"

"I'm not implying. I know your alibi was bullshit so don't come off high and mighty with me, and stop threatening me!" With that I hung up.

After my heart stopped racing I called Lisa.

"Lisa, I had another call from your dad."

"I'm sorry. He just caught me at a bad time. It won't happen again."

"Alright, don't worry about it."

As I was hanging up, Jack called.

"I am so happy it's you." I went on to tell him everything that happened including my altercation with Jason Kane.

"You really told him that?"

"I did. My heart was beating so fast I thought I was going to give myself a heart attack."

"Well he deserved it."

"If he did kill his wife he knows I'm on to him."

"If he did it's going to be almost impossible to prove, even if he did lie about his alibi. With only circumstantial evidence it's going to be very difficult to make your case. Go back over everything you learned so far. Maybe something will jump out at you. Also it might be a good idea to go over the police reports again."

"Unless someone decides to confess, what do I have to lose."

"That's the spirit."

"How are things going with Jake?"

"Except for the firm's Monday morning meetings to discuss any new cases or to talk about current cases, we haven't seen much of each other so far."

"How's my bike?"

"She's fine. I fed her some straw from the barn. I'll take her out for a ride later."

"I guess I had that coming."

"Sleep tight and don't worry. Everything will work out."

CHAPTER 28

As soon as I got up the next day I plugged in the coffee maker, took a shower and pulled out the police file on Rebecca. After going through it again I decided to contact Detective Cooper since there were some things I wasn't clear about.

"Hello."

"Detective Cooper, it's Tracey Marks. We spoke a couple of weeks ago on the Rebecca Kane murder."

"Hi Tracey, how's it going?"

"That's what I'm calling you about." I wasn't sure how much to tell him even if he was no longer working for the police department.

"I have a couple of questions."

"Shoot. I'll see if I have any answers for you."

"Is it unusual that there was no forensic evidence at the scene?"

"From what I remember there was a partial fingerprint but not enough to work with. But to answer your question, there might not have been much of a struggle. If that's the case that could be the reason there wasn't any other physical evidence. It was winter and if the killer had gloves on that also would reduce the chances of any physical evidence."

"I see. I noticed there was one interview with a Mrs. Rogers who said she heard the Kane's in a shouting match. There didn't appear to be any follow up questions. Also, there were only three neighbors interviewed. Was there a reason?"

"I'm not sure. I know I usually assigned those neighborhood interviews to my police team helping me with the investigation. It's possible when they were canvassing some of the neighbors weren't home and they never went back."

"It's probably not important," I said.

"Did you find out anything?" Detective Cooper asked.

"Apparently there was someone Rebecca was seeing at the time of her death."

"That's interesting. How did you find out?"

"One of her friends told me. She was away at the time Rebecca was murdered so she was never questioned."

"What's your vibe on him?"

"Not sure. He was in love with Rebecca. There was still pain on his face when he spoke about her. I can't rule him out. I still like the husband for it but we'll see."

"If you have any other questions feel free to call."

"Thanks."

After hanging up I took out my corkboard and 5x7 index cards. I added the names Simon Mack and Jacqueline Donovan to my list of suspects. Off to the side I tacked up cards with the names of Miguel Cortez, Howard Stein and Danielle Kane. Though I had reached out to Miguel Cortez I had the feeling there was something he was hiding or afraid of. I thought I would pay him a visit at some point. As far as Danielle Kane is concerned, if she wasn't with her husband the night

Rebecca died, I wouldn't expect a confession, but I would like to see her reaction.

In the meantime I was interested in tracking down the neighbors living on the Kane's block during that time period. Except for Janice Rogers and two neighbors that lived across the street from the Kane's, I had no clue who the other neighbors were. Hopefully Janice Rogers is still living next door.

Time for good old fashion PI work, canvassing the block. I drove to Jason Kane's brownstone and found a parking spot at the end of the street. I rang the bell where Mrs. Rogers had lived twenty years ago. My fingers and toes were crossed.

"Hello." A young man, probably in his early thirties answered the door. Not a good sign unless it was her son.

"Sorry to bother you. I'm looking for a Janice Rogers who used to live here."

"I bought this place from her about five years ago."

"Would you happen to know where she went?"

"What's this about?"

"I'm looking into the murder of a woman who lived next door," I said handing him my card.

"When was she murdered?"

"Twenty years ago, but now the family would like to reopen the investigation since her murderer was never caught."

"But the Kane's have been here longer than twenty years."

"It was Mr. Kane's first wife, Rebecca."

"Wow! Was it a break-in?"

"The police didn't think so."

"Did they suspect the husband?"

This conversation was getting out of hand.

"I don't know. Did Mrs. Rogers mention where she

was moving to?" I said, trying to get him back on track.

"I think she said some place in North Carolina."

"Would you happen to know approximately how old she would be?"

"Maybe in her sixties."

"Was she married?"

"I don't think so."

"Well I appreciate all your help."

"Good luck."

I walked to the brownstone to the left of the Kane's. No one was home. I left my card in the door. I thought I would try a couple more houses while I was here.

As I was walking to the next place, I saw an elderly gentleman walking his dog. When I got up closer I pegged him for maybe eighty years old or thereabouts.

"Hi, sorry to bother you," I said.

"No bother. When you get to be my age and don't have much to do, I welcome a pretty young lady to talk with."

"You're not old."

"Well I'm not young."

"You got me there. I'm Tracey, by the way."

"I'm Morris. Nice to meet you."

"Likewise. I was wondering if you've lived on this block for a while."

"Almost forty years."

"Would you happen to remember a woman by the name of Rebecca Kane that was killed about twenty years ago?"

"Sure. It was the talk of the neighborhood back then. The police even suspected Mr. Kane. So why does a young lady like yourself inquire about a murder?"

"I'm a private investigator hired by a family member to reopen the case."

"That's interesting. Would you like to come in for a

cup of coffee?"

"I never refuse coffee." He seemed harmless enough.

Morris' place was beautiful. My eyes were everywhere.

"I love your place."

"Thank you my dear but I owe it all to my late wife."

"Oh, I'm sorry."

"I am too. She was the love of my life and as you can tell a wonderful decorator. I have someone come in a few times a week to make sure I don't make a mess of the place."

We went into a room right off the kitchen. It had a white hardwood floor, two white wicker chairs with cushions in a floral design, and an off white needlepoint rug with a rose colored border. There were potted and hanging plants that added warmth to the room.

"How do you take your coffee?"

"Black, no sugar please."

After handing me a cup of delicious smelling coffee, Morris sat down on one of the chairs while I sat opposite him on the other chair.

"What can you tell me about Rebecca and Jason Kane?"

"I thought they were an odd couple though I can't say why. They once had a party and my wife and I were invited. It was a lovely party."

I wasn't sure if Morris had any information that was relevant or he was just a lonely man who wanted the company.

"What I meant by odd is that anytime I saw them together, they didn't seem that happy. I think Rebecca was a little drunk at the party. She wasn't mingling with her guests."

"And you remember that from more than twenty years ago? I can't remember what happened yesterday."

"It was something I observed, and with her murder it probably stayed with me."

"Did something happen at the party?"

"Not really, though she was having an argument with her brother. They were in the kitchen by themselves and I was standing right by the door."

"Did you hear what they were arguing about?"

"No, but Rebecca seemed awfully mad."

"Did the police ever question you?"

"Nope, they never did."

"Would you happen to know where one of your neighbors, Janice Rogers, moved to?"

"It was North Carolina. Would you like more coffee?"

"No, I'm good, thank you. Do you know where in North Carolina?"

"I have her address. We exchange Christmas cards every year. She was a lovely neighbor. Never married. Had a super high powered job. She was so kind to me when my wife passed on."

"Do you think I can have her address? I'd like to talk with her."

"I can do better than that. I can give you her telephone number."

"That would be even better."

"Did you speak with Cindy yet?" he said.

"Who's Cindy?"

"Rebecca's friend. They would sometimes take their kids to the park together."

"Does she live around here?"

"She used to but she moved after her divorce. Janice might know where she lives now."

"Do you recall Cindy's last name?"

"Can't say as I do."

I stayed a while. He was so kind and I didn't want to

seem like I was in a hurry to leave. We chatted. Morris told me about his career as an architect. Apparently he was involved in designing some pretty famous buildings. As he talked, I realized what an interesting man he was.

Walking back to my car I thought how lucky I was to bump into Morris. My mother used to say never judge a book by its cover. Besides Morris being delightful company, it turned out his information might be very helpful to my investigation.

Instead of going back to the office I went home and typed up the conversation I had with Morris. I wondered what the fight between Rebecca and her brother was all about. I guess it could have been any number of things, including family stuff.

After making myself some scrambled eggs and toast, I called Janice Rogers. It went straight to voice mail and left her a message.

About an hour later I changed into my running clothes and headed to the park. There were tons of people taking advantage of the nice weather. Sunbathers were stretched out on the grass, some in shorts and others wearing bikinis. Laying out in the sun has never been appealing to me. Even on a beach you'll find me under an umbrella.

On the way back I stopped at my neighborhood pizza place and ordered a couple of slices to go for dinner later. I had finished the last of my ice cream the other day so I headed over to the Corner Sweet Shoppe.

"Hi Mr. Hayes."

"Hi Tracey. Just in time to try my latest combination. Let me know what you think?"

"Yum, mocha with peanut butter. That should go over well with your customers."

"How's your nice young man?"

"Jack's good. Maybe next time he's in the city we'll

stop in."

"Here you go," Mr. Hayes said, handing me a pint of pistachio ice cream.

"See ya soon," I said waving goodbye.

When I got home I noticed a missed call from Janice Rogers.

"Mrs. Rogers, this is Tracey Marks. Thank you for returning my call."

"I spoke with Morris about an hour ago and he told me you were investigating Rebecca's murder."

"Yes, that's correct. Do you have a few minutes to speak with me now?"

"This is fine. At the time it was so upsetting. I think people got the wrong idea about Rebecca and that was a shame."

"What do you mean?"

"I believe they thought she was a cold fish and maybe she did appear that way, but I got the impression that Rebecca was not a happy person, though I'm no therapist."

"Did she confide in you?"

"Not really."

"In your initial interview you told the officer that you heard the Kane's arguing. Did they argue a lot?"

"I can't say how often, but when they did, it was a real screaming match."

"Did Rebecca ever talk to you about her husband or her marriage?"

"Never. And I didn't want to be one of those nosy neighbors."

Too bad, I thought to myself.

"Morris mentioned a woman named Cindy who Rebecca sometimes hung out with. Would you happen to know her last name or where she moved to?"

"Cindy Marshall. I believe she's still living in the

city."

"Did she ever remarry?"

"Not that I'm aware of."

"How do you like it in North Carolina?" I asked, trying to be polite.

"I love it here. Charlotte is a lovely city. I'm so happy I'm no longer living in New York."

"Well thank you for your time."

Now I knew why there was nothing else reported from the original interview. Besides hearing loud arguments, Janice Rogers didn't have any other information that would have been significant to the investigation.

CHAPTER 29

I stuck the pizza slices in the oven to warm up while I took a quick shower. I made a salad to get something healthy in my body and poured myself a glass of wine.

Now that I was recharged, I opened up my computer and did a search for Cindy Marshall. There was one that matched. Cindy was around fifty and living on the west side.

I picked up my phone and called her.

"Hello."

"I'm trying to get in touch with Cindy Marshall."

"Yes, this is she."

"My name is Tracey Marks and I'm investigating the death of Rebecca Kane."

"Really! That was over twenty years ago. Why are you looking into her death now?"

"I was hired by her daughter Lisa to reopen the case. Do you think we can meet? I have some questions which I would rather ask in person."

"I'm in meetings most of the day tomorrow. If it's not going to be too long, I could possibly see you say around 12:30. There's a coffee place two doors down from my building. You can't miss it."

"Thank you."

Mrs. Marshall gave me her work address before hanging up and a brief description of herself.

I then called Susie.

"Hi," I said when she answered the phone. "Am I interrupting anything?"

"We were just cleaning up from dinner."

"Can I interest you in some lunch on Saturday? I won't keep you out that long."

"Mark gave the thumbs up. Anything to get me out of the apartment."

"I'll meet you in front of your building at high noon."

I was glad Susie agreed to have lunch with me. I miss our time together, and I'm keeping my fingers crossed that she's decided to go back to work on Monday.

When I got into bed I called Jack.

"How's my big, strong man doing?"

"You sure you have the right number?"

"So hilarious. I made a playdate with Susie for lunch on Saturday."

"That's encouraging."

"I hope so. You miss me?"

"Absolutely. I was thinking about you just before you called."

"Oh yeah. What kind of thoughts were you having?" I said.

"The kind dirty old men have."

"What would you know about dirty old men thoughts?"

"I like to think I have some imagination."

"Talking about old men, I met this elderly gentleman today who lured me into his house by offering me a cup of coffee."

"If I knew that was all it took I wouldn't have tried so hard."

"I met him quite by accident. He was walking his dog on the block where Jason Kane still lives. I was doing good old fashion PI work, talking to the neighbors."

"Did he enlighten you about the Kane's?"

"As a matter of fact he did." I filled Jack in on the conversation I had with Morris.

"Well it seems like I might have competition with this guy Morris. Should I be worried?" Jack said. I could picture him smiling.

"Why don't we leave that open for now. We'll see how things go."

"Playing both ends. Smart lady."

"What are you up to this weekend?" I asked Jack.

"My friend has tickets to a Boston Red Socks game. We're leaving early in the morning. Depending on what time the game finishes, we might stay over."

"That sounds like fun. I don't know much about baseball. My father was a Mets fan. I think he would have preferred to root for the Giants but as you know they left New York for sunny California so he became a Mets fan by default."

"Why don't you come up here next weekend. We can bike if you're up for it."

"I'll give it the old college try. I'm meeting with this woman Cindy Marshall tomorrow. I'm hoping Rebecca confided in her, though it seems like whatever was going on with her, she kept it to herself."

"Keep at it. Something will shake out."

"I hope so."

"Sleep tight."

"Ditto."

CHAPTER 30

I was waiting for Cindy Marshall outside of the coffee place the following day. I spotted her walking towards me. Cindy was petite, her straight blonde hair trimmed close to her ears. She was wearing business attire.

"Hi," I said as she approached me.

"Why don't we go inside," Cindy said.

We found our way to a cute table that had striped yellow and brown cushions on the chairs. When the waiter came over I ordered a cappuccino and croissant and Cindy had the same.

"So you're looking into Rebecca's death. It was a shame they never found out who killed her back then."

"Did you have any suspicions of who it might have been at the time?"

"I can tell you she was going to divorce her husband. That may have given him a motive."

"Unfortunately, someone gave him an alibi at the time," I said.

"I've seen enough TV shows to know that alibis don't mean much."

That was an interesting comment, I thought to myself. According to the police, at the time they thought Jason had an airtight alibi, but now we know his alibi was bogus. Maybe if the police had talked to Cindy they would have tried harder to poke holes in Jason Kane's alibi.

"Were you and Rebecca close?"

"I wouldn't say close. We went to the park sometimes with the kids and had dinner together maybe once a month."

"Did Rebecca mention any problems she was having with anyone besides her husband?"

"Not that I'm aware of."

"Her brother told me that they weren't on good terms before she died. He thought Rebecca should have been paying more attention to her daughter. He felt she was neglecting her," I said.

"It's true Lisa spent a lot of time with the nanny, but I'm not sure I would say she was neglecting Lisa. I know she took on someone to run the dress shop so it would give her more free time with her daughter."

It doesn't mean she spent that time with Lisa, I said to myself.

"Did you know Rebecca was having an affair?"

"Yes, she told me."

"What did she say?"

"Just that she couldn't stand her husband and wanted out of the marriage."

"Was he abusive?"

"No, nothing like that, though he was a control freak or that's what Rebecca told me. Besides he was having his own affair."

"Did Rebecca tell you that?"

"Yes, but I didn't get the impression that she cared."

"Was there anything worrying Rebecca that you can recall?"

"Not that I can remember."

"Well thanks for meeting me. If you think of

anything else here's my card."

On my walk over to Jason Kane's offices to see his law partner, Howard Stein, I thought about the conversation I had with Cindy. She really didn't know anything more than I had already found out. Either Rebecca was tight-lipped or nothing was going on in her life except for her indiscretions.

I rode up to the seventh floor where the offices of Kane and Stein were located.

"May I help you?" the receptionist asked me.

"I would like to see Howard Stein. My name is Tracey Marks."

"Do you have an appointment?"

"No, but can you tell him it's about Rebecca Kane."

The receptionist had a funny look on her face as though she wasn't sure what I was talking about. She picked up the phone and repeated what I said to Mr. Stein.

"Mr. Stein is waiting, second door on the right."

Mr. Stein got up to greet me and we shook hands.

"Ms. Marks, take a seat."

Mr. Stein was medium height and on the stocky side. He was completely bald, which suited him.

"Thanks for seeing me. I know you're a busy man so I won't take up too much of your time. I'm not sure if Mr. Kane told you that someone was looking into the death of his first wife Rebecca."

"He mentioned it."

"Were the two of you partners back then?"

"Not right away. My father had started the firm but he retired a while ago. Now it's just the two of us."

"So you knew Jason before he married Rebecca?"

"I was his best man."

"Can you tell me about their relationship?"

"The one thing I can tell you for a fact is that Jason had nothing to do with Rebecca's death."

"How can you be so sure?"

"I know Jason."

"Did you know he was having an affair while he was married to Rebecca?"

"Yes. That doesn't make him a killer."

"That is true. But it doesn't make him husband of the year either."

Mr. Stein did not comment.

I wasn't sure how much I wanted to stir the pot and tell him about Jason's false alibi for the night of his wife's death.

"At the time there did seem to be quite a bit of circumstantial evidence against Mr. Kane."

"You could see it that way though he did have an alibi."

"Only if the person who gave him that alibi was telling the truth."

"What are you implying?"

"I'm not implying anything, but we do know that sometimes people lie."

"I think we're finished here," he said getting up out of his chair. My signal to do the same.

"Well thank you for your time Mr. Stein." He did not shake my hand on my way out.

I wondered if Mr. Stein was going to relate our conversation to Jason.

Before calling it quits for the day, I thought I would make an impromptu visit to David Martin's wife, Gabriele. I knew they lived on the Upper East Side in the eighties. I thought I would take my chances and see if she was home.

The doorman at Gabriele Martin's building picked up the phone and I assume spoke to Gabriele since a moment later I was told to go right up. They lived on the ninth floor. There were seventeen floors to the building.

When the door opened I was looking up at a stunning woman with long straight dark hair and a flawless complexion. Her willowy body moved gracefully as she showed me into the living room. The room was very modern with beautiful artwork on the walls.

"Please sit. David told me you were looking into Rebecca's death."

"Did you know Rebecca?"

"Oh, I guess no one told you. I introduced Rebecca to Jason."

That was a surprise.

"How did you know Rebecca?"

"We met at the Fashion Institute. I knew Jason from some friends and introduced them."

"So you met David through his sister?"

"Yes, but we didn't date until maybe a year or two after Rebecca and Jason were married."

"Were you aware of any problems between Rebecca and David?"

"Not that I knew of. Why do you ask that?"

"Oh it's probably nothing. David had mentioned that he wasn't a fan of the way Rebecca was bringing up Lisa. He didn't think she was spending enough time with her daughter."

"I don't remember David being upset with Rebecca. I know their parents were not around much when David and Rebecca were growing up."

"David told me he wasn't talking to Rebecca at the time of her death," I said.

"Now I remember, you may be right. It was so long ago I had forgotten that they had argued about Lisa," Gabriele said, fumbling over her words.

I knew she wasn't telling the truth but decided not to say anything, though I was curious why she was lying.

"Did you know of any problems between Jason and Rebecca?"

"Rebecca was probably going to divorce him. She knew he was cheating on her, and I also believe Rebecca had a problem with all the money Jason was spending, none of which he earned. It was Rebecca's family money."

"Do you think he killed her?"

"To tell you the truth I can't say one way or the other."

"Well I appreciate your honesty. Do you think Rebecca was jealous of David because their parents brought David into the business and not her?"

"I don't think Rebecca was interested in the business. She always wanted to open up a dress shop."

"Yet, she had someone run the business for her on a day-to-day basis. Would you happen to know why?"

"I know she was going into the store at least two days a week, and she spent several weeks in Paris and Italy buying merchandise for the shop each year. You can't run a store by yourself. There's too much to do. By having someone take care of the day to day she didn't have to worry that things weren't running smoothly when she wasn't there."

"That makes sense. And I can understand why your husband felt the way he did knowing how much time Lisa was being raised by a nanny instead of her mother."

"I think Rebecca did the best she could," Gabriele said.

"I appreciate your time and thank you for clearing up some things for me. By the way did the police question you when Rebecca died?"

"No, but I'm pretty sure they questioned David."

On the way down in the elevator it was clear that David had lied to me about the reason he and his sister were not speaking when she died. I had to find out why.

CHAPTER 31

I didn't get home till almost 6:00 pm. I stopped at the fish store and decided to buy a piece of filleted Branzino. I thought I would give it a try since I had never made it before.

After changing into my sweats I tackled the fish. Google said I could pan fry it in some butter and olive oil. I did as instructed and was pleasantly surprised when the kitchen didn't catch on fire and the fish didn't burn. While I was waiting for my fish to cook, I quickly made a salad and poured myself a glass of wine.

While I was eating I made some notes on the case and what my next steps would be. So far I wasn't any closer to finding out who killed Rebecca than when I started. Was I missing something? Maybe I had to dig deeper into the possible suspects I had. But without any forensic evidence and a twenty year old murder, who's going to admit to killing Rebecca. If I was the doer, I certainly wouldn't. I was hoping Susie might have some ideas.

I woke up to blue skies but a chilly morning. In a few more days it'll be October. Though serious runners brave the weather, whatever it may be, I have to say anything below forty degrees, I would rather go to the gym.

I ran my three mile loop and on the way back I stopped for a coffee. It was starting to warm up by the time I reached my building.

"Hi, Miss Tracey, I thought that was you earlier leaving the building."

"Hi Wally. What are you doing here today, isn't it your day off?"

"James called in sick. I don't mind and I get to see your smiling face."

"You always know the right thing to say. Well enjoy the nice weather."

"I certainly will."

Susie was just coming out of her building when I arrived.

"Mark gave me specific instructions not to come home before 5:00 pm. What can I take from that?"

"You need fresh air plus he's probably tired of you hanging out at home."

"What a nice husband," Susie said with a half smile.

We walked over to the French café a few blocks away. We waited a couple of minutes before we were seated.

"I decided to go back to work on Monday."

"Well this calls for a celebration. How about mimosas all around?"

The waitress came over and I ordered my usual, French toast and bacon very crisp. Susie ordered an omelet with home fries. We each ordered a mimosa and coffee.

"I thought maybe half days to start, and then I'll see how it goes," Susie said.

"That's a good idea. I don't think your boss will mind."

"Are you kidding, he'd be thrilled as long as my body was there. We'll see how long that lasts."

"I think I'm more suited to working on my own, not having a boss."

"That's for sure. You should go to law school and then we can open up our own law firm."

"Or you can become a PI and the firm can be Marks and Jacobs."

"Why is your name first?"

"Because it's beauty before age and besides, I'm the more experienced one."

"I see. Well now that you've had your fun, what's going on with the case?"

"Here you go ladies," setting down our mimosas and coffee. "Your food will be out in a few minutes."

"Thank you," I said.

"I've got three possible suspects, no evidence and a twenty year old murder. Otherwise everything's dandy."

"So who are the three suspects?"

"Rebecca's husband, Rebecca's best friend Jacqueline and the third is Rebecca's lover."

"Why the lover?"

"He was madly in love with Rebecca and would have married her, but from what I learned she had no intentions of marrying him. I got the feeling that may have angered him just a bit."

"Why Jacqueline?"

"Rebecca slept with Jackie's husband back then, and the nanny that took care of Lisa overhead Jacqueline screaming and threatening Rebecca."

"Jacqueline's ex sounds like a prince. What else did you learn?"

"At the time of Rebecca's death she and her brother David were not speaking. From what he mentioned, he was upset at Rebecca because he felt she had been neglecting her daughter. But when I spoke with David's wife, she had no recollection of that fight."

"It was over twenty years ago so that seems reasonable."

"It would, but then she changed her story and happened to remember that's what they fought about."

"That's interesting. Something made her change her mind."

"I think David and Rebecca fought for another reason. But why make up something, why not just tell me the truth?"

"Maybe he was embarrassed. I wondered if David's mother might know," Susie said.

The waitress brought our food and filled our coffee cups.

"That's a thought. Also, there was this guy working at the warehouse at the time of Rebecca's death. Though I spoke to him briefly, he sounded frightened."

"How could you tell?"

"He cut me off and hung up. I noticed he had an accent, maybe from Mexico."

"If he's illegal that would be a good reason. He hears private investigator and he gets scared."

"Good point. I'll have to try and question him."

"Tread lightly. Try not to frighten him."

"Talk to me. What's going on with you?" I said.

"You know before I was pregnant I wasn't sure if I wanted a baby, but when it happened something changed. It's hard to describe. And when I lost the baby I had never felt such an emptiness. It took me by surprise. I realized how much I wanted this baby."

"I'm so sorry sweetie," I said, reaching for Susie's hand.

"I'm not sure I could go through that again."

"But now you know how much you want a child. I

know there are no guarantees but it doesn't mean it will happen again. I'm sure the doctor has told you it's fairly common, and women go on to deliver healthy babies. Anyway it's probably way too early to decide anything now."

We finished up and took a walk over to Central Park.

"So when is your first appointment with the therapist?" Susie asked as we were leisurely walking through the park.

"Monday at 5:00 pm. I have to tell you I'm not looking forward to it. I wouldn't even know where to begin."

"Not to worry, she'll put you at ease."

"What if I'm incurable?"

At that point Susie was laughing hysterically. It almost brought tears to my eyes.

"It's not like you're dying. If you are 'incurable' it will still be fine," Susie said in between fits of laughter. "You'll still have me."

"Well that's true."

"But I think you're going to be surprised. It might take a while, hopefully not before you're old and gray."

"I can always count on you to cheer me up."

"It's funny how it's easier to cheer someone else up than yourself."

I didn't say anything.

After meandering for about two hours, we stopped for a drink at Cafe Fiorello near Lincoln Center.

By 5:15 I wore Susie out and we walked back to her building where we hugged and said goodbye, but not before she made me promise to call her right after my therapy session.

CHAPTER 32

First thing on Monday morning I called Sylvia Martin, David and Rebecca's mother. She agreed to see me at her home in Bronxville at 11:30 am.

When I arrived I followed Mrs. Martin into the same room we sat in the last time I was there.

"Can I get you a cup of coffee or something else to drink?"

"No, I'm fine thank you."

"Since we last spoke have you learned anything new?"

"I can tell you that I have been interviewing several people, some of whom were never questioned by the police, but I can't provide you with any of that information."

"I see. So what did you want to talk to me about?" There was irritation in her voice.

"I was told that at the time Rebecca died, Rebecca and David were not speaking. Were you aware of that?"

"Have you asked David?"

"I have but I was wondering if you knew?"

"To tell you the truth I had no idea they weren't speaking. What did David tell you?"

I decided to share that with Mrs. Martin to see her

reaction.

"David said he felt Rebecca was neglecting Lisa and confronted his sister about it. They got into a fight and Rebecca stopped speaking to him."

"If that's what he said, I have no reason to doubt him."

"Can you think of any other reason why they wouldn't be talking?"

"Why would I?"

Something about Mrs. Martin's tone changed. It was very subtle. I wondered if she was hiding something.

"Were they close?"

"Rebecca and David led different lives. Rebecca had Lisa and the clothing shop and David was busy learning the business. Nothing more than that."

"I just thought maybe Rebecca and Jason and David and Gabriele socialized together."

"I can't tell you if they did. Why is this important?"

I didn't want to tell her I thought her son was lying.

"It's probably not."

"I'm not a stupid woman Ms. Marks. Do you think my son is lying to you?"

"I don't know."

"Apparently you have some reason to believe he is. Please don't beat around the bush."

"I'm not." I wanted to leave it at that, but I said: "I have my doubts whether David was completely honest with me. I'm not convinced that would be the reason the two of them were not talking."

Mrs. Martin seemed to be lost in her own thoughts and did not respond. I didn't know what else to ask her. I was just about ready to leave when she said:

"Do you think my son killed his sister?"

"At this point I have no idea who killed Rebecca."

"I can't imagine David hurting Rebecca. It's

preposterous. I hope you find out who did."

Driving back I was curious about the change in attitude of Mrs. Martin when I confronted her about David. But to lose a child and then to possibly think your only other child was the killer is almost unimaginable. Let's hope that's not the case.

I picked up a turkey sandwich and coleslaw before going back to the office. I had a couple of hours before I was due for my therapy appointment. I had to keep busy so I wouldn't think about chickening out, which is what I wanted to do.

In writing up the conversation with Mrs. Martin, I didn't learn anything new except she appeared to have no clue what was going on with her kids. Maybe most parents don't. I'm not the expert in that department.

I was feeling antsy so I went across the hall to Cousin Alan.

"Hi Margaret."

"Tracey, always so lovely to see you."

"Well aren't you the chipper one. Did my cousin give you a raise?"

"I wish. No, nothing like that. Jaden got an A on his math exam. He's been failing so we got him a tutor, and we're glad to see it's money well spent. An Einstein he's not, but who is?"

"That's great. Happy to hear it."

"Knock and go right in."

"Hey there."

"Come, sit down. What's going on?"

"Not much. Case is driving me a little crazy. No one wants to admit killing Rebecca."

"Well they are just plain rude."

"I think so. How's my little man?"

"Getting bigger every day. He keeps asking for you."

"I'll call Patty and stop by."

"Anything else on your mind?"

"Nope." I wanted to ask him about our family or lack of, but something held me back.

"Next time Jack's here why don't you come over for dinner?"

"Well since he's in love with Patty and her cooking, that won't be too difficult. I gotta go. Give Michael a big hug and kiss from me."

"Will do. Be careful."

"Always."

At 4:30 I drove over to the Upper East Side where Dr. Davidson's office is located. I found a parking spot two blocks away. As I was walking to her office my palms started to sweat. Thoughts of turning around were going through my head. I've gone this long without it and I'm doing okay, why rock the boat? But I kept my feet moving towards her office.

When I walked in the receptionist Sandy took the forms I had filled out at home. She told me the doctor would be right with me.

A minute later a door opened and a woman who I assumed was Lily Davidson called me in.

"Nice to meet you Tracey. Please call me Lily. Why don't you have a seat."

Ms. Davidson was a woman in her sixties. She looked like anyone's grandmother, not a young sixty. Somehow it made me feel more comfortable.

"I thought you're supposed to lie down on a couch."

She smiled. "There are some forms of therapy where you lie down but I prefer having eye contact with the client."

"So what now?"

"Why don't you tell me why you're here?"

"I'm scared to death to be in a relationship."

"Can you say a little more about that?"

"Where do I begin?"

"Anywhere you like. There are no rules."

"Until now I've never been in a long term relationship, and I've never been preoccupied with having a boyfriend. I'm not sure why."

"Tell me a little bit about yourself."

"I was an only child. I didn't have any friends growing up but that was my fault. I liked being by myself. I talked to kids when I was in school but I never invited anyone to come home and play with me."

"Did anyone ask you?"

"Not that I can remember. It wasn't until I was in high school when I met Susie."

"Tell me about that?"

"Her desk was next to mine in math class. It was only because she kept pestering me that I spoke with her. And also I was terrible in math and she was a whiz at it."

"Did you become friends?"

"We did. Susie is my best friend, actually my only friend, and the closest person in my life."

"Was there something about her that you were drawn to?"

"I guess it was her personality. She is so different than me."

"In what ways?"

"She's upbeat and bubbly and annoying."

"Why was that appealing to you?"

"I had never met anyone like that before. I am just the opposite, more reserved and cynical."

"Tell me about your family."

"Susie and my Cousin Alan and his wife are my family. And now their son, Michael."

"What about your parents?"

I started to feel sad and my eyes were welling up.

"They were wonderful parents. My father died when I was thirteen and my mother died when I was twenty."

"That must have been very difficult for you losing both parents at such a young age."

Tears were slipping down my face.

"They were everything to me. I was lucky to have them."

"How did your parents die?"

"My father had a heart attack. I was sitting at the kitchen table doing my homework and my father was cooking dinner, my favorite, macaroni and cheese. I heard this loud thud and when I looked up my father was on the floor. I couldn't move. I screamed and my mother came running in. After that it was a blur."

"Do you remember how you felt after he died?"

"I was sad a lot and I felt sad for my mother. I think she tried to be cheerful for me but I knew it was an act. My mother got breast cancer when I was seventeen. She battled until she died three years later."

"You know Tracey, it's understandable how losing both your parents at a young age, especially because they were your entire life, can shape the way you look at the world around you. It can be scary. And forming attachments might be difficult. We like to think we're unique but we're not. I can assure you that what you feel and your thoughts, there are other people with the same feelings and thoughts.

"I think this may be a good time to stop. Would you like to come back next week?"

All I could do was nod my head in the affirmative.

I couldn't believe how exhausted I felt after the session. When I got home I undressed and slipped on a tee shirt. I looked for something to eat. I had leftover shrimp and broccoli from yesterday and some brown rice. I heated it up, dumped it all into a bowl and sat down to eat.

Afterward the only energy I had left was to read my Michael Connelly book in bed. My phone rang as I was trying to keep my eyes open.

"Hi Jack."

"You sound tired. Everything alright?"

"Yeah. I didn't sleep that great last night. How was the ball game?"

"Boston won. It was a close game but we pulled it out. How is Susie feeling?"

"She decided to go back to work today, at least part time. I miss you."

"You sure everything's okay?"

"I'll call you tomorrow. I just need a good night's sleep."

"I love you."

"Me too."

I hated lying to Jack. I felt bad. Maybe I should tell him about the therapy. In the meantime I promised Susie I would call her.

"Hey it's me. How did your first day back go?"

"It was okay. I was busy trying to catch up with my cases. At least I didn't have to interact with clients. How did the therapy go?"

"I guess it was good. I'm just exhausted."

"Let's talk tomorrow," Susie said.

After we hung up I read for a little while longer. I could feel my eyes closing so I turned off the light and conked out.

CHAPTER 33

In the morning instead of running in the park, I went to the gym and did my usual routine, working out with weights, twenty minutes on the treadmill and then push-ups and sit-ups.

After showering and dressing I walked back to my apartment and picked up my car. I decided to pay an unannounced visit to Miguel Cortez, the man who worked in the warehouse. There was something going on with him and I needed to find out what it was.

The GPS guided me to his building in Queens. I was hoping someone in the building would buzz me in since I didn't want to give Mr. Cortez the opportunity to deny me entrance. I saw his name on one of the buzzers but instead rang several others until someone buzzed me in. Don't people know they should ask who it is before letting someone in? I could have been a burglar or a rapist or an axe murderer.

I walked up to the third floor and knocked on his door. I saw someone look through the peephole and then opened the door slowly but with the chain on. It was a woman, somewhere in her forties, short and stocky.

"May I help you," she said with an accent.

"Is Miguel in?"

"What do you want?"

"I need to speak to him about Rebecca Kane. I promise you he's not in trouble."

The door shut and I heard footsteps walking away. I guess she didn't believe me. I was about to leave when I heard a lock turn and the door open.

"Come in," she said, releasing the chain.

"Thank you."

I heard water running in the bathroom.

"Miguel will be right out."

A few moments later Miguel walked into the living room.

"Who are you?" he said harshly.

"My name is Tracey Marks. We spoke on the phone. I promise you I'm only here to talk with you about Rebecca Kane. I'm not here to cause any trouble."

Mr. Cortez was short and slender with dark brown hair and an olive complexion.

"Please sit Ms. Marks," Mrs. Cortez said. "Can I offer you a cup of coffee?"

"Yes, thank you. Black is fine."

"I have no idea who killed Rebecca," he said. "I only met her once. She came to the warehouse to speak with her brother."

"Before she died Rebecca and David weren't speaking. Do you have any idea why?"

"I'm sorry. I can't help you," he said nervously.

"Are you afraid of someone? I can tell you this conversation goes no further. It's been over twenty years since Rebecca died. Her daughter Lisa has a right to know who killed her mother and that person needs to be punished."

"I told you I have no idea who did it."

"I believe you but was something else going on?"

Mrs. Cortez handed me a cup of coffee.

I could see Mr. Cortez was debating whether to say something.

"I don't want any trouble and I don't want the cops involved."

"I understand. What you say to me is strictly confidential."

"Rebecca came to the warehouse. I heard her shouting at her brother."

"Could you hear what they were saying?"

"I heard Rebecca yelling something about the toys, but I don't know anything else except that she was very angry."

"Did Rebecca threaten David?"

"I didn't hear the rest of their conversation."

"Do you remember how long after Rebecca was at the warehouse she was killed?"

"Maybe a few weeks, maybe less. I don't know exactly."

"Do you think David could have done it?" I asked.

"I have no idea."

I had the feeling Mr. Cortez was holding back, but I knew I wasn't going to get anything further from him. Obviously he didn't want to get involved. It was very possible he was here illegally. I had no reason to raise the subject with him.

As I was walking to my car I spotted a coffee shop on the corner. I went in and sat down at a booth. When the waitress came over I ordered two eggs on a roll and a cup of coffee. I thought I could kill two birds with one stone, eat and mull over what Miguel Cortez told me.

I now knew David lied to me, and I believe David's

mother may have been holding back on what she knew. I didn't think it was about Rebecca's parenting, though parent of the year was probably never in the cards for Rebecca. It had something to do with the business, something that made Rebecca mad enough that she went to the warehouse to confront her brother. Now all I need to do is figure out what that was.

While I was biting into my egg sandwich I thought of someone who might know the answer.

CHAPTER 34

I took out my phone and dialed his number.

"Hello."

"Mr. Mack, it's Tracey Marks. We spoke not too long ago."

"Yes, I remember. What can I do for you?" he said, not sounding very friendly.

"I'm sorry to bother you but something has come up and I thought you might be able to help me. Is it possible to come over sometime today?"

"Well if you think it's important. You can come now if you like."

"I'm in Queens so I'm not sure how long it will take me."

"I'll be here."

I finished eating and set my GPS to Simon Mack's address. When I arrived Mr. Mack looked a lot better than the last time I saw him. For one thing, he was clean shaven.

When we sat down I said to Simon: "Any luck finding a job?"

"Actually yes. I start next Monday. It's a sales job."

"That's great. You must be happy about that."

"Sandra and I are both happy."

I assumed Sandra was the woman Simon was living with.

"The last time I was here I had asked if you knew anything about an argument Rebecca had with her brother and you said no. Can you tell me if there were any problems you were aware of with David back then?"

"It was so long ago I guess it doesn't matter anymore. Without his parents' knowledge David starting using a different company in China to import some of their toys."

"Why was that a problem?"

"Because the company he was buying from had lead based paint in their toys."

"Why would he do that?"

"It's all about money. He was paying a lot less for the toys. I discovered it quite by accident as I was going through the invoices. David was trying to hide his tracks but he slipped up."

"Did you tell anyone?"

"I told Rebecca. She was furious."

"Did you tell his parents?"

"No. Rebecca wanted to handle it. She didn't want her parents to know what David was doing. She thought she could take care of it by herself."

"And did she?"

"Eventually it got resolved but there was no way Rebecca's parents weren't going to find out about it. His parents had to clean up his mess and it was pretty tense between them for a while."

"How come they didn't fire David?"

"It's their son and they were willing to give him another chance. I have to say he cleaned up his act."

"Do you think it's possible he could have killed Rebecca if she threatened him?"

"It crossed my mind, but when the police focused their investigation on her husband, I kind of forget about David."

"Do you remember what the time frame was when you first told Rebecca and when she was killed?"

"I'm just guessing. Maybe two weeks, if that long."

"So why did you originally tell me that you didn't know why Rebecca and David weren't speaking?"

"I didn't feel it was necessary to open up that can of worms. I'm sorry."

"Why did you leave the company?"

"It wasn't about that. It was about Rebecca. I just couldn't work there anymore. It was too painful."

"Well I really appreciate your honesty. I hope everything works out for you."

"Thank you."

I have to say, I wasn't prepared for what Simon Mack just told me. No wonder David and his mother were lying to me. Now what? I didn't think I had any other choice but to confront David Martin and listen to what he had to say. The suspects kept piling up.

It took me almost two hours to get home. There was bumper to bumper traffic almost all the way back. The ride was not only long but with nothing scenic to look at, it was also boring. I parked my car in the garage and walked three blocks to pick up half of a roasted chicken for dinner.

It was after 7:00 pm by the time I finished eating and cleaning up. I brought my glass of wine into the living room and called Jack.

"Just thinking about you," Jack said when he answered the phone.

"Oh yeah. Let me guess what you were thinking. You

have the most fabulous, sexiest, gorgeous girlfriend any man could want."

"How did you know?"

"A lucky guess. Listen I wanted to tell you I wasn't completely honest with you last night. I was tired but not because I didn't get a good night's sleep the day before."

"I'm listening."

"I went to see a therapist but I wasn't going to tell you because I was afraid if it didn't work out and I was a lost cause, I didn't want you to know."

"First, I'm really proud of you that you decided to see someone. I know you might think it's a sign of weakness but it's the opposite. You can't always fix everything by yourself."

"Even though I told you unless I decide to share something with you, I would rather not discuss it."

"I completely understand. As far as it not working out that shouldn't be a worry of yours."

"I know you said therapy helped you," I said to Jack.

"It did. It helped a lot. It gave me the ability to move forward with my life. I just don't want you to get discouraged if things don't change right away. It takes time so give it a chance."

"Thanks. By the way I have some very interesting news to tell you."

"I'm not sure I can handle any more news."

"Very funny. Anyway, it turns out Rebecca's brother David was importing toys from China that had lead contained in the product."

"Really. Did his parents know?"

"They found out eventually and had to clean up David's mess."

"How did you find out?"

"Because I'm a great detective." I explained to Jack how after speaking with Miguel Cortez, I thought if anyone might know it would be her lover Simon Mack since he worked in their corporate office."

"Well, I am impressed. Good thinking. So what now?"

"Beats me. I've now got four possible suspects. My great detective skills only take me so far. I thought you might have some ideas."

"I remember watching a Hercule Poirot Mystery on TV where he lined up all these suspects in one room and announced who did it."

"Any other ideas smarty pants?"

"Let me sleep on it."

"How's work there?"

"Just finishing up some cases. We have a big trial coming up but other than that, I'm pretty caught up."

"Well I'm going to put on my thinking cap and try to come up with something. Sleep tight," I said.

"You too."

I called Susie after I hung up from Jack.

"How was day two of work?" I asked Susie when she answered.

"The same as day one, just getting caught up. Tomorrow I have a new client coming in. Not sure I'm in the mood to hear about their problems."

"I know you'll rise to the occasion."

"Hopefully, otherwise I might tell the client where to go and that might not be pretty."

"I told Jack I went to see a therapist. I hated lying to him."

"And?"

"He was proud of me. I told him not to ask me any questions. I'll volunteer information if I choose."

I then went on to explain to Susie what I had learned today from Miguel Cortez and Simon Mack.

"The plot keeps getting thicker."

"That's all you have to say?"

"Well at some point you might have to confront David Martin."

"Not now?"

"If he did do it, you think he'll just confess?"

"No, but…"

"Talk to some other people first. Word will get around and David Martin will come to you. And what about the husband? He had a lot to lose if Rebecca was divorcing him."

"I didn't forget about him. I just have to keep all my options open."

"If I come up with any great ideas, I'll let you know," Susie said.

"Okay, love you."

Before going to bed I made a list of each person I suspected and wrote down their possible motives. Any one of them could have murdered Rebecca in the heat of passion, but which one?

CHAPTER 35

The rain was coming down pretty heavy when I woke up. My clock said 6:10 am. I was struggling to get out of bed. I wanted to stay under the covers and listen as the rain beat against my bedroom window, hoping it would lull me back to sleep. Ten minutes later I was up and went to turn on the coffee maker. In the meantime, I showered.

As I sat down to breakfast, I was thinking about my therapy session. There was something calming about Lily, though I hated to admit it. I still had my doubts whether therapy could help with my commitment problems but I was willing to give it a try. For how long, I couldn't say.

In between my spoonfuls of Cheerios, I jotted down a couple of names of people I needed to speak with that might have additional information about what was going on between Rebecca and her brother. One was Rebecca's assistant at the dress shop, Samantha Gerard.

On the dot of 9:00, I called Mrs. Gerard.

"Hello."

"Mrs. Gerard, it's Tracey Marks. Something's come up and I need to ask you some questions. Would it be possible to meet with you sometime today? I'll only take a few minutes of your time."

"If you really feel it's necessary. Can you come by around 11:30?"

"Yes. Thank you. See you then."

I thought about calling Rebecca's friend Jacqueline Donovan. I wasn't sure she was speaking to Rebecca at the time Rebecca found out what her brother was up to. I guess a phone call couldn't hurt.

I called Jacqueline and it went straight to voice mail. I left a message for her to call me back.

The rain was down to a light drizzle by the time I left my garage. I found a parking spot a block away from Mrs. Gerard's apartment building.

"Thank you for seeing me," I said as I walked into Samantha Gerard's apartment.

"So what can I help you with Ms. Marks?" she asked as we were seated in her living room.

"I've recently learned that Rebecca found out that her brother David had been importing toys from China that contained lead in them. Did she mention anything to you?"

"Let me think. A couple of weeks before Rebecca died she came into the shop and I could tell something was wrong. She was in a very bad mood. I asked her if she was alright. She never really answered but it was obvious something was going on."

"Did she say anything at all?"

"It was so long ago. I'm sorry."

"Are you sure she didn't say anything, maybe something that didn't seem important at the time?"

"Wait," Mrs. Gerard said. "I do recall something. I remember because it was a Tuesday and that's normally one of the days Rebecca came into the shop since I only worked half days on Tuesdays. She seemed anxious and distracted and told me I needed to work the rest of the day. I wasn't happy about it. Actually I was pretty mad. I asked her why and she said she had to drive to New Jersey and talk with someone. She didn't say who and I didn't ask."

"Do you remember what time she left?"

"I think around noon but I can't say for sure."

"Well thank you again."

Getting into my car I thought that may have been the day Rebecca went to the warehouse to confront her brother.

I heard my phone ringing.

"Hello."

"Ms. Marks, it's Jackie returning your call."

"Hi Jackie. Something's come up and I had a question for you. How long before Rebecca died did the two of you stop speaking to each other?"

"Why are you asking?"

"It has come to my attention that Rebecca's brother became involved in something he shouldn't have, and Rebecca was quite upset with him. Did you know she was angry at her brother?"

"I think I had mentioned to you that I thought they had some sort of disagreement but that's all I know. I have no idea what it was about."

"And how long was that before she died?"

"A couple of weeks, no more than a month, I think."

"Okay. Thank you."

"Please let me know if you find out who killed Rebecca."

"I will."

After hanging up my gut was telling me Jackie had nothing to do with Rebecca's murder. The timeline was off. Of course I couldn't be totally sure, but I think I can cross her off my list of suspects, at least put a pencil through her name.

Before speaking directly to David Martin, I thought I would pay another visit to Sylvia Martin. My thought was that she would tell her son about my visit.

I drove up to Sylvia Martin's home in Bronxville. It was 2:00 pm when I rang her doorbell. The housekeeper answered.

"Hello, I'm Tracey Marks. We met before. Can you please tell Mrs. Martin I need to see her?"

"Of course, please come in."

I waited in the foyer.

"Hello Tracey. I wasn't expecting to see you."

"Yes, I'm sorry but it was last minute and I have to speak with you."

Mrs. Martin led me into the living room. It was filled with antiques. I sat on a gold colored velvet sofa and Mrs. Martin sat opposite me on an identical sofa.

"What is so urgent that you couldn't call?"

Not a very good way to start.

"During my investigation I learned that your son was importing toys from a company in China that had lead in their product. Rebecca found out and was furious. It seems before telling you or your husband she wanted to handle it by herself. I believe she confronted David."

"How did you come by this knowledge?"

"I can't tell you, but I can assure you I wouldn't be here if I didn't think it was true."

"My husband and I did find out and the situation was quickly rectified."

"I'm sure it was. My concern is what transpired between your two children. You originally told me you had no idea why they weren't speaking, but that wasn't true, was it?"

"I felt there was no reason to tell you since my son had nothing to do with Rebecca's death."

"How can you be so sure?"

"I know my son."

"I'm not saying he intentionally did it. It could have been an accident."

"My son has assured me he had nothing to do with his sister's death."

There wasn't any point in arguing with Mrs. Martin or asking her any more questions since I would just be spinning my wheels. Even if she had her doubts about her son's involvement, she wasn't going to share them with me.

CHAPTER 36

I left Mrs. Martin sitting in her living room. I showed myself out.

I was starved. I went into the Town of Bronxville and parked my car. I threw some quarters in a meter and walked across the street to a place called Pete's Tavern. It was kind of dark inside. I sat at a table and ordered a burger and fries.

I took out my computer and typed up the conversations I had with Samantha Gerard and Sylvia Martin. I was hoping Mrs. Martin was going to call her son and tell him about our meeting.

It was 3:45 by the time I finished eating. Instead of going to my office I decided to head home. On the way back I heard my phone ringing. I didn't recognize the number.

"Hello."

"This is David Martin. I need to see you now."

"I'm driving, what can I do for you?"

"You know darn well why I'm calling. I know you spoke with my mother. We need to talk now."

"I can meet you at my office in an hour." So much

for going home.

"I'll be there."

Actually I was surprised Mr. Martin called so soon, but I was glad he did.

Mr. Martin walked into my office at 4:45. I decided to skip the niceties and didn't ask him if he wanted anything to drink. I waited for him to speak when we sat down.

"I'd like to know what's going on here! You barge in on my mother and you accuse me of killing my own sister! Does my niece know what's going on?" he said, yelling at me.

"It's my investigation and I take it wherever it leads me. I don't need anyone's permission. I'll be glad to talk with you if you calm down."

He didn't appear to be happy with the way I was speaking to him. I didn't care.

"You should have come to me first. There was no need to upset my mother. I would have told you what you wanted to know."

"I do recall when I spoke with you there was no mention that Rebecca was angry because you were importing toys containing lead. If I remember correctly, you said the reason Rebecca wasn't talking to you was because you accused her of being a neglectful parent."

"She was a terrible mother."

"But that's not why she was angry with you."

"Okay, let's get everything out in the open. It was true Rebecca was angry with me because of the lead in the toys, but I had nothing to do with her death."

"Why don't you tell me exactly what she said to you."

"She came to the warehouse and started yelling. She was angry and said I was ruining the business."

"Did she threaten you?"

"She said she was going to tell our parents if it wasn't taken care of immediately."

"And how were you proposing to do that? It doesn't seem that simple to me."

"I didn't know right then. I needed time to think about it."

"I bet that didn't go over well with your sister. Did she give you a deadline?"

"I told her I would take care of it."

"And did you?"

"It wasn't that simple. The easy part was no longer dealing with the company. The hard part was how we were going to handle the toys already shipped to the stores."

"What about the ones that could have been sold already? The truth is you couldn't fix the problem by yourself. How much time did Rebecca give you, a week, two weeks? When it still wasn't resolved she had it and told you she wasn't going to give you any more time so you killed her. Maybe it was an accident. She slipped on the bathroom floor and hit her head."

"I didn't kill Rebecca. I swear. It was true I didn't want my parents to find out but I eventually told them and Rebecca was still alive when I did."

"I only have your word."

"My mother will vouch for me."

"Pardon me if I don't take your mother's word for anything when it comes to you."

"There must be someone else you can ask."

"That's not my job. You find someone else."

"I know it was a horrible thing I did."

"What about the kids? Did you ever think about them? I bet Rebecca was thinking about Lisa and how she could have ingested the lead. What possessed you to work with a company that had lead in their products?"

"At first I didn't know. I thought I was helping my parents by importing the toys for less money."

"But you found out eventually?"

"By that time it was too late. Are you going to tell the police?"

Until I had proof I had no intention of going to the police, but I wasn't going to tell him that.

"Can you give me any reason why I shouldn't?"

"I swear I had nothing to do with my sister's death. I don't know what I can do to prove it to you."

"I'll see you out."

"By the way, you might want to look into Rebecca's assistant who was working at the clothing store Rebecca owned. Rebecca had told me she was going to get rid of the store. Where would that leave her assistant?"

I didn't answer Mr. Martin as he walked out.

Mrs. Gerard mentioned something about an agreement she had with Rebecca. I believe she said it was only a verbal agreement.

I gathered my backpack and computer and locked up.

CHAPTER 37

By the time I got home I was tired. I scrambled up some eggs, defrosted a sesame bagel and put on a pot of decaffeinated coffee.

While I was eating I thought about the conversation I had with David Martin. As far as I could tell his sister was pressuring him and maybe the stress was too much and he cracked. He confronted Rebecca at her house and somehow in a struggle she slipped or maybe he intentionally killed her. Was he trying to shift the blame to Rebecca's assistant? That would be my guess. And if he did kill Rebecca, why would he admit it? That was a problem.

After dinner I showered and slipped on a pair of boxer shorts and a tee shirt. I was reading in bed when my phone rang.

"Hello."

"Tracey, it's Lisa. I got a call from my Uncle David and he was quite upset. He said you accused him of killing my mother."

"I'm sorry this investigation is causing problems for you but I have no control over that. Did he tell you why your mother was angry at him?"

"Yes, but do you really think he killed my mother?"

"At this point I have no idea. Sometimes I have to handle a situation the way I see fit. How the person reacts to it, I can't predict. I suggest you try not to let anyone upset or pressure you in any way. I know it's difficult."

"I hear you. I'll try to keep that in mind. I'm sorry to have bothered you."

"Don't be. I know it's hard. Call me any time."

"Thank you."

I was angry at David Martin for pressuring his niece. Was he trying to persuade Lisa to stop the investigation? That would be my hunch.

As I was drifting off to sleep thoughts of toy soldiers popped into my head.

In the morning I went for a run. After showering I dressed and headed for my office but not before stopping at the Coffee Pot.

"Tracey, it feels like I haven't seen you in forever."

"It's the case I'm working on. I've been spending less time in the office and more time in the car."

"Well then you deserve one of our special muffins."

"I thought they were all special."

"Yes, but this one comes with extra love."

"Sounds yummy. The kids doing okay?"

"Ask me at the end of the day."

"See ya."

I was sitting at my desk contemplating how to approach Samantha Gerard while eating my special cranberry walnut muffin. Now that I was thinking about this so-called verbal arrangement Mrs. Gerard told me about, I don't remember her telling me there was any written agreement. I was curious if Samantha Gerard made it all up.

I picked up the phone and dialed Lisa's number.

"Hello."

"Lisa it's Tracey. How are you doing today?"

"Better. I thought over what you said, and I won't let anyone's feelings get in the way of your job."

"I'm glad. I have a question for you. Do you know anything about an arrangement or agreement your mother had with Samantha Gerard, the woman who managed your mother's store?"

"No. Was there something in writing?"

"I have no idea. Would you happen to know the name of the lawyer who drew up the contract on the shop for your mother?"

"I don't but I can get it for you and call you back."

"That would be great Lisa. Thanks."

Before talking with Mrs. Gerard I wanted to know if anyone else knew about this verbal arrangement. I'm having doubts as to whether Mrs. Gerard had any type of agreement with Rebecca. I was also interested in finding out if Rebecca had contacted a divorce attorney before she died.

About an hour later Lisa called me with the name of the attorney her mother retained to negotiate the contract for her clothing store.

I found a telephone number for Max Greenberg, attorney specializing in contract law, and called him.

"Max Greenberg's office."

"My name is Tracey Marks and I would like to make an appointment to see Mr. Greenberg."

"He has an opening a week from this Tuesday."

"Actually I need to speak with him regarding a personal matter. Can you tell him it's about Rebecca Kane. He handled a matter of hers over twenty years ago."

I was put on hold for a few minutes.

"Ms. Marks, Mr. Greenberg can see you at 3:00 today."

"Thank you."

I called Susie.

"Hey, how are you?" I said when she answered.

"I haven't killed anyone yet so that's something."

"Does your boss have you working too hard?"

"No, but I think for a few weeks I'm going to take Friday's off. I need an extra day to myself."

"So does that mean I can bribe you to have breakfast with me tomorrow?"

"Only if it's your treat."

"Why not. I'll bill the client for it since your services are of great value to the case."

"Yes, that is very true."

"Is 10:00 am okay?"

"I'll meet you at the French café."

I was at Mr. Greenberg's office a few minutes before our scheduled appointment. His office was located on the east side on 38th Street in a brownstone.

"Hello, I'm Tracey Marks. I have a 3:00 appointment with Mr. Greenberg."

"I'll tell him you're here."

When Mr. Greenberg greeted me I was kind of surprised. He looked much younger than his sixty plus years. I could tell he worked out. His body was lean and his biceps were clinging to his shirt.

"Come in. Take a seat."

I sat across from him.

"I haven't heard Rebecca's name in a million years. What's going on?"

"I've been hired by her daughter Lisa to find out who killed her mother."

"After all these years. So how can I help you?"

"Did you draw up the contract for the lease on the clothing store when Rebecca originally bought it?"

"I did."

"Do you know if she was planning to sell the store?"

"I believe she was but was killed before she had a chance."

"Did she tell you why she wanted to sell the shop?"

"Not exactly. Though she didn't say, I got the impression she was interested in pursuing other avenues. The shop was becoming too much for her. It took a lot of her time."

"That doesn't seem to make too much sense since she had someone who was taking care of the day to day operations."

"I can only tell you my impressions. They may be completely wrong."

"Rebecca had someone named Samantha Gerard manage the store. Can you tell me if Rebecca mentioned a verbal agreement she may have had with this woman where upon if Rebecca was going to sell the store, her assistant would have first opportunity to buy it?"

"That doesn't sound familiar but it's been a long time."

"Do you still have Rebecca's paperwork? Maybe you made notes about this agreement."

"It's most likely in the file cabinet I have in the next room where I keep all the old files and some other stuff."

"Would you be able to check to see if you still have Rebecca's file?"

He pressed a button on his phone. "Melissa, can you please check if we have Rebecca Kane's file in the cabinet?"

"She'll look and let me know in a few minutes," Mr. Greenberg said to me.

"One other question. Would you happen to know if Rebecca was planning on divorcing her husband?"

"I don't know for sure. She did ask me for the name of a divorce attorney I would recommend."

"And did you give her that person's name?"

"I did. I believe it was Philip Slater."

"Is he still practicing?"

"I'm not sure. I think he may be retired."

"Would you happen to know where I could possibly get in touch with him?"

"As far as I know he's living in Boca Raton, Florida. I had wondered why Rebecca's husband was never arrested. Would you happen to know why?"

"It was all circumstantial and he had an alibi."

"It sounds as if you poked a hole in that alibi."

"I can't really say but I'm looking into several people."

I heard a knock on the door.

"Thank you Melissa," he said, handing Mr. Greenberg the file.

I sat and waited while Mr. Greenberg went through Rebecca's file.

"I have to say, I don't see any notes about a verbal arrangement, but I don't think that's something that I would have marked in the file since we're not talking about a written agreement. I guess it would be hard to prove whether Rebecca was lying to Mrs. Gerard or Mrs. Gerard was lying to you."

CHAPTER 38

The same thought occurred to me as I left Mr. Greenberg's office. I took a taxi back to my office. First thing on my agenda was to get in touch with Philip Slater to find out if Rebecca had spoken with him about divorcing her husband Jason.

I found a number for him in Boca and called. A woman answered.

"Hello, I'm looking for Philip Slater."

"Does he know you?"

"Can you tell him it's regarding a woman named Rebecca Kane who died over twenty years ago."

"Hold on a moment."

I heard her shouting his name and telling him to get on the phone.

"Hello," Mr. Slater said when he picked up.

"Mr. Slater, my name is Tracey Marks. I'm sorry to bother you. I'm calling from New York about a woman named Rebecca Kane."

"Why does that name sound familiar?"

"She may have come to you inquiring about divorcing her husband. Also, she was killed over twenty years ago and it was all over the papers."

"Yes. Now I remember. Can I ask why you're interested in whether she was planning on divorcing her husband?"

"I was hired by Rebecca's Kane's daughter to look into her death."

"Now it's all coming back to me. The police suspected her husband."

"Yes, but he had an alibi. I was told by one of Mrs. Kane's friends that she was planning on divorcing her husband."

"How did you get my name?"

"I spoke with Max Greenberg."

"How is Max?"

"I can only tell you he was alive and well when I left him."

"Glad to hear it," he chuckled. "She did come to me about divorcing her husband. At that meeting she made another appointment in order for us to discuss the matter further, but she never showed. I later found out she was murdered."

"So she was planning on divorcing him?"

"It would appear so."

"Do you recall anything from the conversation you had with her?"

"Do you mean if she said anything about her husband?"

"Yes, anything."

"I don't remember going into specifics at our meeting. Sorry I can't be of any further assistance."

"That's alright. Well thank you for your time."

"Say hello to New York for me."

Well now I knew for sure that Rebecca was going to divorce her husband. He certainly had enough reasons and no alibi, but so does Rebecca's brother and now possibly Samantha Gerard, Rebecca's manager at the clothing store. Any other people want to add their names to my list, I said out loud. You're all welcome.

On my way home I called Patty.

"Well hello there. How are you?" Patty said when she answered the phone.

"I'm okay."

"You don't sound okay. Are you sure?"

"Just busy with the case. How's my little man?"

"I thought the terrible two's don't start until two."

"That's funny. He's probably just advanced for his age."

"Now that's funny. Well there's a spare room where you can stay until he's at least three."

"How about if I take him off your hands next Saturday? This weekend I'm going up to Jack's."

"That sounds lovely. Say hello to Jack."

"Will do. Give Michael a big hug and kiss for me."

Before stopping home I went to the seafood place near me and picked up a container of shrimp and corn chowder.

After showering and putting on my sweats, I made a salad, heated up the soup, and poured myself a glass of wine. I was reading my book but I was having a hard time concentrating. I kept thinking about Samantha Gerard and whether she lied to me. With the only other person who knows the truth dead, how will I figure it out?

I heard ringing from my backpack. I got up and reached into my bag for my phone.

"I'm so happy to hear your voice," I said to Jack.

"Oh boy, that bad a day?"

"I can't wait to see you tomorrow."

"I hope I can live up to your expectations."

"You will. I'll tell you what's going on when I see you. I'm going to meet Susie for breakfast and then I might come directly to you."

"Just let yourself in. I'm not sure when I'll be home but I'll try to sneak away early. Sleep tight."

"Ditto."

When I got up the following morning I went directly to the gym. When I got back home I packed an overnight bag and went to meet Susie for breakfast. Susie was waiting when I got there.

"Why don't we sit outside while the weather is still nice," Susie said.

"Sounds good to me."

The waitress seated us and we ordered. I had my usual, French toast with bacon very crisp, and Susie had an omelet. We both ordered coffee.

"I'm happy you came out to breakfast with me," I said to Susie. "I miss our after work outings."

"I miss them too. My emotions are still all over the place. One minute I'm doing fine and the next I feel so sad. I hate to keep leaning on Mark since I know he's hurting also. He tries not to show it but sometimes I can see it on his face."

"You have me always. Maybe it would be good if you and Mark can help each other."

"When did you become so wise?"

"That's what happens when you have a therapist."

Susie laughed. It was nice to hear.

"So one session and you're a guru in the field of therapy?" Susie said. "By the way when's your next session?"

"Monday. I'm still anxious talking to someone besides you about my stuff."

"I'm sure it'll get easier."

The waitress brought our food and coffee.

While we were eating, I told Susie what had transpired since the last time we talked about the case.

"Well you've been very busy," Susie said.

"But not getting any further in finding out who killed Rebecca Kane."

"But, a lot further than the police did twenty years ago. That's a big accomplishment."

"But how can I prove who the killer is even if I think I know?"

"I can't tell you right now but something will happen."

"Let's hope I'm not shot at or stabbed again."

"You do seem to have a propensity for those things happening to you."

"Thanks a lot."

"You're welcome."

"I thought I would pay an unexpected visit to Samantha Gerard on Monday. I doubt she'll come clean and admit there was no arrangement between her and Rebecca."

"It's possible Rebecca was stringing her along and told her she was going to give her the opportunity to buy the store if she was planning on selling it."

"How will I know if she's telling the truth?"

"I think the only thing you can go on is your gut. Pay close attention when she's answering you. If she's lying there will be something in her expression or mannerism that will give her away."

"I hope you're right."

"Me too."

CHAPTER 39

Susie and I stayed another hour chatting and then I walked her back to her apartment building and went to pick up my car.

The ride up to Jack's place was uneventful. It was 4:00 when I inserted his house key in the front door. I yelled out to Jack even though I knew he wasn't home yet. I went upstairs to the bedroom. I must have fallen asleep since the next thing I knew Jack was lying next to me, gently stroking my arm.

"Hi. I must have fallen asleep."

"Now I don't have to carry you up the stairs to have my way with you."

"Stop talking and begin."

An hour later we were lying quietly wrapped in each other's arms. It's at times like these that I get scared something's going to happen to change everything. I tried to push those thoughts out of my head.

"I missed you," Jack said to me.

"You sure it's me you missed and not my sexual prowess in bed?"

"Can I have a minute to think about it?"

I playfully punched Jack in the arm.

"I definitely missed you," he said as he kissed me deeply on the lips. "Do you want me to start dinner?" he asked.

"Let's wait a bit," I said as I kissed him back.

Half hour later we both went downstairs to start dinner.

"So what are we having this evening? You know I so look forward to your culinary skills."

"I thought tonight we would have barbecued short ribs."

"Oh boy, I can't wait."

We sat outside on the patio enjoying a glass of Merlot while eating dinner. I hoped my loud sounds of pleasure as I ate my ribs weren't disturbing Jack. As we were eating I gave him the run down on what was going on with the case. He listened without asking me any questions. When I finished he didn't say anything until he did.

"So you have three viable suspects."

"That's all you got to say? Actually five if you count Jacqueline Donovan and Simon Mack, though neither of them are my primary suspects."

"I'm very impressed with your investigative skills."

"Keep going."

"They all have motives. You have to keep pressure on each of them. Just don't get discouraged. I don't think anyone could have uncovered as much as you have. Be patient, something will break."

"What's for dessert?"

"How about some pie a la mode?"

Jack made coffee and we had apple pie with vanilla ice cream. I was stuffed by the time I put the last bite of my pie a la mode in my mouth.

I woke up the next day to the smell of coffee. The

clock said 9:45 am. I couldn't believe I slept that long.

"Hey sleepy head, want some coffee?" Jack said as he sat down on the bed.

"It must be the air up here, that or you put something in my food last night. I haven't slept this late in ages."

"It must be the company."

"It must," as I took a sip of coffee.

"You have two options at the moment, breakfast or me," Jack said

"You do drive a hard bargain," as I pulled Jack on top of me.

"Excellent choice."

About forty-five minutes later we were seated in Jack's kitchen. He was flipping some pancakes while I watched.

"So what are my choices for the day?" I asked Jack.

"I thought we would go biking around the area. I bought you a helmet since you didn't have one."

"How thoughtful. Okay you win. We'll give it a whirl."

Four pancakes and two cups of coffee later, Jack and I hit the road.

"I thought we would venture into Lenox. They have several art galleries that are really interesting."

He lead and I followed. It was a pretty ride. Lots of green and flowers along the way. After a while I felt more relaxed though I did have to be careful of cars. About half way we stopped and sat on a bench. Jack handed me a water bottle that he pulled out of his backpack.

"So how do you like biking so far?"

"I'm enjoying it. I'm glad I run since I'm not sure my legs could handle all the pedaling otherwise."

"We've biked almost five miles. Another five and

we'll be in Lenox."

"Nothing like starting out slowly."

"I figured you could handle it," Jack said as he kissed me lightly on the lips.

"Oh you did, did you. I hope there's a great lunch at the end of this ride."

"I promise it will be worth the wait."

Since we were going at a fairly slow pace it took us another forty minutes to arrive in Lenox. Jack found a bike rack in town where we were able to chain up the bikes.

Instead of having lunch right away, we walked around the town and went into some of the art galleries. I'm not an art connoisseur but some of the paintings we saw were beautiful, though very expensive, but it was fun to look. One of the galleries displayed only modern paintings. It reminded me of the paintings I saw in Molly Kane's art gallery.

The Town of Lenox is very charming. Besides art galleries and a book store, it had several specialty and gift shops, one that included Jewish ceremonial items, fine art and jewelry from Jerusalem. I saw a very unusual Mezuzah that I purchased for Susie. A mezuzah is made of wooden, plastic or metal that holds a parchment scroll that has two biblical passages. It is affixed to a Jewish home and represents a visible sign and symbol to all those who enter that a sense of Jewish identity and commitment exists in that household.

"I'm hoping it will give Susie some faith."

"She'll love it. It's beautiful."

An hour later we walked into Bistro Zinc to have lunch. The place was very busy but we managed to get one of the last empty tables.

A young man dressed in a white shirt and black cotton khakis came over. He looked just old enough to be a college kid.

"Can I get you something to drink?"

"I'll have a glass of Sauvignon Blanc."

"And I'll have whatever beer you have on tap."

"I'll leave you the menus."

"Jack, I noticed a couple at the table to your right pointing at us and whispering something to each other."

"Unfortunately, this is not New York City. There are people up here that are not used to seeing bi-racial couples. Just ignore them."

"I guess I shouldn't be so surprised. Born and raised in New York I must be a little naïve to what goes on in the rest of the country. Doesn't it bother you?"

"I just look at them as being ignorant. They're not worth my time. How is Susie doing?"

"She's like a seesaw. She fluctuates. She could be fine one minute and sad the next. When I told her that she and Mark should be helping each other, she was amused that I was such an expert after one therapy session."

The young man returned with our drinks. I kept sneaking peeks at the couple who had stared at us. I wish I could be as benevolent as Jack.

"Do you know what you'd like to have?" the waiter asked, bringing me back to the present.

"I'll have your house salad and the trout meunière."

"I'll have the same," Jack said.

"I have to admit I felt pretty comfortable talking to the therapist. She has a way of putting me at ease."

"I'm glad. In order for therapy to work you have to be open to talking even if it makes you uncomfortable."

"I get it. I just hope I can overcome my fears."

"It's not as if I don't have any fears. I do. I just don't let them stop me from getting what I want," Jack said, looking at me with his big, brown eyes.

Lunch was delicious. We spent the rest of the

afternoon going in and out of the shops and made a stop at the Patisserie for coffee and dessert.

By the time we arrived home, it was after 7:00 pm. We were both still full from our late lunch and dessert. Jack opened up a bottle of white wine and we sat outside drinking and nibbling on cheese and crackers.

"You know you're going to spoil me with all this fresh air and good food."

"That's the idea."

"It's working."

After polishing off almost a bottle of wine we went upstairs, shared a shower and fell into bed. I didn't remember much after that.

On Sunday we sat on the patio and played chess in between lunch and dinner.

When we kissed and hugged before I left on Monday morning, Jack said he would like to come down the following weekend. I was surprised since we normally see each other every other weekend. I didn't ask him why, but I told him I would like that also.

On the way back I was planning my strategy for when I confronted Samantha Gerard. My first thought was that I should just show up at her place. Then I had second thoughts about that. Either way she would figure out where I was headed with my line of questioning. In the end I decided not to call first.

CHAPTER 40

I parked my car one block from Samantha Gerard's building. The doorman told me he had seen Mrs. Gerard leave about an hour ago. Now what?

Before the doorman had a chance to ask who was looking for her, I left.

I was hungry since Jack sent me on my way with just a bowl of cereal and milk. I walked a couple of blocks till I found a coffee shop. Since there was no one up front to seat me, I made my way to a booth.

"Can I help you?" the waitress asked me.

"Sure. I'd like an egg sandwich with crisp bacon on a roll, a side of home fries and coffee."

"Coming right up."

She wasn't kidding. Five minutes later my food appeared with my coffee.

Do I now go to plan B which is to call Mrs. Gerard? I might as well. With the doorman having to ring up, she's going to know it's me anyway. No way getting around it unless I wait outside for her. For all I know she could be waltzing into her place as I'm sitting here.

When I finished eating I went back to Mrs. Gerard's apartment building. A different doorman was on duty.

"I'm here to see Samantha Gerard."

He picked up the phone. Apparently she still wasn't home since I didn't hear him talking.

"She's not answering. Was she expecting you?"

"I was passing by and thought I would see if she was in."

I decided to wait since I had nothing pressing for the rest of the day except for my therapy session later. I was glad I had made a pit stop before leaving the coffee shop.

An hour later I was just about to leave when I saw Mrs. Gerard across the street, down the block from her building. I crossed over and approached her.

"Oh, hi Ms. Marks. What are you doing here?"

"I'm sorry to interrupt your day, some things have come to light that I needed your help with. I wonder if we could go upstairs."

"Is this very important? I'm supposed to meet someone in about an hour."

"I'll be quick. I promise."

We went up to her apartment and sat in the kitchen.

"How can I help you?"

"I remember you mentioned an agreement between you and Rebecca. What was the agreement about again?"

"There's not much to tell. It was a verbal agreement. Rebecca told me if she planned on selling the store she would give me the opportunity to buy it before offering it to anyone else."

"You didn't have anything in writing?"

"No. I was just an employee. I couldn't demand anything from Rebecca, but as I had told you I trusted her and thought she would keep her word."

"How did you wind up with the clothing store?"

"The landlord approached me after Rebecca died and asked if I was willing to enter into a new lease since he knew that I had been managing the store."

"I spoke with Rebecca's brother. He mentioned that Rebecca was going to sell the store?"

"Yes, she told me. I was very surprised."

"And she kept her word and offered the store to you?"

"Yes."

"That's not exactly what her brother said. He told me Rebecca had another buyer in mind."

That wasn't true but I wanted to see her reaction.

"He's lying to you!" she said in an angry voice.

"What reason would he have to lie?"

"I have no idea. You'd have to ask him that."

"The problem is the arrangement you had with Rebecca was verbal so you're asking me to take your word for it?"

"I'm not sure what you're getting at?"

I wasn't sure myself.

"I told you exactly what transpired between Rebecca and myself. I don't know what else to tell you."

"You can tell me what really happened since I'll find out if you're lying to me. If Rebecca did have another buyer I can easily check with Rebecca's attorney involved with the transaction at that time." I was bluffing and I hoped it worked.

Mrs. Gerard's shoulders slumped.

"It's true what I said about a verbal agreement, but Rebecca didn't care. She decided that she was going to sell the store to someone who was able to pay her more money than I was. Was I angry? Yes, but I didn't kill her. Fortunately there were no signed contracts at the time of Rebecca's death and I was able to negotiate a new lease with the landlord."

"I'd say you were one lucky lady."

"What is that suppose to mean?"

"Just that it was fortunate for you that Rebecca died when she did."

"Fortunate or not, I did not kill Rebecca."

Unfortunately Susie was wrong. I left Mrs. Gerard's place not knowing whether Samantha Gerard was lying to me or not. I was no further along in figuring out who killed Rebecca than when I started. I just had more suspects.

I drove to the Upper East Side for my appointment with Lily Davidson.

I was sitting in the waiting room anxious because I didn't know what I was going to say to her.

"Tracey, c'mon in."

I sat down in the same chair as I did the last time I was here.

"Have you ever had anyone not talk for the whole hour?"

"Are you worried you won't have anything to say?"

"It had crossed my mind."

"Well don't worry about it. Something will come to you."

"Let's hope." I noticed Lily smile.

"Last time you were here you told me a little bit about the day your father died. Can you tell me a little more about that?"

"What else do you want to know?"

"Do you remember what you were feeling at the time?"

"I think I was numb. I wasn't feeling anything. I just sat there. I didn't run over to my father and try to help him. I was screaming for my mother at the top of my lungs."

"And what would you have done to save him?"

"I don't know, but I was a coward."

"You were only thirteen and scared. You know you couldn't have saved your father."

"He was the best father in the world and he was gone in an instant right before my eyes."

"Did you feel abandoned by him?"

"Why would I feel that way? It wasn't his fault," I said, though I knew there was some truth to what she said, as my eyes started to water.

"Do you remember what you told me in our first session? The reason why you're here."

"It was about my fear of being in a committed relationship. It's not that I don't know that I'm afraid to get close to someone because I'm afraid they'll die."

"It's one thing to know something intellectually. It's our feelings about the issue that you have to work through. Until you deal with those feelings, your fears will stay with you."

"So how do I figure out my feelings?"

"There's no easy answer. Can you talk a little more about after your father died?"

"I remember I didn't want to go to school."

"Why is that?"

"I was afraid to leave my mother. I thought if I wasn't with her something bad would happen."

"Did you think she might leave you like your father did?"

The tears were streaming down my face.

"Our time is up. Why don't you think about what we discussed and I'll see you next week."

CHAPTER 41

Driving home my mind was numb. It felt like I was on overload. When I got back I took a shower and made myself a tuna fish sandwich. I sat on my gray and beige striped club chair that's in my bedroom and turned on the TV. I set my wine on the table next to my chair.

I didn't want to think of the case or my therapy session. I turned on the TV and watched a rerun of the show Friends, which always made me laugh. By 10:00 pm, I was sleeping.

While I was getting ready to go to the office the following day I decided I would see Jason Kane. I wanted to finally confront him about his false alibi and what I found out from Rebecca's divorce attorney.

I stopped for my usual coffee and muffin before going into the office. As I was sitting at my desk sipping my coffee, I picked up my phone and dialed Susie's number.

"Hi," Susie said.

"Are you at work?"

"I'm on my way. How was your weekend?"

"Nice. I'm officially a biker. It was fun. How are you doing?"

"I'm okay. Mark and I talked. I'll tell you about it when I'm not rushing to get into work. By the way how did therapy go?"

"We'll talk soon. Love you." I decided not to say anything to Susie about the Mezuzah until I saw her in person.

I contemplated calling Jason first but decided against it. I thought a random visit was in order.

After taking care of some administrative paperwork piling up along with some bills, I took an Uber over to Jason Kane's office.

"Hi," I said to the woman behind the receptionist's desk. "I'd like to see Mr. Kane."

"Do you have an appointment?"

"No. Tell him it's Tracey Marks and I need to see him."

"Please have a seat."

How I hate that line. Ten minutes passed and I was having a hard time sitting still. He was probably getting even with me for our last encounter at my office. Finally a young woman approached me.

"Ms. Marks, please come this way."

"What's your name?" I asked, trying my best to make small talk.

"Felicia."

Felicia walked me to Jason's office and told me to go right in.

"I wasn't expecting you," Jason said as I walked into his office.

"Some things have come up that I need to discuss with you."

"Sit," he said. "What's going on?"

I noticed he had photos of Danielle and Lisa on his

desk.

"I recently spoke to an attorney by the name of Philip Slater."

"Doesn't ring a bell."

"Of course not, he was Rebecca's divorce attorney."

"I'm not following."

"She went to him because she was intending to divorce you, but didn't get the chance since she was murdered before she had the opportunity."

"Well that's news to me."

"Of course it is," I said sarcastically.

"If she was planning to divorce me she never mentioned it."

"We only have your word for that, don't we?"

"I guess we do. So you think I killed her because I found out she was going to divorce me?"

"I do. Your wife was worth millions. If she was to divorce you, you'd be a struggling attorney and from what I found out about you, that would certainly hamper your lifestyle."

"Maybe, but I didn't kill Rebecca."

"So you say."

"If you had proof you would be contacting the police and not talking with me."

He was right about that.

"Well that might happen sooner than you think. It turns out I learned recently that the alibi you gave the police was bogus. Your client Eric Jordan lied for you."

I could see fear in Jason's eyes.

"Look, it's true I lied to the police but it was only because I knew how it would look if they found out I was seeing another woman."

"Yes, Mr. Jordan told me that's what you said. I guess your wife could corroborate your story. It was Danielle you were seeing at the time, wasn't it?"

He didn't answer me for a moment. Then he said: "Of course she could."

"Well thank you for your time. I'm sure I'll be speaking with you again."

Walking toward the elevator I thought my conversation with Jason Kane went quite well. I bet Mr. Kane was on the phone with his wife at this very moment.

CHAPTER 42

I heard my phone vibrating as I got off the elevator.

"Hi Patty."

"How about coming over for dinner tonight? Why don't you come a little earlier if you can, any time after 5:00?"

"That sounds great. It'll give me more time with the little man."

It was almost noon when I looked at my watch. I wanted to see Danielle Kane before she had too much time to think about her story.

She picked up on the fourth ring.

"Hello."

"Mrs. Kane, this is Tracey Marks. Can we meet this afternoon? There are a few questions I need to ask you."

"I have several appointments today. Can it wait a day or so?"

"I think it would be in your husband's best interest if we talk as soon as possible."

"How about at 2:00 pm at your office?"

I gave Mrs. Kane my address before hanging up.

Mrs. Kane arrived at my office a few minutes after 2:00.

"Please sit. Can I offer you something to drink?"

"I'm fine thank you."

Mrs. Kane did not look like she wanted to be here, though I have to say she was impeccably dressed.

"When I first spoke with you, you told me you had met Jason a few months after his wife died. That wasn't true, was it?"

"No, it wasn't," she said looking uncomfortable.

"Why did you lie?"

"I thought it would look bad if you knew we were seeing each other while Rebecca and Jason were still married."

"I see. Well that's understandable," I said, trying to lure her into a false sense of security.

"Where were you the night Rebecca died?"

"I was with Jason after his dinner meeting with his client."

"What time was that?"

"I'm not quite sure," she said, not looking directly at me.

"Well why don't you take a guess?"

"Maybe around 10:00 pm."

"Till when?"

"Around midnight."

"Where did you meet?"

"At a bar near the restaurant Jason was at."

"Do you remember the name of the bar?"

"No I don't."

"Did you take a cab together when you left the bar?"

She didn't answer right away.

"Maybe you walked," I suggested.

"Yes, that's right. Well actually now I remember. Jason walked home and I took a cab back to my place."

"How come Jason didn't go back to your place?"

"It was late and it would look too suspicious if he

came home in the middle of the night."

"That makes sense. That's all the questions I have. Thank you for coming in."

Danielle Kane got up and left.

I was pretty sure she was lying. If she was with him she would have remembered every detail of that night.

I packed up and left the office. On the way home I stopped at my favorite French bakery and bought some pastries for the grownups and butter cookies for Michael.

At home I quickly changed into my running clothes and did my three mile loop around the park. As soon as I returned I showered, dressed and took an Uber over to Patty and Alan's place.

When Patty opened the door, Michael was standing next to her, hugging her leg. I handed Patty the box of pastries and picked Michael up. He was in his pajamas and smelled as only a baby can after a bath.

"My little man, you are getting so big. When did you start standing on your own?"

He giggled as I twirled him around.

"So my main man, how are your parents treating you?"

Michael giggled again.

"Tell your cousin Tracey we treat you like a king. I wish I was treated as well when I was growing up," she said as we were walking into the kitchen.

We heard the door open.

"Dada," Michael shouted.

I put Michael down and he ran to his father. So much for feeling special.

"I thought little boys are supposed to cling to their mother," Patty said. "Not my boy. He's definitely more attached to Alan."

"Are you jealous?" I said to Patty smiling.

"Maybe just a little."

"Hey Tracey," Alan said giving me a quick hug.

"Michael, why don't we go up to your room and pick out something to play with?" I said.

Michael scurried up the stairs and I followed. First we played with his LEGO set. We attempted to build a bridge which didn't look half bad when we finished. Then I read Michael a story.

"Hey you guys," Patty said as she came into the room. "It's bedtime Michael."

Patty and I settled Michael into his crib and went downstairs.

Alan was opening up a bottle of wine when I walked into the kitchen.

"Something smells delicious," I said.

Patty made a pork tenderloin, roast potatoes and a salad. We sat down to eat in the dining room.

I greedily took slices of pork and a big spoonful of potatoes and then filled my bowl with salad.

"How's Jack?" Patty asked me.

"He's fine."

"Is something the matter?" Patty said. "You seemed a little hesitant when I asked."

"I went to see Lily Davidson. You didn't tell me how upsetting it could be."

"Anytime you dig into your past it might be hard. I'm not going to pry but you know you can tell us anything without judgment," Patty said.

"Do you remember much about my father?" I said, looking at Alan.

"Of course I do. Don't forget I have a few years on you. I loved him. I remember the time my parents sent me down to your summer house to spend with you and your parents. I got to know him pretty well."

"Remember when the three of us used to go out on the boat fishing," I said. "You couldn't believe a girl could bait a hook without squirming. If I recall you were the one feeling a little squirmish about baiting the hook."

"In my defense, it was my first time," Alan said.

"You teased me about it."

"That's because I was jealous though I couldn't admit it then. What I do recall was the first time you dragged me to the ice cream shop in town. I really didn't want to be seen with an eight year old girl."

"I bet you forgot all about my age when you were licking the best ice cream on the planet at the time."

"She was always obnoxious," Alan said, looking at Patty with a twinkle in his eye.

"I envied you because you had such a great dad and mine wouldn't give me the time of day."

"I didn't know that," I said.

"Why would you? It's not something I wanted anyone to know."

"I guess looking back makes me feel sad, but I want my relationship with Jack to go forward and it can't if I'm stuck."

"Is he pressuring you?" Patty asked.

"No. He's been really good about it, but I know it can't stay this way forever."

"It may never be easy for you, but at least you might get to the point where it won't stop you from going forward," Patty said.

"Can we change the subject?"

"Sure," Alan said. "We were thinking about taking a vacation."

"With Michael?"

"That's what we were debating. Patty's parents would love to take care of him."

"So what's the problem?"

"It's leaving him for a week that I'm concerned about. We only left him once overnight with my parents," Patty said. "We'd love to go someplace like California or New Mexico but we don't want to travel that far or go someplace where we have to travel by plane."

"Why don't you go someplace for three or four days. It'll give you a little break but you won't have to go far or take a flight."

"Any suggestions?"

"Well there's always Washington, DC or Maryland. Or you can go north to Maine or Vermont."

"That's not actually a bad idea. Thanks Tracey," Alan said.

"Any new developments with the case?" Patty asked.

"It's complicated. I have suspects but no concrete evidence against anyone. My client remembered very few details from that night. She was only three. I'm pretty sure she saw her mother's dead body on the bathroom floor but blocked it from her mind."

"Poor thing," Patty said.

"By the way, are we still on for Saturday? I'll take the little man off your hands for the day. Jack is coming down so they'll be four eyes watching Michael."

"I trust you even if there were only two eyes watching him," Patty said.

"Thanks, I'm ready for dessert."

CHAPTER 43

Two days later I was sitting in my office enjoying my first cup of coffee of the morning when the phone rang.

"Tracey Marks."

"Ms. Marks, this is Felicia from Jason Kane's office. We met the other day."

"Oh yes. What's going on?"

"I need to speak with you. Is it possible to meet at some point today?"

"Sure, just tell me where and what time."

"I'm leaving early today and would rather meet you someplace that's not near my office. There's a café right across from Grand Central on 42nd Street where we could meet. Is 3:00 okay?"

"Yes, I know the place. I'll be there."

When I hung up I wondered what that was all about. Felicia sounded nervous. I picked up the phone and dialed Susie.

"This is early for you," Susie said when she answered.

"Can I lure you away for lunch?"

"You don't have to try hard. I'll see you at 12:00 at Gino's."

Susie was already seated at a table when I arrived. I kissed her on the cheek as I sat down.

"You look good," I said to Susie.

"What you really mean is I don't look as horrible as the last time you saw me."

"Absolutely not, though you do have a little more color in your face."

"Say hello to Bobbi Brown Hibiscus Pot Rouge."

"Damn it looks good. I gotta get some of that."

"I spoke to Mark. I told him we can't keep our feelings to ourselves. We need to rely on each other."

"What did he say?"

"I think he was relieved. I didn't realize how much losing the baby had affected him."

"You're going to make me cry," I said.

"Are you ready to order?" the waiter asked.

"Definitely. I'll have your rigatoni pomodoro and a house salad."

"And I'll have the same," Susie said.

"Anything to drink ladies?"

"I'm working, so unfortunately no," Susie said.

"I'm working and I'll have a glass of your house wine."

"On second thought, I'll have the same. What the heck."

"Living dangerously. Good for you."

"Mark and I are thinking of taking a vacation."

"Now?"

"In a few months. We were deciding where to go."

"Maybe the four of us can go on vacation together." I had mentioned that Jack brought up the subject of vacationing.

"I'll ask Mark and maybe you should run it by Jack. Fill me in on the case."

I did. I caught Susie up to speed including the phone call from Felicia.

"So let me get this straight," Susie said. "Originally Jason Kane gave his client as his alibi. You discovered Kane was never with his client after dinner that night. Kane was meeting a woman. Then Jason's current wife, Danielle told you that she and Jason didn't start dating until after Rebecca died. When you met with Jason to confront him about his bogus alibi, he tells you he was with Danielle. When you spoke to Danielle again she said she originally lied to you because she thought it would look bad that she was seeing Jason while he was still married to Rebecca. Do I have that right?"

"You do. Now I get this call from Kane's secretary wanting to meet with me."

"So what are you thinking?"

"That there are a few more twists to this whole story."

"Tell me more about Rebecca's assistant that managed her shop."

"Apparently there was some sort of verbal agreement that if Rebecca sold the store, her assistant would have first dibs to buy it. I have only her word that there even was a verbal agreement. But for argument's sake let's say there was a verbal agreement. That puts suspicion on Samantha Gerard."

"And if Rebecca reneged on the deal and decided to sell the store to someone else, would that make Mrs. Gerard mad enough to kill Rebecca?" Susie said.

"What a mess, and that doesn't even include Rebecca's brother David who was buying toys in China containing lead."

"You do have quite a conundrum on your hands."

Our wine and food came. We both dug in.

"Look, you've come this far. Something is going to

show up. It's just a matter of time."

"I do hope you're right," I said.

"Let me know what the secretary has to say. This should be interesting."

"Oh by the way, I almost forgot. When I was in Lenox I saw this for you and couldn't resist." I handed Susie the wrapped Mezuzah I bought for her.

"This is so beautiful. I love it," Susie said. "I can't wait to put it on our door."

Tears were slowly seeping from her eyes.

I was so happy she liked my present. I was practically in tears. Susie and I hugged outside the restaurant since we were going in opposite directions.

At 3:00 I met with Felicia outside the café.

"Let's go inside," she said, looking kind of jumpy.

The place was huge. We sat at one of the tables in the back and we both ordered coffee.

"You have to promise me that whatever I tell you doesn't get back to my boss. I can't get fired."

I couldn't promise her since I didn't know what she was going to tell me.

"Without knowing what's going on, I don't know how to answer you."

Felicia started to get up. "I'm sorry I can't stay."

"Wait Felicia, I promise."

Felicia sat back down. I waited till she was ready to talk. I was praying I wouldn't regret promising without even knowing what secret I had to keep.

"When you left the office the other day, Mr. Kane called his wife."

My heart was beating faster.

"He said something like, 'that Marks woman just left my office; she knows my alibi was bogus; I told her you were with me; just stick to that story and we should be fine.'"

"Was there anything else you recall?"

"His wife must have been upset since I heard him say to her not to worry about it. What does this all mean? Should I be worried?"

"Calm down. You have nothing to be concerned about."

"Remember you promised not to say anything. If I lose my job I'll know it's because of you."

"It'll be fine. Thank you for telling me. You did the right thing."

When we left I could see the worried look on Felicia's face.

Walking to the subway, I contemplated how I was going to keep my promise to her.

CHAPTER 44

I took the train to my office and wrote up the conversation I had with Felicia. Then I packed up and left for the day.

On the way home I called Susie and told her what Felicia said. I knew I had to confront both Jason and Danielle. But how could I do that without Jason realizing Felicia was the one who told me.

I changed into my running clothes when I got back and did my three mile loop, all the while thinking about what I could say to Jason Kane without him getting suspicious.

I showered and changed when I got home and called Jack.

"Hi babe. Everything okay?"

I told Jack about my meeting with Felicia.

"It sounds like he had no alibi for that night, unless…"

"Unless what?"

"He could have been lying to Danielle because he was with someone else. Maybe he gave her a cock and bull story where he was that night."

"I never thought of that. Any other ideas?"

"Besides that he may have killed Rebecca?"

"Yeah, besides that?"

"Nothing that comes to mind at the moment. So how are you going to handle it?"

"I think I came up with something that won't get Kane's secretary involved. By the way, I told Patty I would take Michael on Saturday."

"Michael I can handle."

"Are you trying to say I'm too much for you?"

"I'm saying being with you is always an adventure."

"Good save. On another topic, I met Susie for lunch today. She said they're thinking of taking a vacation in the next couple of months. Are you interested in a foursome?"

"I've never even had a threesome. Don't you think I should work my way up to a foursome?"

After I stopped laughing, I said: "So what do you think?"

"If we agree on a vacation spot, I'm all for it."

"Good to know."

"I'll see you bright and early on Saturday."

"Looking forward to it."

My plan was to pay an unannounced visit to the Kane's. I thought I would surprise them tomorrow night. Then I remembered Jason leaves his office early on Friday afternoons to spend the weekend at Spring Lake. Maybe I can catch them before they go. I was thinking of calling Felicia to see what time Jason leaves the office but I decided not to involve her. I'll show up at his place by noon tomorrow and wait.

I parked about three quarters down the block from the Kane's the following day. I brought snacks in case I got hungry.

At 2:15 I saw Jason Kane walk up the steps to his brownstone. I waited a minute and then rang the doorbell. Jason Kane opened the door.

"What the hell do you want now? We're on our way out."

"This will only take a few minutes."

"Come in," he said in a harsh tone.

Mrs. Kane walked into the living room.

"Mrs. Kane, when I spoke with you yesterday you lied to me. As a matter of fact you both lied. You weren't very convincing that you were with Jason that night."

"How dare you!" Danielle said.

"Actually I'm tired of all your lies. You have both, let's say, been less than honest with me from the beginning. Either you tell me the truth right now or I'm going to the police to let them know that you had no alibi for the night Rebecca was killed."

I saw the look on Jason Kane's face. He looked as if the wind had gotten knocked out of him.

"What I'm about to tell you, I don't want Lisa to find out," Jason said.

"I can't guarantee you anything. Just tell me what it is."

"I was meeting with a private investigator that night. I hired him to watch Rebecca. I had my client lie for me because I didn't want the information about Rebecca to come out."

"And what information is that?" I said, annoyed with all his bullshit.

"I began to suspect that my wife was sleeping around, and I wanted to know what was going on with her. This PI told me she was picking up guys at bars and going back to their place or to seedy motels. If this had come out eventually Lisa would have found out when she got older, and I couldn't let that happen. That's why I was upset when Lisa hired you."

"So what you're saying to me is that after you left

your client that night you met with this private investigator."

"Yes, that's exactly what I'm saying."

"Do you have any documentation from this person? A report, photos, anything?"

"No, I got rid of all of it."

"So you want me to now believe this PI is your alibi, but you have no proof?"

"I know that doesn't sound good but it's the truth, I swear."

"What is this guy's name and where can I find him?"

"It was over twenty years ago. I'll have to see if I could locate his name."

"You can't remember his name?"

"Not right at this moment."

"I'm feeling a little generous. I'm going to give you until Monday at 5:00 pm to get me his name. If I don't have it by then I'm going to the police with all the information I have. You don't want them knowing what you've covered up."

"I know why you might not believe me but I lied only because of my daughter."

"Then prove it."

I turned and walked out.

I couldn't believe what Jason just told me. Either he's the greatest bullshit artist ever or he's telling the truth. I didn't know which to believe. Is it possible Rebecca was as promiscuous as Jason wanted me to believe? I wonder if Rebecca's friend Jackie knew what was going on and did Simon Mack have an inkling?

CHAPTER 45

When I got back to the car I called Jackie and left a message. Then I called Simon Mack. He answered right away.

"Hello."

"Simon, this is Tracey Marks. How are you?"

"I started working."

"That's good. Listen Simon, something's come up that I have to ask you about."

"Go ahead."

"Rebecca's husband just told me that he had hired a private investigator to follow Rebecca. It appears that she was picking up guys at bars and sleeping with them. Did you have any clue about her behavior?"

"I can't believe this."

"At this point I don't know if there is any truth to what he said. I'm trying to find out."

"If Rebecca was promiscuous, I had no clue."

"As far as you know when she left you she went home?"

"Yes, I had no reason to believe otherwise."

"Again, I have no proof if what her husband told me was the truth. I'm sorry but I had to ask you."

"It's okay. It was a long time ago," he said. I could

hear the sadness in his voice.

As soon as I hung up, my phone rang. It was Jackie.

"Hi Jackie. Thanks for getting back to me so soon."

"What's going on?"

"I just spoke with Jason Kane. He told me he had hired a private investigator to conduct surveillance on Rebecca."

"Why?"

"He said he had reason to believe she was sleeping around."

"Well we knew that."

"But what he found out from the PI was that she was picking up guys at bars and going home with them. Did you know anything about this behavior?"

"I knew she had no qualms about sleeping with my husband, but if she was sleeping with a lot of men she never said anything to me. Rebecca kept a part of herself secret. I realized that, but it didn't interfere with our friendship until I found out she slept with my husband. What has this got to do with the case?"

"I'm not sure at the moment."

I didn't want to tell Jackie that it may have been Jason's alibi for the night his wife was killed.

"Thanks Jackie."

When I hung up a horrible thought came to me. If what Jason Kane told me was true, that leaves the possibility that she could have picked up a psycho who could have killed her. I sort of dismissed that thought since according to what Jason told me, the private investigator said Rebecca never took men home to her house, though it is possible one of them found out where she lived.

I parked my car in the garage and went upstairs to my apartment. I needed to work off all my frustration. Instead of taking a run I went to the gym. I worked out really hard with weights and then ran on the treadmill for forty minutes.

On the way home I stopped at a bookstore and picked up a Sue Grafton mystery book. As soon as I got in I took a quick shower, poured myself a glass of wine and called Susie.

"What's going on?" she said before I had a chance to speak.

"You are not going to believe this. Jason Kane told me he hired a private investigator because he was pretty sure Rebecca was fooling around. It turns out his new alibi was this PI he met with the night Rebecca died. The PI told Jason that his wife was picking up men at bars and going to either cheap motels or their places. Of course he couldn't remember the PI's name off the top of his head. I gave him till 5:00 pm Monday to give me the name of this guy or else I was going to the police."

"How did he react to that?"

"I could tell he was scared. Oh, and the reason he originally lied to the police about his real alibi was because he never wanted his daughter to find about her mother. What do you think?"

"That's one hell of a whopper if it's not the truth. You'll find out on Monday or maybe sooner."

"What happens if he comes up with the name of this PI but it turns out this guy is dead?"

"Let's take one step at a time."

"I talked to Jack about the four of us going on a vacation. He was fine with it as long as we could agree on a place to go," I said.

"I'll talk to Mark and see what he says."

"Love you, talk soon."

After eating I spent the rest of the evening reading my book.

The next morning I got up early to do some cleaning before Jack arrived. As I was putting on the coffee maker I heard knocking at the door.

"Hey," I said pulling Jack in.

"You smell good," Jack said hugging me.

"You sure it's not the coffee that smells so wonderful?"

"Pretty sure."

"Since we're picking up Michael at 11:00 let's go directly to bed. The coffee will have to wait."

"I think I could deal with that," Jack said smiling, as he followed me into the bedroom.

Forty-five minutes later we were wrapped in each other's arms.

"So what are the plans with Michael today? Got any ideas?" Jack asked.

"Lunch and maybe the zoo. What do you think?"

"I would love to go to the zoo. I haven't been to one in years."

"This is for Michael. Keep that in mind."

"I'll try to contain my excitement."

After breakfast we took an Uber to Alan and Patty's house.

"Hi guys," Alan said as he opened the door. "Come in. Patty's getting everything ready."

"I thought we were taking Michael for the afternoon. Am I missing something?"

"When you have a kid you have to plan for all contingencies. Like a boy scout, always be prepared."

"There's the little man," Tracey said.

"Tracey," Michael said running to me.

"Say hello to Jack."

"Okay, everything's ready," Patty said, attaching Michael's diaper bag to the stroller. "Try not to kill my kid."

"Don't worry we'll bring him back in one piece. Enjoy the day."

With Michael in the stroller we walked across town to Central Park. When we got to a place where we could relax on the grass, Jack opened up his backpack and took out a small blanket and a rubber ball.

"Were you a Boy Scout since you definitely came prepared?"

"I told you I've been around little kids."

I watched as Jack and Michael played with the ball. It was more like Jack rolling it to Michael and Michael trying to pick it up. I was enjoying the back and forth. I marveled at how much Jack was engaged with Michael and how much he was enjoying himself. I tried not to let myself think about what the future would look like if Jack and I lived together. I doubt if children were in the cards.

At some point I joined in on their little game. Michael pooped out after a while and I gave him his water bottle. The three of us were sitting on the blanket. I took Jack's hand and held it.

"I think it's lunch time," I said.

We walked over to the Boat Basin Café and we were seated by the hostess. Jack and I each ordered a hamburger and French fries. Though we knew Michael wouldn't eat a whole burger we ordered one for him also. Jack had a beer and I had a lemonade.

When the burgers came we took Michael's out of the bun and cut it up into tiny pieces along with cut up French fries, and placed the food on the tray that was attached to his stroller. Patty packed a juice bottle that we gave to Michael.

Michael was having a grand old time eating his

burger and fries, and Jack and I had some good laughs watching him eat.

Before going to the zoo we parked ourselves on a bench since we could see Michael's eyes were starting to close. He was sound asleep two minutes later.

"Did you bring anything for us to play with?" I asked Jack.

"Nothing that wouldn't get us thrown in jail most likely."

"I see. You know Michael adores you," I said.

"That's because I'm only with him very infrequently."

"Well I adore you and I'm with you quite a bit."

"I haven't shown you my dark side yet." Jack said.

"I find it hard to imagine there's a dark side to you. If anyone in this group has a dark side it would be me."

"Oh yeah?"

"Yeah." I said kissing him on the lips.

"Michael might wake up and tell on us if we're not careful," Jack said.

"I dare him."

Twenty minutes later I saw Michael's eyes pop open.

"Hey little man," I said as I picked him up and sat him on my lap. "Did you have a nice sleep? You want to see the monkeys now?"

Michael gave me a big grin.

"Do you think he's wet?" I said to Jack.

"There's only one way to find out."

"I'm going in Michael. You are wet, aren't you. Don't you think since you're both guys you should change him?" I said looking sheepishly at Jack.

"Alright Michael it's just us men."

We laid Michael down in his stroller and Jack changed him. Then we went to the zoo, but not before buying Michael a cup of ice cream from the Good

Humor cart inside the park.

It was after 6:00 by the time we walked back from the zoo.

When Patty opened the door, I said: "I don't know about Michael but I'm pooped."

"How was he?"

"Michael was great," Jack said. "I didn't hear one complaint from him."

"You guys must have the magic touch. He'll sleep good tonight. Would you like to stay for dinner?"

"Thanks, but I would probably fall asleep at the table. We'll take a rain check," I said.

After saying goodbye, Jack and I took a cab back to my place. Instead of grabbing some dinner out we brought in Chinese food.

A shrimp was dangling from my chopsticks when I said to Jack: "The therapist asked me something I wasn't expecting. She asked me if I thought I could have saved my father."

Jack kept quiet.

"Deep down I thought I could have saved him if I hadn't froze. I know it doesn't make sense."

"To a thirteen year old it makes perfect sense," Jack said.

My eyes started to water. I quickly changed the subject.

"Oh, with taking care of Michael today, I completely forgot to tell you about my conversation with the Kane's."

I caught Jack up to date with what transpired.

"Well you have to give it to the guy he tells a good story."

"Do you think there might be any truth in it?"

"I suppose. It's certainly easy enough to check out

once he gives you this guy's name."

"What if he can't recall or the guy's dead?"

"You'll figure it out."

"You and Susie both said the same thing."

"Well then it must be true."

"You are awfully sure of yourself mister."

"Right now the only thing I'm sure of is what I want to do with you for the next hour or so."

"Well we better hurry before I fall asleep."

CHAPTER 46

On Sunday Jack and I had a late, leisurely breakfast and then took the train to Greenwich Village where we spent time going in and out of the shops. At one point we stopped at a bar. I had a glass of wine and Jack had a beer. It was a pleasant way to pass the time.

We wound up in Soho where we went into a little Italian place and had dinner. We were home by 9:00 and sleeping by 10:00 pm.

Monday morning Jack left at 7:00 since he had an early meeting with a potential witness. I was a little anxious waiting for Jason Kane's phone call. I should have given him till 10:00 this morning instead of later today. I still wasn't sure if he was telling the truth or not. I was hoping he would call before my 5:00 therapy session.

I was in the middle of finishing up my report to send to my client when my phone rang.

"Tracey Marks."

"Ms. Marks this is Jason Kane. I found the private investigator's name. If there is any way you can keep Lisa out of this I would greatly appreciate it."

"What's his name?"

"Walter McKensie."

"Where is he located?"

"I'm not sure. I think his office was down in the twenties on the west side. I was only there once. Last time I saw him was the night Rebecca died."

"Do you remember how old he was?"

"I can only guess. Maybe he was forty-five or fifty."

"Keep your fingers crossed I can find him," I said and hung up.

If Kane was correct this guy could be sixty-five or seventy now. I don't even know if he'd still be in business.

I started with an internet search. There was no listing under private investigators with his name. Now what? Call the New York State Licensing Board. I got their number and called. It turns out this guy is no longer licensed but they had an address for him from about five years ago. I was informed that he was sixty-eight years old.

The address from five years ago was in Yonkers, New York, a town in lower Westchester County. I conducted an in-depth database search on Walter McKensie. It appears that Mr. McKensie is currently living in Vermont. I guess he wanted the country life.

When I checked to see how far it was from New York to Brattleboro, Vermont, it turned out to be about a five hour drive. I didn't want to call McKensie. I needed to see him in person. I decided to leave in the morning.

I made a couple of phone calls and booked a room at a Hampton Inn in Brattleboro. I packed up and made it just in time for my therapy session.

"Come in Tracey," Lily Davidson said.

I sat for what seemed like forever without saying

anything.

Finally I said, "I don't know what to talk about."

"Just say anything that comes to mind."

"I agreed to go on a vacation with Jack."

"You mentioned in our first session that you are currently in your first long term relationship. Can you tell me about Jack?"

"Jack is also a private investigator. I met him on one of my cases that was in the Stockbridge area in Massachusetts. He was helping me on something and there was instant sexual attraction, at least on my part. I don't usually sleep with someone I just met but I did anyway. At the time I was seeing someone, but for me, I didn't think we were exclusive and the truth is I didn't care."

"Tell me more about Jack?"

"It's hard to put into words. He's different than the other guys I've been with."

"How?"

"He's the complete opposite of me."

"That's interesting. You also said that about Susie."

I thought about that for a moment.

"How is he different?"

"He's easy going and I'm not. He's the first person I've been with where I feel I can be myself. He doesn't judge me."

"Those are really good qualities in a person. So what do you think is stopping you from going forward with your relationship?"

"Fear always pops up for me."

"What do you think is behind the fear?"

"If we were living together, he wouldn't want to be with me."

"So far that doesn't seem to be a problem."

"That's true, but we do have sort of a long distance

relationship."

"And he wants more?"

"He does."

"And what do you want?"

"I don't know."

"I think we need to spend more time figuring out what that fear is from."

"I thought it was about being afraid to lose someone I'm close to because of my parents."

"That could be part of it. But I'm also wondering if you might feel that you don't deserve to be in a loving relationship?"

That struck something inside of me but I wasn't sure why.

"Sometimes children who lose a parent at a young age believe it was because of something they did wrong and not the circumstances. I think agreeing to go on a vacation with Jack is a baby step in the right direction. Why don't we stop here."

Could there be any truth to what Lily Davidson said?

CHAPTER 47

When I got on the road the following morning I called Jack and Susie to let them know I was heading to Vermont and why.

My GPS directed me to the New York State Thruway, then to U.S Route 7 North into Vermont. I reached the Hampton Inn in Brattleboro by 1:30 pm. I checked in and asked where there was some place close by to have lunch. I was told the Putney Diner served breakfast till 3:00 pm.

The Putney Diner looked different than the diners in New York. This had more of a cozy atmosphere. It was brighter, with small wooden tables instead of booths.

I sat down at one of the tables and a waitress with a name tag on her uniform that said Melinda greeted me. She was tiny, maybe twenty-five with straight blonde hair pulled up in a ponytail.

"Hi there," Melinda said, with energy that could wake up the dead. "Can I get you a cup of coffee while you're looking the menu over?"

"That would be great, thank you."

A minute later Melinda brought over my coffee.

"So what can I get you?"

"I'll have an omelet with Swiss cheese and bacon

crisp with a side order of home fries and whole wheat toast."

"Are you by any chance from New York?"

"I am. Have you ever been?"

"No, but my boyfriend and I are thinking of going this spring. We're going to get tickets for one of the Broadway plays. Can you recommend a show?"

"It depends what you like, musical or drama?"

"I really like musicals."

Why did that not surprise me?

"Though I can't say firsthand, I know from reviews that the shows, Come From Away, Dear Evan Hansen and Oklahoma you might enjoy."

"Thanks, I'll keep that in mind."

When Melinda came back with my food I inquired about downtown Brattleboro. She told me it had a lot of bookstores, art galleries and places to eat. She suggested Elliot Street Fish & Chips for dinner. In reading a little bit about the town it said it was located on the Connecticut River. I wasn't sure if I would have a chance to browse through the shops.

After eating I thanked Melinda and headed over to Walter McKensie's place. It turned out to be a farm house in an isolated area surrounded by acres of land. There was a gravel road leading up to the house.

I knocked on the side of the screen door and shouted hello. The woman who came to the door was probably in her sixties, with soft skin and large blue eyes.

"May I help you?"

"I'm looking for Walter McKensie. Does he live here?"

"That depends on why you're looking for him," she said in a joking manner. "Why don't you come in."

I walked into the kitchen that smelled of freshly baked bread.

"My name is Jennifer. Walter is my husband. How can I help you?"

"Tracey Marks. Here's my card."

"A female private investigator."

"I'm working on a twenty year old murder case that took place in New York City. I've been asked by a family member to investigate since the killer was never found. One of the people I'm looking into gave your husband as his alibi for that night."

"I see. Well Walter is down by the lake fishing. If you follow the path you'll run right into him. I have to warn you he's kind of forgetful these days."

"Thank you."

Walking down the path I was hoping Walter was still able to remember meeting with Jason Kane. I spotted him sitting on a folding chair with his fishing pole. I didn't want to sneak up on him so I called out his name and he turned towards me.

"Well hello there young lady. Come and join me. Pull up a rock. Sorry I don't have an extra chair."

"This rock will do just fine. I'm Tracey Marks. I'm a private investigator from New York."

"I'd introduce myself but you already know my name."

"That's true. Would you happen to remember a man by the name of Jason Kane? About twenty years ago you did surveillance on his wife Rebecca. You may recall she died not long after."

"Sounds vaguely familiar. My memory is not so good these days. Do you know how to fish?"

"I do. My father taught me. We used to rent a cottage in North Carolina during the summer months. I could tell you exactly what type of bait to use depending on what you're fishing for."

"Well you're my kind of gal. I love fishing. Used to

be strictly a city boy, but when I decided to retire I thought the missus and I would try something different. You couldn't pay me to move back."

"Though I'm strictly a city gal myself, I can understand how you would like it up here."

"So Tracey, what's going on?"

"Rebecca Kane was murdered about twenty years ago and the police never found out who killed her. They thought it was her husband, the man who paid you to follow his wife around, but he had a solid alibi. It turns out that alibi was bogus."

"So who you working for?"

"I was hired by Rebecca's daughter. She wants to know who killed her mother even if it turns out to be her father."

"He gave you my name?"

"He did. It took me a few minutes to find you."

"So I'm his alibi now, is that it?"

"That about sums it up."

"You got any other suspects?"

"I do, but I'd like to eliminate the husband if I can."

"I'm pretty sure I remember him. I do remember his wife; she was beautiful."

"He said he met you around ten the night his wife died. You were going to show him what you found out on her."

"Not sure about the time but I did meet him that night."

"How can you be so sure?"

"Only because that was the night she was killed. Hard to forget that."

"Would you still happen to have photos from your surveillance and any reports?"

"You mean any photos I took?"

"Yeah and any reports?"

"I have a box in my attic. The file might be in there."

"Do you know if you made a notation of the time you met with Jason Kane?"

"Can't say. So how did you get into the business? I think I met one other female PI back then."

"Kind of fell into it. Not sure that was my goal at the time."

"I think I got something on my hook."

Walter reeled a nice looking trout in. I noticed there was another one on ice.

"Are you heading back today?"

"I booked a room at the Hampton Inn for the night. I figured I probably wouldn't want to drive back later."

"My wife's a great cook. I'm sure she'd love to have you stay for dinner."

I was eyeing the trout and my mouth was watering.

"If the smell of her bread is any indication I'd have to say yes."

"When we head back we'll take a look in the attic and see what we find."

"I appreciate that."

"Maybe you can tell me more about the case over dinner."

Walter caught another fish before he called it quits for the day.

"If you hang around tomorrow we can go out on my boat and you can show me your fishing prowess young lady."

"I would love to but I probably should head back early. My friend Jack would love it up here."

"Well maybe you can come back another time with him."

"Thanks. Maybe we will."

We walked up to the house. I helped him carry his chair and the fishing pole.

"Jennifer, we got company for dinner."

"If that's alright with you ma'am?"

"I would love to have the company. It's rare that we have a guest for dinner."

"Can I help you?" I asked Jennifer.

"If you'd like you could cut up the tomatoes, red peppers and mushrooms."

"I'm going up to the attic to see if I have the file you're looking for," Walter said.

"No you're not. It's too much for you to climb up there," Jennifer said in a stern voice.

"I'll do it," I said. "It shouldn't be that difficult to find if it's there."

Walter yanked down the attic steps and I climbed up. "Are the boxes marked?" I said when I got up there.

"They should be," Walter shouted up.

After surveying the boxes I found the right one. I opened it with anticipation, hoping Rebecca's file was in there. Bingo. I pulled it out of the box.

"Did you find it?" Walter asked.

"Yes. I'll be right down." I opened up the folder and there were numerous photos. Also handwritten notes. I climbed back down and couldn't wait to look through the file.

While we were eating I explained what I had found out so far.

"It sounds like you put a lot of work into it. How come Mr. Kane lied about his alibi if he was with me?"

"He said he never wanted his daughter to find out about her mother."

"The poor thing," Jennifer remarked.

"At this point I have suspects but no way to prove who did it. I'm not even sure if it was a male or a female. And now with the possibility of Rebecca sleeping with the wrong guy, it complicates things."

"Sometimes I miss the hunt," Walter said.

"How many years were you a private investigator?" I asked.

"Over thirty."

"Walter seems to forget all the times he would come home and complain about the work. It was grinding and the hours were terrible. Do you remember all the nights you spent following people around?"

"Yeah, it could be a pain sometimes, but I did enjoy it."

"This fish is amazing," I said. "You wouldn't by any chance give me your secret recipe?"

"Oh my dear there is no secret. When the fish is so fresh it makes a difference. Trout should always be pan fried."

"My boyfriend is going to be so jealous."

After a delicious dessert of apple pie and ice cream, Walter and I looked through the file.

"I don't see anything in the file about what time you met with Mr. Kane that night."

"I might not have marked it down since it was our last meeting. The meeting might have lasted maybe fifteen minutes, give or take five minutes or so."

"The coroner said Rebecca Kane died between 8:00 pm and 12 midnight. If you only saw him for approximately fifteen minutes that might have given him enough time to go home and kill his wife. Would it be possible to take the file with me? I could mail it back to you."

"I don't see why not."

"Thank you."

I said goodbye and thanked them for their hospitality. It was almost 10:00 pm when I got back to the Inn.

CHAPTER 48

I took a quick shower and fell fast asleep. In the morning I gathered my stuff and was out the door by 7:30 am. I decided to stop at the diner for breakfast before heading home.

The diner was pretty full. I guess they get a good breakfast crowd. I was shown to a table by a young waitress named Kathy. Apparently Melinda doesn't work the early shift.

"I'll have an order of pancakes with a side order of bacon very crisp and coffee, please."

After Kathy brought over my coffee, I took out Rebecca's folder. Walter had certainly taken a lot of photos. There were some of Rebecca at bars with guys drinking and dancing. She appeared to be drunk in some of the photos but it was hard to tell. She certainly was beautiful with her thick long red hair and large green eyes. She could have been a model.

There were other photos, some where she was entering a house or an apartment with a guy. It looked like Walter must have taken some shots near a window since there were close up photos of Rebecca in bed with a guy. From the dates on the photos, it appeared Walter was following her for about three weeks, enough time to reveal Rebecca's promiscuity.

I closed the file when I saw Kathy coming over with my breakfast.

"Refill?"

"Always, thanks."

When Kathy left I opened up the folder again. The dates on Walter's notes coincided with the dates of the photos. Walter made a detailed list of all the bars Rebecca frequented, the addresses of the guys she went home with and the motels she went to. I wondered if she was a nymphomaniac. I kind of felt sorry for her. I saw a small notation that Walter met with Jason Kane at 10:15 the night of Rebecca's murder. Unfortunately it didn't mention when the meeting was over. If Walter was right and the meeting lasted about fifteen minutes, Jason would have had enough time to kill Rebecca.

I used the ladies' room before leaving and was back in my office by 2:10 pm. The first thing I did was call Jack. He texted me back that he was really busy and would call me later.

I felt stuck and wasn't sure what to do to determine who killed Rebecca. While I was reflecting on this thought, my phone rang.

"Hello."

"Tracey, it's Lisa."

"You sound upset. Is everything alright?"

"I've been remembering some things from that night. I think it might be because of the hypnosis."

"That's great. So why are you upset?"

"The more I remember, the more frightened I get."

"Why?"

"Because it may be my father. I know that I told you I wanted to know the truth no matter what. Now I'm not so sure."

"You might be jumping the gun. Why don't you tell

me what you recall?"

"The strong smell in the hallway by my mother's room, I think it was cologne and not a perfume scent."

"Anything else?"

"One other thing, the other voice I heard besides my mother's, I believe it was a man's voice. I'm just not sure if it was my father's voice."

"This does not mean it was your father. It just tells me it was most likely a man who killed your mother."

"But who else would want to hurt her?"

"Let me worry about that."

"Is there anything you can tell me?" Lisa asked.

"The best I can say is that I'm making progress, but can't say anything else at the moment."

I had no reason to mention my trip to see Walter McKensie unless I had to. Though Lisa was my client and had a right to know what I found out, for the time being I thought I would keep her mother's affair with Simon Mack a secret.

"Well as soon as you do, please let me know. This whole thing has me on edge."

"I will, I promise. Please try not to worry. I know it's not easy."

After hanging up I thought about what Lisa said. This might narrow the list of suspects, though the killer might have been someone Rebecca slept with for one night.

I packed up and left the office. I thought I'd go for a run to relieve all the stress I felt coursing through my body. On the way out I bumped into Gary Roberts, the criminal attorney who now occupies Max's office.

"Hey Tracey, how are you?"

"I'm okay, just on my way out."

"I won't keep you. I thought one of these days we could go for a drink."

I wasn't exactly sure what that meant. Was he just being friendly or was he hitting on me?

"Let's talk another time," and I left.

You would think I'd be better at reading people, but I had no idea if it was just an innocent remark because we both had an office on the same floor or there was more to it. I decided not to give it any more thought at the moment.

By the time I finished my run, my stress was at a minimum. On the way home I stopped at the Corner Sweet Shoppe for my ice cream fix and then picked up some Thai food.

As I was getting out of the shower I heard my phone ring. It took me a minute or so to find it under a pile of my running clothes.

"Hello."

"You sound out of breath," Jack said.

"I was just getting out of the shower when you called, and the phone was hidden under a pile of clothes."

"How was the trip?"

"Very interesting." I went on to tell Jack about my day in Brattleboro.

"It sounds like it was very productive and a bonus of a great home cooked dinner."

"The fish was amazing. I am now an expert at pan frying trout."

"You do learn fast. So what was your takeaway after looking through the file on Rebecca?"

"This woman definitely had a problem, if you could call too much sex a problem."

"Well normally I would say no, but from what you've told me she did seem to entertain a lot of guys."

"I guess that is a problem. Anyway, getting back to Walter's notes, unfortunately, I can't eliminate Jason

Kane. He still had enough time after meeting with Walter to kill Rebecca, and after looking at the photos, that might have made him mad enough to do the deed. And there's more. I spoke with Lisa and she remembered two more pieces of the puzzle. One, the strong scent by her mother's bedroom was cologne and not perfume. Also she was pretty sure the other voice she heard that night was a man's voice."

"So now we can narrow down the suspects."

"Unless it was a guy she slept with."

"Let's put that aside for now."

"I feel as if I'm at an impasse. I don't know what to do to lure the real killer out."

"Why don't you give everything you know to the police? Let them sort it out."

"Who knows if they're even interested in a cold case. They have enough active cases to handle. I need to finish this for Lisa. The only way I can think of right now is to bait each one of them. Threaten them, anything to get the real killer worried."

"It's too dangerous."

"I just don't see any other alternative."

"Promise me you'll have your gun on you at all times and you'll be super careful."

"I promise. Believe me I do not want to die. Besides I'm so looking forward to seeing the Grand Canyon."

"Not funny."

"This is such a comforting conversation. Maybe it's time to make out a Will, though besides a few dollars in my bank account, there really isn't anything."

"Well I wouldn't mind the hallway table."

I laughed.

"You have a key. Just come in and take it before anyone knows I'm gone."

"Be safe."

"Always."

CHAPTER 49

I called Susie as I was getting ready to eat.

"I was just thinking about you," Susie said.

I explained what I learned from Walter and my conversation with Jack.

"I want the living room chair and your mom's dishes."

"What the hell. I'm not even dead yet and you and Jack are planning what you have your eyes on. I won't forget this," I chuckled. "How are you doing?"

"What's the saying, one day at a time. By the way I spoke to Mark and he thinks the four of us on a vacation together would be fun."

"That's fantastic. I'm glad you guys are coming."

"Wait. Is there something going on you're not telling me about?"

"I don't know. It's just that I've never been away for a week or ten days with someone."

"But it's Jack."

"I know who it is. That's the weird thing. I'm comfortable with him so I don't know why I'm apprehensive about this."

"Maybe it's because it might mean a step closer to a commitment which scares you."

"Thank you Lily Davidson."

"You're welcome. I'll talk to you tomorrow. Love you."

"Me too."

If I wasn't so tired I'd think about what Susie said. She might be right.

The last image in my head before falling asleep was the image of Rebecca Kane staring up at me from her bathroom floor, blood all around her.

Something cold against my face woke me. It was pitch black in the room.

"Wake up Tracey."

The voice sounded familiar. It was Jason Kane's voice. I quickly became fully alert.

"How the hell did you get in here?"

"That's the first question you ask with a loaded gun pointed at your head?"

I was trying to remain calm but it was impossible. I was freezing and sweating at the same time.

"Sit up. I want you to look at me when I pull the trigger."

He turned on the lamp sitting on my nightstand. I sat up. He moved the gun away from my head and was now pointing it directly at me. I was trying to think. I wanted to stall him but my mind was frozen.

"I told you to back off but you wouldn't listen. You had to keep digging and digging. It's your fault. And because of that you're going to die."

"Why couldn't you just divorce Rebecca? Why did you have to kill her?"

He laughed.

"You are so naïve. You were right. She was planning on divorcing me. I would have gotten nothing."

"With the photos you had of her, a judge would have given you custody of Lisa and awarded you alimony."

"Again, you are naïve. With all her family money there was no way I was going to win custody of Lisa."

I was trying to stall him.

"Look, it's an old case. Chances are nothing is going to happen to you. There really is no proof that you killed Rebecca. I'll forget about this if you walk out now."

"You know I can't do that. I know what you're trying to do and it's not going to work. As soon as I leave here you would head straight to the police, but nice try."

"I know we can work something out. Rebecca was a bitch. She treated everyone like garbage."

"Shut up," Jason yelled.

His hand was shaking. My only salvation was to rush him. I'd probably be dead before I got to him but I had to take that chance. I lunged forward. The last thing I heard was the sound of the gun going off.

My eyes popped open. Sweat sticking to my tee shirt. When I realized it was a dream, I felt such relief. I got up and walked into the bathroom. I splashed cold water over my face. I was still shaking as I tugged off my shirt and panties and turned on the shower. I got in and let the cool water run off my body.

The dream felt so real. Maybe my mind was trying to tell me that Jason Kane was the killer and to be very careful.

I tried going back to bed but it was impossible. The clock said 4:00 am. I turned on the TV thinking the sound would lull me back to sleep. After tossing and turning for what seemed like forever, I gave up and went into the kitchen and switched on the coffee maker.

As I was drinking my coffee I was trying to come up with a plan on how to bait the killer into coming after me. I wasn't exactly happy being a target but there didn't seem to be any other solution. Though I had no real proof on Rebecca's husband, her brother or her lover, Simon Mack, I had to find a way to convince them I did, or maybe I just had to convince them they were a viable suspect, and I would go to the police with what I had.

I was at the office by 8:00 am after stopping to get a muffin and a coffee. I took out the folder with the photos of Rebecca and looked through them again. I decided I would pay a visit to Rebecca's brother David first. It seemed as if he had a lot to lose if it was found out he was importing toys with lead in them. I didn't think Rebecca would let her brother get away with what he was involved in, especially since it might destroy the family business and the money Rebecca would inherit.

Around 11:00 am I left and went to see David Martin at his office.

"Hello," I said to the receptionist. "I'd like to see David Martin and I don't have an appointment. Please tell him it's Tracey Marks."

"One moment please."

She picked up the phone and I heard her talking to someone but couldn't hear what she was saying. A few minutes later I heard David Martin call my name.

"Why don't you come into my office?"

When I sat down David said: "What the hell do you want now? I've answered all your questions."

"It seems as if Rebecca was being surveilled."

"By whom?" he asked

"I can't tell you that."

"What does that got to do with me?"

"It appears that you and Rebecca got into some pretty heated arguments. I'm assuming it was over the issue of the lead in the toys."

I thought a little white lie wouldn't hurt.

"I know you told me that got resolved, but here's my dilemma. I only have your version of what happened. Unfortunately, your sister is not here to corroborate your story."

"My mother can."

"You don't expect me or the police to take your mother's word for it."

"Why would you get the police involved?"

"David, you are my prime suspect."

"What about the woman who managed Rebecca's clothing store? I told you about her," David said, raising his voice.

"It seems that your niece has remembered a few things from that night and it was definitely a man's voice she heard in her mother's bedroom."

"Well what about her husband? He had a lot of reasons to kill my sister."

"It seems he has a rock solid alibi."

Another fib.

"Look, I didn't kill her, I swear."

"Unless you have some other proof besides your mother, I'll have to go to the police with what I know."

"I'm begging you. I didn't do it."

I got up and left.

I was wondering as I walked out of the building whether I came on too strong to David. He might want to kill me even if he didn't murder Rebecca. That wasn't my problem unless it became my problem.

CHAPTER 50

I picked up a turkey sandwich and fries before heading back to the office. As I was munching on a fry my phone rang. A number I didn't recognize.

"Tracey Marks."

"Ms. Marks, this is Sylvia Martin. I was wondering if you could make the time to see me this afternoon. I have something to discuss with you."

It sounded more like an order than a request.

"Can you tell me what this is about?"

"I'd rather discuss it in person."

"I can be at your place around 3:00 pm."

"I'll expect you then," Mrs. Martin said before hanging up.

So David called his mother as soon as I left his office. I wondered how she thinks she is going to handle the situation. I was eager to find out.

I rang Mrs. Martin's doorbell on the dot of 3:00. The housekeeper accompanied me to the same sitting room I was in the last two times I was here. It never tires me to look out onto the back of the house with the lush trees and the blue sparkling water from the swimming pool.

"Thank you for being so prompt," Mrs. Martin said

as she came into the room. "Please sit Tracey."

"What is this about?" I asked.

"It seems my son David is not in your good graces. I understand you are accusing him of killing my daughter."

"It appears your son was engaged in the illegal importing of toys that contained lead and Rebecca found out."

"Yes, and my son came to my husband and myself and confessed to what he did. He told us that he was not aware of the situation until a few months after he was in business with this particular company in China."

"That may be true but he must have had some inkling why the price was much cheaper than it had been with the original company you were doing business with."

"He was just learning the business. It was stupid on his part. He should have talked to us first."

"Yet he didn't tell you about the change until after his sister confronted him."

"The situation was resolved so he had no reason to kill Rebecca."

"Maybe that's true but I think I'll let the police sort that out."

"I thought you would say that. Excuse me for a moment."

A few minutes later Mrs. Martin came back into the room.

"This is for you," handing me a check for $25,000.

"Wow, that's a lot of money. What is this for?" I said playing dumb.

"I told you when you first came to me that I wanted the person who murdered my daughter to be found and hopefully punished. I hope this is enough money to keep looking since I know my son is innocent."

"I'm sorry. I can't take your check or your word for it that your son is innocent," handing the check back to her. "I already have a client who's paying me."

"Yes, my granddaughter. If you won't take my check I am asking you that you do not get the police involved unless you are one hundred percent sure my son is guilty."

"I can't promise you anything but I will think about it."

"Thank you for coming my dear."

Well that was interesting I thought, as I was driving back. She was baiting me to see if I would take the bribe. When she knew I wouldn't, she was smart in trying to get me to back off for the time being. Mrs. Martin was a shrewd woman. No wonder she had such a successful business.

I had no intention of getting the police involved at the moment. I still had two more suspects on my list that I needed to speak with. I was hoping one of them killed Rebecca. If not, I was out of ideas and out of luck.

It was almost 5:00 by the time I got home. I changed into my sweats, poured myself a glass of wine and sat down on my living room couch. The phone rang as I was contemplating what to say to Jason Kane to rattle him.

"Hello."

"Ms. Marks, this is Walter McKensie."

"Hi, how's the fishing?"

"Excellent."

"I'm sorry I didn't get a chance to send the folder back yet."

"Take your time. That's not why I'm calling. On some cases I wrote annotations about the people who hired me. As you know you have to be careful that they have no intention of harming the person they've hired you to conduct surveillance on. I forgot about the notebook where I've written notes about certain people. It appears I was kind of leery about Jason Kane."

"Why is that?"

"Something about the guy bothered me. He seemed very eager to get dirt on his wife."

"That seems normal. That's why he hired you."

"Actually most guys would rather find out that their wife isn't cheating."

"Ah, maybe he was planning on blackmailing her," I said.

"That's a possibility. It did cross my mind."

"So even if she did divorce him he could use the blackmail card to extort money from her," I said.

"One other thing. When I met him that night he seemed to be in a hurry. He took the manila envelope I gave him that contained the photos of his wife but wasn't interested in making conversation. Normally people are interested in talking about what I found out. They usually ask questions."

"This helps. Thank you Walter."

"Let me know when you and your gentleman friend would like to pay a visit. The missus has no interest in fishing, and every once in a while it's nice to have a fishing buddy to shoot the breeze with."

"We will definitely get up there one of these weekends. Please say hello to your wife for me."

"Will do. Good luck with the case."

My mind was reeling. What if Jason went back to the house, showed his wife the photos, gave her an ultimatum, money or the photos come out. They argued and somehow she winds up dead. It's a good theory, only if it's what really happened.

CHAPTER 51

I picked up the phone and called Jack.

"Hey, I was just going to call you."

"I've heard that line before."

"Would I lie to you?"

"Can I have a minute to think about that?"

"Well as much as I'm fascinated by this stimulating conversation, what's going on?"

I told Jack about Walter's impressions of Jason Kane.

"Didn't Kane tell you the reason he gave a false alibi was because he didn't want his daughter to find about her mother's sexual activities?"

"It could still be true. If the blackmail was successful the photos didn't have to come out."

"I guess that's one take of the situation."

"The evidence keeps piling up against him."

"All circumstantial. Keep an open mind."

"I will. I spoke to Susie and she said that Mark's on board with us all vacationing together."

"Great, as long as we're not sharing a room with them." I could imagine the smile on Jack's face.

"Do you see a problem with that? I think Mark is very sexy."

"I guess I'll book my room for one."

"Over my dead body."

"That's my girl."

"Maybe we can get together with them next week and plan it. It should be fun," I said.

"I'll talk to you tomorrow. Love you."

"Ditto."

When I woke up the following morning instead of going into the office I thought I would ride out to Long Beach and wait for Simon Mack to come home. I didn't want to involve his girlfriend so I had to think of how to get him alone.

Since I wasn't in a hurry I went for a run. When I got back Wally was at his post.

"Hi Wally."

"Miss Tracey. Haven't seen you in a few days."

"Trying to keep out of trouble. I guess we're missing each other."

"Thomas, my youngest is having a baby."

"Congratulations. You must be so happy."

"It's about time he settled down. It took him a long time to find a wife."

Though Thomas is Wally's youngest he must be almost forty by now.

"When's the baby due?"

"Not for a few months."

"You'll have to take lots of pictures of the baby."

"You bet I will. It's going to be a little nippy today."

That's Wally's polite way of telling me to take a jacket.

"See ya later Wally."

By the time I showered and had breakfast it was almost 10:00. I filled my backpack with a couple of protein bars and a bottle of water. I didn't forget to take a jacket before leaving.

The traffic out to Long Beach was horrendous. It took me almost an hour and a half till I parked my car across from Simon's house. I saw one car in the driveway but didn't know if it was his or his girlfriend's car. I decided to see who was home.

I knocked on the door and a woman who was probably Simon's girlfriend came to the door.

"Can I help you?"

"I was looking for Simon. Is he home?"

"What is this about?"

I didn't want to reveal too much.

"I'm working on an old case, and Simon knew the family I'm investigating." I gave her my card.

"Did he know you were coming?"

"No, it was last minute."

"I see. Well to tell you the truth Simon moved out last week."

"Do you know where he moved to?" Well this was certainly a surprise development.

"No, but he said he would stop by to pick up his things and his mail."

"Last time I spoke with him he mentioned that he was working. Do you know where?"

"I'm not sure I should give you that information."

"If for some reason I'm not able to get in touch with him, could you please tell him I need to speak with him. It's important."

"I will."

"I don't mean to pry but can you tell me why Simon moved out?"

"I think you should talk to Simon."

"Was he drinking again?"

She gave me a weird look.

"You'll have to talk to Simon."

When I got back to the car I called Simon. It went straight to voicemail where I left a message. What if he doesn't call me back? I should have insisted that I needed his work address. It was pretty apparent after talking to him a few times he never really got over Rebecca. Maybe bringing up the past triggered something in Simon. He seemed fragile to me. What now?

I got out of the car and knocked on the door again.

"I'm really sorry to bother you again but it's really important that I get in touch with Simon."

"I'm assuming you have his telephone number."

She wasn't going to tell me where Simon worked.

I was sitting in my car debating what to do when my phone rang.

"Simon, is that you?"

"Hi Tracey. I'm at work. What do you want?"

"Something on the case has come up and I need to talk with you."

"Look, this is a bad time. I'm staying with a friend and works been crazy."

"I can meet wherever it's convenient for you. Just let me know the time and place and I'll be there."

"I'll call you back," and he hung up.

I still had no idea where he was working or who he was staying with. Well there wasn't anything I could do about it at the moment. Maybe it was time to pay a visit to Jason Kane.

When I looked at the time it was almost 12:30. Since it was Friday I knew he would be leaving the office early. I wondered if I could catch him at the office before he left.

I found a parking spot near his building and rushed up to his office. I was out of breath as I exited the elevator.

"Is Jason Kane in?"

"He is but he's on his way out."

"I need to speak with him before he leaves. Tell him it's Tracey Marks."

Before she had a chance to let him know, he was walking towards the door leading to the elevator.

"Mr. Kane," I said, as I approached him.

"What are you doing here?"

"I need to speak with you. It's important."

"It will have to wait till Monday."

"I'm sorry it can't wait. Either we have this conversation in the hallway or we can go back into your office."

"Are you giving me an ultimatum?"

"Yes. You can either decline my request or I'm going to the police right now with what I found out."

He was furious. If we weren't in a public place, I'm not sure what he would have done.

"Make it quick," he said as we walked back into his office.

"I went to see the private investigator you hired to follow Rebecca. He said you were in quite a hurry after he provided you with the photos of your wife."

"And your point?"

"You had enough time to kill your wife."

"This is absurd."

"Maybe it was your intention to blackmail her."

"That's crazy. I would never do that."

"It seems things might have gotten out of hand and you fought and she fell. Maybe it was an accident. You didn't mean to do it."

"I don't know how many times I can tell you I didn't kill my wife. She was already dead when I got home."

"So you say."

"If you saw the photos you know that it's possible any one of a number of men she slept with could have killed her."

"For what reason?"

"How do I know. Maybe the guy was a psycho and followed her home."

"That's a possibility but unlikely. You were the one with the strongest motive. She was going to divorce you. That's why you hired the PI, to see what dirt you could get on her. Maybe even try to get custody of Lisa. But it all went to hell when she refused to pay you."

"If the police started investigating again they would find out about all your lies, starting with the false alibi you gave them, the reason they didn't prosecute you in the first place."

"If you go to the police I'll be ruined even though I'm innocent."

"Do you have any way to prove you're innocent?"

"Probably not."

Jason Kane did not look well. He was turning white.

"I think I'm having a heart attack. My chest, it's killing me."

I quickly dialed 911.

"Jason, an ambulance is coming. Look at me. You're going to be fine."

I ran to the front desk to tell them an ambulance was coming for Jason.

When I went back into his office I knelt down and took Jason's hand, praying the ambulance would hurry up. I kept talking to Jason like you see on TV, hoping to keep him calm.

The next thing I knew the ambulance was here and taking Jason out on a stretcher.

"What hospital are you taking him to?" I said.

"Mt. Sinai."

I told the receptionist to call his wife and that he was being taken to Mt. Sinai Hospital.

My heart was racing as I was driving to the hospital. What kept going through my mind was the thought that I might be responsible if Jason died. My palms started to sweat and my hands were shaking as I gripped the steering wheel with all my might. Over and over I kept saying, "please don't let him die."

I dumped my car into a parking lot and went into the hospital. I was told Jason was being admitted and I should wait in the emergency room. About fifteen minutes later I saw Danielle Kane rushing in.

"Danielle?"

She turned in my direction.

"What happened? Is he alright?" she said, tears streaming down her face.

"I don't know. He said his chest was hurting."

"Were you with him?"

"Yes," I answered. I hope my face didn't show the guilt I was feeling.

"What did you say to him?" she shouted.

"It doesn't matter now."

I didn't want to be in the same room with her so I walked outside and called Susie.

"Susie, I think I may have killed Jason Kane."

CHAPTER 52

"Take a breath. What do you mean?"

"I went to his office and confronted him with everything I found out. I threatened to go to the police. Then he began turning white and he said his chest was hurting. He thought he was having a heart attack. I'm at Mt. Sinai Hospital. His wife is here and she started yelling at me."

"Calm down. You probably didn't kill him. Even if you did you're not to blame. People get accused all the time and they don't have heart attacks. It's possible he had an anxiety attack or if he did have a heart attack there was probably something wrong with his heart anyway."

"Which I brought on. And I don't even know if he killed Rebecca."

"You were just doing your job."

"I need to make sure he's still alive before I leave."

"Okay, but stay away from his wife. Do you want me to come and wait with you?"

"No. I'll call you as soon as I find out anything."

When I went back inside I didn't see Danielle.

"Excuse me," I said to the receptionist, "Jason Kane was admitted. Can you tell me what floor he's on?"

"As far as I know he's taking tests."

"Would you be able to tell me where his wife Danielle is?"

"What is your relationship to Mr. Kane?"

"I was with him when he started having chest pains. I called for an ambulance."

"I sent her up to the second floor. She's probably waiting there for the results of her husband's tests."

"Thank you."

I was debating whether to go up to the second floor. I didn't want to upset Danielle but I felt I had a right to know what was going on.

I entered the main entrance of the hospital and found my way to the elevators. When I got off on the second floor I was pointed in the direction of the waiting room. Danielle was on her cell phone with her back to me. When she turned around I saw the look of loathing in her eyes.

I sat down on the opposite side of the room hoping Danielle wouldn't come over. Unfortunately, that was not to be.

"What the hell are you doing here? Haven't you caused enough damage?"

"I'm really sorry. I didn't mean to cause any harm to your husband but I needed some answers."

"I don't want you near my husband ever again."

"I can't promise you that."

At that moment, the doctor came out.

"Mrs. Kane?"

"Yes," she said.

"Your husband is completely fine. All the tests were negative. He may have had a panic attack which can mimic a heart attack. We'll keep him here overnight and he'll be released in the morning if nothing else shows up. Has he been under a lot of stress lately?"

"A little," she said, looking over at me.

"I'll talk to him about trying to reduce his stress. In the meantime you can go in and see him."

Danielle did not look at me as she went into her husband's room. I breathed a sigh of relief and was glad to leave the hospital.

On the way to pick up my car I called Susie.

"It was just a panic attack, thank heavens," I said when Susie answered.

"Well I'm glad for your sake he didn't have a heart attack, but if it turned out he killed his wife maybe that would be a little justice."

"I can't disagree. What are you guys up to this weekend?"

"Maybe a movie, dinner, the usual. You want to join us?"

"No, I think I'll relax. I've had enough excitement for a while. Are you still working on a lighter schedule?"

"For now. I'll give it another few weeks. Do you think I'll ever feel normal again?"

"It depends what you mean by normal. I never feel normal, but yes you will, I promise."

"If you change your mind and want to meet us for dinner, just call. In the meantime go home, pour yourself a glass of wine and relax."

"Will do. Love you."

I did exactly as Susie said when I got home. I poured myself a glass of wine, heated up leftover Thai food and turned on the radio to listen to some soft rock music. I wasn't in the mood for anything too heavy. I quickly undressed while my food was heating up and got into my sweats.

I wondered if Jason's panic attack was from guilt over his wife's death. Short of any physical evidence there appeared to be overwhelming circumstantial evidence against Kane. Before going to the police I wanted to speak with Simon Mack. He was the last suspect on my list. Patience was not my strong suit, and waiting for Simon to call me back was a bit unnerving.

After dinner I took a hot shower and got into bed with my Sue Grafton book. My eyes were closing when I heard my phone ring.

"Hey Jack."

"You sound tired."

"I was kind of nodding off. The day, to say the least, was very stressful."

I filled Jack in on the events of the day.

"Are you okay?"

"I am now. I was a basket case until I found out Kane was fine."

"Maybe a guilty conscience put him in a state of anxiety."

"There is so much circumstantial evidence against him, but I'm just not sure."

"What about David Martin, Rebecca's brother?"

"Maybe. Until I speak with Simon I'm reserving judgment. And at this point since I have no idea where he lives or works, I have no choice but to wait till he contacts me again."

"And if he doesn't?"

"I don't want to think about that right now."

"I've been checking on places to stay near the Grand Canyon. It turns out there are lodgings in the state park where we can stay. Also we can take a mule ride all the way down to the bottom of the canyon."

"Aren't we the adventuresome one."

"Let me see, you've been knifed, shot at, vandalized and I'm probably leaving out something else, and you can't handle going down into the canyon on a mule?"

"When you put it that way it doesn't sound so terrifying."

"The other alternative is hiking down which takes pretty much a whole day and it's not exactly a walk in the park."

"The mule is sounding better and better."

"Go to sleep. I'll talk to you tomorrow. Sleep tight."

"Ditto."

CHAPTER 53

It was a treat getting up on Saturday morning knowing I didn't have anywhere I had to be. Actually until I heard from Simon Mack I had no plans. If I didn't hear from him by Monday, I would have to figure out a way of getting Sandra, Simon's ex-girlfriend, to tell me where Simon works.

I spent the weekend being mostly a homebody, cleaning my apartment, reading and watching movies on Netflix. I hadn't heard from Simon, and by Monday morning I was beginning to think he was avoiding me when my phone rang.

"Hello."

"Tracey, it's Simon."

I came to attention.

"Simon, I'm glad you called."

"I'm house sitting for a friend who lives in Great Neck. Can you be here by 11:00 am?"

"Sure."

Before hanging up Simon gave me the address. I quickly showered and dressed, and had some cereal before leaving. According to the GPS I had to take the

Long Island Expressway to exit 33. The Expressway is notorious for traffic but it was the most direct route.

On the way over I was thinking of what I could say to Simon to lure him into believing he might be a suspect. When I pulled up to the house I was surprised. It was more like a mansion. I was curious what the inside looked like.

I parked in the circular driveway and rang the bell.

"Hi Simon." He didn't look too good. I could smell a hint of alcohol on his breath.

"Come in."

"Wow. This place is beautiful."

We sat in a room that looked like a mini botanical gardens. There were all types of plants everywhere. Now I know why this person needed a house sitter. It would take someone hours just to water all the plants. A moment later a giant dog came bounding into the room.

"This is Red. He's an Irish Setter."

"He's beautiful."

Red came over and smelled me and then turned and sprinted out of the room. Should I be insulted?

"So what did you find out?"

"It seems that Rebecca's daughter remembered a few things from that night."

"Like what?" His eyebrows shot up.

"Lisa heard a man's voice with her mother. Also there was a strong scent of cologne by her mother's room."

"Did she recognize the voice?" Simon asked. I picked up a hint of concern.

"Unfortunately, not at the moment. But you never know. Her memory could come back at any moment."

"I recently found out for sure that Rebecca was being followed by a private investigator her husband had hired. It appears Rebecca was hitting the bar scene and picking up men and going home with them."

"That can't be true. I would have known about it," he said.

The look on Simon's face revealed he wasn't as confident as he wanted me to believe.

"Why would you? I'm sure it wouldn't be something she would want you to find out about."

"It just wasn't the Rebecca I knew." There was definitely anger behind his words.

"You told me yourself that Rebecca had no intentions of marrying you."

"That's what she said but maybe after she divorced her husband she would have changed her mind."

"Why would you think that after what she told you?"

Simon didn't answer me.

"Maybe you found out what Rebecca was up to. You confronted her but she didn't care what you thought. This infuriated you..."

"You're way out of line!" he said raising his voice. "I had nothing to do with Rebecca's death. I loved her."

"I'm sure you did."

"I suggest you look at Jason Kane. It was his wife that was fooling around."

Did I detect some hostility towards Rebecca in his voice?

"And if it wasn't for his alibi back then the police would have arrested him," he said.

"Can I ask why you're no longer with Sandra?"

"It just didn't work out."

"Have you started drinking again?"

"That's really none of your business."

"I think I'll let the police sort out this mess," I said as I was leaving, hoping it would scare him enough if he did kill Rebecca.

I would have liked the two minute tour of the house

but I didn't think that was in the cards now. I showed myself out.

On the way back to the city I couldn't help but feel Simon knew more than he was telling me. It was the first time I heard anger in his voice expressed towards Rebecca. If he did kill Rebecca, did I give him enough bait to trap him? Time will tell.

CHAPTER 54

When I got back I went for a run. With everything going on, I almost forgot that I had a therapy session at 5:00 pm. I started to have doubts whether therapy could really help me. The only reason I haven't stop was because of Jack. I wanted to see if we had a future together and what that would look like. I knew I wanted to be with him but didn't know if I could go the distance. Maybe I was a little bit like Rebecca. I kept my dark side hidden, but sometimes it revealed itself.

I was sitting inside Lily Davidson's office.

"So how are you doing today Tracey?"

"I'm in the middle of a case, and to say the least, it's frustrating."

"Your work must be very interesting."

"It can be. In the last couple of years I've been working on more challenging cases. What I realize about myself is that I like the danger. I've never said that out loud before."

"Can you say more about that?"

"I've been shot at, attacked with a knife, run off the

road, threatened and my office has been vandalized. And that's just a few incidents. I've also wound up in the hospital twice. Yet it doesn't even enter my mind that I should stop."

"As I had told you, Jack wants me to go on vacation with him. And when he mentioned riding on a mule down into the Grand Canyon that scared me more than being attacked. Not sure what that says about me."

"Does anything come to mind?"

"I don't know."

"Do you think your fear of commitment and the danger you place yourself in, have any connection?"

My mind was mulling over what Dr. Davidson said.

"I'm not sure."

"It might be something to think about."

I guess she wasn't going to give me the answer.

"Is it possible the danger might represent comfort to you and keeps you from dealing with your feelings about your commitment issues?"

"So you're saying I welcome the danger as a way of not dealing with my feelings."

"I think there's a theme and it all stems from the loss of your parents. Danger can make you feel alive as a substitute for getting close to someone."

"Why don't you think about it some more, and we'll continue the conversation next week."

Could she be right about my need for danger? Could it be a way of avoiding having to deal with my feelings? After my father died it seemed like my world fell apart. It was just me and my mother and I wasn't sure about anything. Though she did her best she was grieving and I felt abandoned all over again. I wanted her to pay attention to me but she seemed withdrawn at times. Eventually we became closer and when she was diagnosed with advanced breast cancer I became numb. Her death was inevitable though I was in denial the whole time. During the period between my father's death and when my mother died I became very self-sufficient. After she died, except for Susie and Cousin Alan, I was alone.

I never thought of my cases in terms of the danger they come with. But there must be an element of truth that it makes me feel alive. I never thought of it that way before. I wanted things to be different. I just didn't know how to make that happen as yet.

Too much thinking is tiring. When I got home I made myself a peanut butter sandwich, grabbed a bag of potato chips and brought both into bed with me.

I allowed my thoughts to wander back to my case. I was still leaning towards the husband but doubts had started to creep in. After talking with Simon, I wasn't sure about anyone, including Rebecca's brother David. I fell asleep thinking about riding a mule down into the Grand Canyon.

CHAPTER 55

When I got up the following morning I went to the gym first thing and then came back to my apartment to change and have some breakfast. I hadn't gone target shooting in over six months. If I was to be prepared I needed to practice in case I became the subject of Rebecca's killer.

When I got into the office I took out my gun from the safe and took it apart, cleaning each cavity of the gun methodically.

I took the train to the Westside Rifle & Pistol Range on 20th Street. When I walked in I didn't recognize the guy behind the counter.

"Hi there, can I get some ammo for my gun?"

"Sure. Is this the first time you've been here?"

"No, but it's the first time I've seen you."

"My name's Roy."

"Nice to meet you Roy, I'm Tracey." Roy reminded me of a westerner, complete with a cowboy hat and boots.

"Where are you from?" I asked Roy.

"Ah, you noticed my dialect."

"Well I knew you weren't from New York."

"I was born and raised in Oklahoma."

"How did you wind up here?"

"Do you want the long or short version?"

"The short version, if you don't mind."

"I met this lady in Vegas. It was an instant attraction."

"Let me guess, she was from New York."

"Yep, and I wasn't going to let her slip away, though I couldn't give up the hat and boots."

"Without being too nosy, are you still together?"

"Almost twenty-six years."

"Wow, that's amazing. What's your secret?"

"She's my best friend."

"You're a lucky guy."

"That I am. So do you shoot for fun?"

"Actually I'm a private investigator so every once in a while I like to practice just in case."

"I hope no one has taken a shot at such a pretty young lady as yourself."

"Not today so far," I chuckled.

"Here you go," handing me a box of bullets. "Stall 12 is open."

"Thanks Roy."

I walked to stall 12. Being here brings back memories of Randy Stewart who I thought I met by chance, though on his part it was completely planned. Not seeing through his façade, I dated him. He wanted to keep me close enough to know what I was up to. In the end I got him and now he's behind bars.

I took out the bullets and loaded each one into each of the chambers. At first a gun can feel heavy and hard to hold, but after practicing, it begins to feel lighter and easier to control.

I spent about an hour aiming at the target paper. Though I was never going to be a bull's eye hitter, I was decent enough. Being comfortable handling a gun was more important.

I returned to the front desk and told Roy I was finished.

"Nice meeting you Tracey. And be careful out there."

"Will do."

On the subway riding back to my office, I thought about what Roy said. I wondered if there was any truth to what he said about marriage, though I guess it's as good as anyone else's.

I found a parking spot close to the office and picked up a turkey sandwich at the deli. I went next door to Cousin Alan before heading into my office.

"Anyone home?" I said out loud since Margaret wasn't at her desk.

"I'm here," I heard Alan shout.

"Where's Margaret?" I said walking into his office.

"She's doing a few errands. She should be back soon. What are you up to?"

"Not much. It seems I'm in a holding pattern. Not sure if my plan to capture the killer is going to work."

"What is the plan?"

"It's probably better if you didn't know. How's the little man doing?"

"He's talking up a storm."

"That's so cute. As soon as this case is over, I could take him off your hands for a day or two."

"Patty would love that. We made arrangements to spend a few days in Stockbridge this coming weekend. Patty's parents will come over and stay at our place."

"Give them my number in case they have a problem."

"Thanks. I'll do that."

"I told Jack I would go on vacation with him."

"It's about time you go somewhere. You need to have some fun, and it will be good to get away and not think about work or what's going on in the world."

"It does sound good when you put it that way. Enjoy your time in Stockbridge. If you need any ideas on what to do, give Jack a call before you go. Have fun and give my little man a big kiss and hug for me."

"Tracey, be safe."

"Always."

I went back to my office, cleaned my gun again before putting it back in the safe and then called Susie.

"Hi. I was thinking about you," Susie said.

"I know you don't want me to keep asking how you're doing, but…"

"Sometimes I'm not sure how I'm supposed to feel."

"Are you up for a drink after work?"

"Absolutely. Mark said he'll be home a little late. I'll meet you at 6:00 pm at the Dead Poet."

"Great. I'll see you then."

I was sitting inside the Dead Poet Bar by 5:45. I ordered a glass of wine while I was waiting for Susie. I was munching on a cashew when I spotted her coming in.

"Hey, over here," I said, as I waved to her.

The waitress came over as Susie was sitting down.

"I'll have a glass of Chianti," Susie said.

"Can I get you anything to eat?" the waitress asked.

"How about if we get an order of chicken wings?" I said to Susie.

"I'm good with that."

"We'll have an order of chicken wings for now, thank you," I told the waitress.

"When I tell you what Jack has in store for us at the

315

Grand Canyon you might change your mind about coming with us."

"What could it possibly be?"

"A trip down into the bottom of the Canyon on a mule."

"I love it. That should be so much fun."

"I should have realized that would be something you'd like to do."

"Though I'm not sure about Mark. You guys can always skip it and Jack and I can go down by ourselves," Susie said.

"I'll warm up to the idea eventually. Why don't we all go out for dinner Saturday and we'll plan the trip."

"Works for me," Susie said.

The waitress brought over our chicken wings and I reached for one.

"You know the new attorney I mentioned that's now in Max's suite? Give me your take on this: I was leaving my office a few days ago and he saw me. He asked if I'd like to get together after work for a drink."

"What did you say?"

"I told him I couldn't talk at the moment since I was on my way out."

"What do you want to know?"

"Do you think he was coming on to me?"

"Maybe. Hard to tell since I don't know the guy at all."

"We have never talked about our personal lives. I have no idea if he's married and he has no idea about my status."

"Are you afraid if you accept, he'll make a pass at you?"

"I just think I should keep our relationship strictly on a professional level."

"So you don't know what to say to him?"

"I guess I don't. It's just awkward."

"Well unless he brings it up again, you don't have to say anything."

"That's true, but what if he does? I'm really bad at this stuff."

"You have no problem confronting a killer but this you have a problem with. Oy vey!"

"I know. Maybe I should talk about it in therapy."

"Any startling revelations you care to share?"

"I'm still mulling over my last session. I'll let you know when I'm ready to talk. In the meantime, not one of my suspects has taken the bait. This case may never get solved. I'd bet the ranch it's got to be one of them."

"It hasn't been that long. Wait, give it time. And on that note I think my witching hour is over."

After paying we walked out together. I had to pick up my car parked near my office. We decided to grab a cab together. I would be dropped off first by my car and Susie would continue on to her place. I waved goodbye as I got out of the cab.

CHAPTER 56

As I was inserting the key in my car door I felt something pressed against my back.

"Get into the car Tracey and don't try anything. I'll shoot you right here."

I did as he said while he climbed into the passenger seat. His gun was pointed right at me. I could smell the liquor on his breath.

"Start the car and drive."

My hand was shaking as I put the key into the ignition.

"Where are we going?"

"Just drive. I'll give you directions."

"Simon, please don't point the gun at me. You're making me nervous."

"I don't think you're in any position to tell me what to do."

My gun was back in the safe. Why didn't I have it on me? His hand didn't seem very steady, and I was afraid the gun might go off.

As we were driving, Simon gave me directions. I had no idea where we were going until we were headed into the Midtown tunnel which takes you into Queens.

"Simon talk to me. What's going on?" The back of

my shirt was sticking to the seat. I was trying to remain calm, but not knowing where we were going was making me more anxious.

"Just keep driving."

"Look Simon I know we can resolve this."

"I said shut up."

My phone started to ring.

"You answer that and I'll put a bullet in your head right now."

My chest was pounding so hard I thought I was going to have a heart attack. That would be ironic after what happened to Jason Kane.

When I saw where he was taking me, I could hardly breathe.

"Park the car here and get out."

I did as he said. We were somewhere in a completely desolate area. I could scream my lungs out and no one would hear me. The animals would probably eat away at me before I was found. I needed to figure out something but my brain wasn't functioning.

I was trying to keep my wits about me. I had only two choices. Go straight at him or keep him talking. The problem was Simon kept his distance so by the time I rushed him, I'd be dead.

"Simon, it's not too late. You can still walk away from this. There is no real proof you killed Rebecca. Can you tell me what happened? I know you well enough that it was probably an accident."

"Rebecca fucked me over really good and my life was ruined because of her."

"What did she do?"

"I followed her one evening after she left me. I saw this other guy following her also. It turns out it was that private investigator you mentioned. He was taking photos of her screwing all these men. The image in my head of her being with these men made me sick. I thought we were going to make a life together after she divorced her husband."

"I'm sorry Simon."

"Too late for sorries."

"What happened?" I said softly.

"That night I went to her place and confronted her. I wanted to know why she needed to be with these men but she had no answer. She asked me to leave. I started to go but then I turned around and followed her into the bathroom. I was just so angry. I reached out and grabbed her. She pulled away, stumbled backward and hit her head. There was blood pouring out of the back of her head. I reached out and checked for a pulse but there was none. I was so scared I ran."

"That means it was an accident. You didn't mean to kill her."

"I don't know if I did or not. Maybe I wanted her dead."

Simon looked like he was on the verge of crying. I started to slowly walk towards him.

"Stay back. Don't take another step." His hand was shaking as the gun was pointed right at me.

"Whether you wanted her dead doesn't matter. It was still an accident. Please Simon put down the gun. You don't need to kill me. I just want to help."

"It's too late."

I didn't believe my eyes as Simon pointed the gun at me, his finger on the trigger and then at the last second he raised his arm and aimed the gun at his head.

"*NO Simon*!" I screamed. "*STOP*!!"

THREE WEEKS LATER

I was packing for my trip to the Grand Canyon. I was expecting Jack at any moment. Our plane from LaGuardia Airport was leaving at 1:00 pm. The four of us were taking a car service to the airport.

I still can't get the memory of Simon out of my head. I keep reliving the scene over and over, Simon's gun pointed at me and then turning the gun on himself and blowing his brains out. That moment when Simon took his own life can never be erased from my mind. For the first time since Jack brought up the idea of a vacation, I was actually happy that I was going away. I didn't realize how much seeing Simon kill himself had unnerved me. There isn't a day that goes by that I don't shudder when I think about him.

I think it was Simon's intention to kill himself all along. He needed me to understand why he was so desperate. I felt sorry for him. Unfortunately for Simon he loved someone who could never love him back. Rebecca had demons no one could have imagined, not her parents or her husband.

When I told Lisa who killed her mother, I decided I wasn't going to be the one to break the news why Simon killed her and hopefully she'll never find out. I did share some of the details about Simon and her mother's relationship with him. Lisa broke down in tears as I was telling her what happened. But mostly there was relief and joy knowing that after all these years the weight that held her down thinking her father may have killed her mother was now lifted.

I heard the knock at the door.

"Hey good looking," I said, as I pulled Jack into the

foyer and gave him a big kiss and wrapped my arms around him.

Fortunately, Wally was able to get Jack a spot in the garage as one of the tenants was going to be out of town for a while.

"I was just finishing up packing. Join me in the bedroom."

"I think this is the first time you asked me to join you in the bedroom without it involving sex."

"Are you disappointed?"

"Of course not. And besides I'll have you all to myself for ten days."

"Well that's not exactly true."

"Close enough."

"Are you positive it's safe to fly?" I asked Jack.

"Absolutely. And if anything happens, we'll be together."

"How comforting. Though I think we should check out the pilot and co-pilot when we get on the plane. Make sure they don't reek of alcohol."

"I'll leave that job to you," Jack said grinning.

"Okay I'm all set. Wait, did I forget to change my telephone message? Did I turn on my auto message for my emails?" Tracey get a grip, I said to myself.

Before leaving I took one more look around to make sure the lights were out and everything was unplugged. I closed the door to my apartment and we headed downstairs to wait for the car service.

THE END

ACKNOWLEDGMENTS

When I wrote my first mystery novel, Looking for Laura, I could not have imagined I would write three more books in the Tracey Marks Mystery series.

Though the main character, PI Tracey Marks is fictional, there are many facets of her life that are similar to mine. Foremost, we are both private investigators. I attribute my love for writing the series to the main characters I have created.

Because this book was written during Covid, it helped me through a terrible time. It gave me purpose and filled my days. During this period my friend Ann Spadafora and I spent hours together walking, having coffee and sitting outside having lunch or dinner in the cold weather with the heat lamps going. She was a captive audience and listened to me while I went on and on about my book. I am grateful for our time together.

Thank you to all my friends for their love and encouragement.

Many thanks to my publisher, Lisa Orban, and my editor, Jennie Rosenblum. Without all their assistance I would be lost.

My gratitude to Susan Greene who has never failed me when I needed her. All of her contributions and insights have helped me to write the Tracey Marks series.

And always a huge thank you to my biggest fan, my daughter Carrie.

ABOUT THE AUTHOR

Ellen Shapiro is a private investigator and the author of four novels of the Tracey Marks Mystery series. Acting on her passion for writing, Ellen enrolled in the Sarah Lawrence Writing Institute where she took courses in creative writing. Her professional experience led her to create the storylines and develop the characters for her novels. In addition to her novels, Ellen has written articles related to her field for both local and nationwide newspapers. She is a member of Mystery Writers of America. When she is not writing or working, you can find Ellen on the golf course yelling at her ball. Ellen resides in Scarsdale, New York.